SILVERCREST ACADEMY

CURSED
SHADOWS

KC KEAN

To taking strength from within, slaying those demons, and smearing your name in their blood.

Boss bitches just got lethal.

ELIVEN REALM

AMBERGLEN

SHADOWMOOR

HAVEN COURT

CREST
EMY

PINEBROOK

DALE

WASTELANDS

LICA REALM

KC KEAN

"One day, you will see yourself how we do, and it's going to be magnificent."

ONE

Raven

My gaze slowly shifts back and forth between two sets of onyx eyes, both framed with even blacker hair. Emotions flicker across Creed's face with every passing second as time slows to a near stop.

Did he just say what I think he...

"Father," he repeats, his brows furrowing as the word falls heavily from his tongue.

There it is again. I definitely heard what I thought I heard, and this man, this *warrior*, is exactly who I believe him to be. How is that possible?

I gape back at the leader of the Battalions, as Erikel called them, taking in his golden armor, which is stained with crimson and copper patterns, each patch deeper than the last.

A pained gasp rattles in my ears, audible over the rest

of the academy's panic and dismay, and I turn my gaze once more, but this time, it's not to check on Creed; it's his mother. Her hand is plastered to her chest, tears tracking down her high cheekbones and dripping from her chin without care. Her eyelids flutter across her brown pupils over and over again, like she can't believe what she's seeing, no matter how long she stares.

Erikel cackles, garnering everyone's attention once again as he spreads his arms out wide. "Excellent. It seems at least some of you are familiar with my monster. Now, how this next part goes will determine how the rest of your... lives unravel." His wicked grin connects with every single person in the hall. It somehow makes the scar that runs down the right side of his face stand out more, reminding us all of the many layers of this man we know nothing about.

Who did we let into the academy?

No, who did *Sebastian* let through those gates?

The whimpers and sobs of fear ebb as we wait for him to continue, but the tension and anxiety only intensify in the air around us.

With every passing second, my pulse thuds wilder in my ears. I can feel the adrenaline in my veins, body zinging with magic as I catch a glimpse of Professor Barton's lifeless limbs splayed out on the floor at Erikel's feet. Erikel's fur cloak is draped over him, hiding most of the blood, but it doesn't disguise the lifeless gray hue of his eyes.

How do I help him?

It's not a matter of if. My magic is drawn to him, desperate to heal his soul and bring him back to the land of the living. I instinctively attempt to take a step toward him again, but my bare feet are still rooted to the floor.

Frowning down at the marble beneath my toes, I exhale slowly, trying to focus on where the magic is coming from. It's not as easy to see it, morph it, and play with it when my adrenaline is running so high and my heart is thundering in my chest. It's not giving me the usual ability to focus, hone in. Instead, I'm scattered and overwhelmed.

My nostrils flare in irritation at my lack of ability, but another sob parts Creed's mother's lips, garnering my attention once again. She can't take her eyes off the warrior at the entrance to the hall, flanked by the Amayans—the faceless men—stoking fear into everyone's hearts. Creed is right there with her, dripping in pain, tarnished with horror, and helpless in the face of a reality none of us believed to be possible.

Continuing around the table, I snarl when I see a smirk teasing the corners of Sebastian's mouth. I want to slaughter him with my bare hands and never give him a chance to come back. He deserves to rot in whatever pit he falls in. Our parents stare at Erikel with apprehension in their eyes and I can't decide if it's mixed with surprise or anticipation of knowing what's to follow.

Eldon stands protectively beside his mother, the frustration of also being locked in place evident on his face as his mother squeezes his hand tight. Zane stares his father down, who remains stoic and unfazed as he waits with bated breath to see what will come from Erikel's mouth next. Brax, however, is plastered against my back. I don't even know how or when he got there, but he's there in all of his protective glory.

Taking a deep breath, I set my sights on Barton but speak to Brax. "I need to save him."

"Save who?" His chest rumbles at my back, calming the rising heat of magic spreading through my veins.

"Barton."

"It's too much of a risk," he grunts in response, and I shake my head as discreetly as possible, careful to make sure Erikel isn't watching us. But he's too busy relishing in the fear he's injecting into the room.

"She's right." My gaze slowly shifts to Rhys, who doesn't look away from Erikel either as he interjects. Zane looks at me, though, confused by the words from his father's mouth.

"It's too much of a risk," Brax reiterates through clenched teeth.

"He's too influential. Everything hangs in the balance

if he dies tonight. All hope will be lost."

"But they'll know," Brax spits, his anger warranted but rocketing far higher than my own, and it's me we're talking about.

Rhys finally takes his eyes off Erikel to find mine. Sympathy crinkles the corners of his eyes as his lips set in a grim line of disappointment.

"I will save you all from death tonight if you can complete one simple task. I want someone to step forth and heal your faithful leader, Professor Barton." Erikel's voice echoes around us. I know what's coming.

Fuck.

The glint in his eyes. He knows. He fucking knows. He just doesn't know *who,* exactly, can aid him.

"The buzz of a necromancer has been zinging through The Monarchy for weeks. If the fuckers from the Basilica Realm are here for something, it's for that reason alone," Rhys states, sending a shiver down my spine as I feel both of my parents' eyes spin to me. I don't pay them any mind, though. I keep my gaze locked on Rhys's as my veins burn with the reality I'm now facing.

The undertone of Erikel's threat is clear. Either the necromancer steps forward, or people start to die. Do I want that on my shoulders?

"You can't heal a dead man," someone hollers from another table, earning a thrum of murmurs of agreement along with it.

Erikel chuckles like he was waiting for such a blatant statement. We're playing directly into his hands, just like he wants.

"I believe your statement to be true. That is, unless you're a necromancer."

I try not to react, but my muscles stiffen at the way the word sounds on his tongue.

"A necromancer? There is no such magic here," someone else adds, and as much as I try to keep my chin up, it's harder than I expect.

"You're wrong. My little soul dancer has until the count of ten to make a decision before the next victim feels the wrath of my warrior."

Fuck.

"Release the magic holding our feet, otherwise no one can help," Rhys declares, turning his attention to Erikel with a sigh.

"Ah, The Monarchy finally speaks. How delightful. Aren't you going to challenge me?"

"I don't think that would be wise of me, do you? I think it's clear to everyone here you have us at your mercy," Rhys replies, cocking a brow at the villainous man who sneers with his chest puffed out, pride clinging to every inch of him.

"Ten… Nine… Eight…"

He doesn't even bother to reply to Rhys, redirecting his attention to hunting down the necromancer. Hunting *me*.

"Hmm, what can we do to incentivize our ultimate healer? Maybe we should bring a victim forward for our warrior to cut down, make the situation all the more real? " Everyone remains silent except for the sound of metal clanging along the floor as the golden warrior steps forward. "Seven… Six… Five… Hmm, maybe we should have him kill his own son. You, step forward," he snarls at Creed, and a moment later, the weight holding my feet in place is lifted.

My eyes dart to Creed, who takes a tentative step forward, and I do the same, trying to stop him even though he's farther around the table, but Brax's arm around my waist stops me in my tracks.

"Let me go," I bite under my breath as Brax pins me to him.

"Who wants to see my fearsome warrior slay his own son? Four… Three…"

"Let me go right now, Brax. He's here for me."

"You're right, he's here for you, but that doesn't mean he gets to have you."

My breathing hollows out as panic dances over my skin, making the hairs on my arms stand on end. "I won't let him kill Creed."

"Raven…" My mother's voice cuts through the air,

barely more than a whisper, but it's enough to interrupt Brax and me.

My gaze locks with hers for the briefest of moments, an array of emotions flashing in her eyes before pain stains her pupils to almost black.

"No takers? Have it your way, then. Stand right here for me. We want to make a show of this," Erikel instructs Creed, who looks directly at me as he follows the order. He shakes his head ever so slightly, but he must be confused as fuck if he thinks I'm just going to let this happen.

I'm not a savior. I'm not a hero, and I have no intention of being one. I'm selfish. I'm greedy. But most of all, I'm in love. With Creed. With Eldon. With Zane. With Brax. And no man, woman, nor beast is going to take what belongs to me. I will slay every other fucker here. I don't care. Just not them.

"It's me." Brax's arm tightens as the words pass my lips, but there's no taking them back now. Not as Erikel stares at me with excitement, even through the hint of caution that flickers across his face. "I'm the necromancer," I add, tilting my chin up as I lock eyes with him.

"Are you? Or do you not want to see this boy's blood painted across the floor?"

Shaking out of Brax's hold, I take a step toward the podium, moving past my parents, who keep their mouths shut as everyone's gaze follows my every move. I don't stop until I'm beside Creed, my hand blindly finding his through the haze.

"You're here for me." The words are like lead on my tongue.

"For you." Erikel peers down at me, intrigue flashing in his dark gaze. I keep my shoulders back as I stare him down, refusing to falter under his presence. "Show me."

I nod. "I will, but first, I want Creed and three other men from that table safely extracted from this room."

Erikel laughs, head tilted back as the sound echoes around the space.

"You don't get to make demands here. You do as I say, and if I find out you're lying, I'll kill you for wasting my time."

My mouth opens, ready to bite back, but Creed squeezes my fingers before I can. "You know we won't leave, Raven. It's a lost cause."

Erikel takes a step back, extending his arm in the direction of Barton as one of the students from Shadowgrim Institute steps forward and drags the fur cloak from his body. Blood frames Professor Barton from head to toe, a thick layer outlining his limp body, and the smell singes my nose as I cringe.

It's too late to back out now. I either reveal myself or die for faking it. Creed releases my hand and I carefully sink to the floor in my long, black-sequined dress. The rhinestones dig into my knees, biting into my skin, but I ignore it as I move to place my hands on Barton's back. Before I can touch him, the student flips him over and yanks the long blade from his body, splattering blood across my face and arms.

"Hey," Zane growls, and I hear a commotion coming from the table I was seated at moments ago, but I keep my gaze focused on Barton.

Now lying on his back, his face looks gaunt and gray. I press my palm against his chest and my magic comes alive inside of me, desperately wanting to mend the broken pieces at its touch. Against my better judgment, my eyes fall closed and the purple orb inside of me tingles from the tips of my fingers right down to my toes.

Silhouettes dance across my vision and an inaudible murmur rings in my ears as my breath lodges in my throat. I feel warm, like I'm basking in a soft glow on a summer morning, before it's gone, leaving me cold and depleted.

Blinking my eyes open, I find Barton lying beside me, the color returning to his face and his chest slowly rising and falling as his heart beats once more.

"It really *is* you," Erikel murmurs in bewilderment, eyes wide as he gapes down at the professor. An evil grin spreads across his face as elation prickles among his men, both students and his battalion. A strange level of excitement and joy at my show of magic that doesn't sit right with me somehow.

Not when I just laid myself bare, exposed myself to the enemy, and did exactly what I've been avoiding. But I would do it all again in a heartbeat to keep Creed safe.

Erikel crouches down beside me, gripping my chin in a painful hold as he stares deep into my eyes. The chaos and noise elevate around me, but I can't focus on anything but the black pits of his eyes. Not a single ounce of warmth glows within him, even his fingertips are icy cold.

"Rest up, little soul dancer. I'm going to be taking *everything* from you."

TWO

Raven

"**O**ur goal here tonight has been achieved. Please, go home and rest. There's a lot to prepare for in the coming weeks. School will continue as normal, just with a few… adjustments," Erikel declares, releasing my chin and staring out at the crowd.

Wait… what?

My eyebrows pinch with confusion as he steps back, his students flanking him on either side as he claps his hands together and disappears before our very eyes. Eldon, Zane, and Brax rush to my side, dragging me to my feet, but my eyes are set on Creed, who stands in the same spot he did earlier. His gaze is fixed on his father, Erikel's warrior, who is staring right back at him.

My heart beats hard in my chest as the warrior takes a moment to search out Creed's mother, the world stopping as they stare at one another, but it's over too quickly as he spins on his heels and leads the rest of Erikel's battalion back through the double doors. The second the wood slams shut behind them all, hysteria breaks out across the room.

"We need to get out of here," Brax grunts against my ear, his hands on my shoulders as the sea of students and their families disperse around the room.

A grunt of pain reaches my ears and I look down to see Professor Burton lifting himself to a sitting position. He presses his palm against his chest, where the wound that killed him had been moments ago, as a confused look takes over his face.

I don't have the energy or patience to catch him up to speed. I saved him. Someone else can deal with this part.

Eldon's hand finds mine and I meet his eyes with a half smile, hoping to look less overwhelmed than I am, but I know he sees right through the attempt. Realization over what I just did is kicking in and the results of that are taking their toll on my body.

"Raven? Raven!" Mama appears before me a second later, tears filling her eyes with worry. Her hands clasp either side of my face as she tries to pull me in, but Eldon and Brax aren't willing to let go. "My darling girl." Tears fill her eyes but not a single drop falls down her cheek.

"How long have you known?" Abel demands, appearing behind her a moment later, and I shrug. Despite his earlier bullshit statement, which was something along the lines of, "You might hate me, but I love you more," I still don't trust him. Not one bit.

"Step back before I make you," Brax bites, his hands dropping from my shoulders and grabbing at my waist as he pulls me back against him, effectively moving me far enough away from my mother that her hands fall dramatically at her sides.

Abel rolls his eyes, silently calling his threat worthless, but he doesn't move closer as I expect him to. Instead, he wipes his hand down his face and glances out at the crowd as they hastily filter through the double doors.

"We should probably be doing the same," Zane states, his shoulder brushing against mine as he steps into my right side.

"Fat chance of that," Abel mutters, his brows furrowing as he continues to watch the mass fight over who is getting out first. "How are we even going to get out of here? The academy is no longer safe."

As if hearing his concerns, another parent by the doors turns and hollers, "The gateways are open. We're free to leave, but no students can pass through."

The room drowns in silence for a split second before all Hell breaks loose and parents start wading their way through the crowd faster, plotting their own escape and leaving their children here to suffer.

I shouldn't be surprised. I shouldn't. But for some reason, I always expect better of people. Is that my version of hope? Clinging to the fact that people will be better, do better, try harder? Fuck if I know, but I don't like the taste of disappointment on my tongue either way.

"What's going on?" Zane asks as his father appears, offering Burton a helping hand and pulling him to his feet.

"He'll want us to spread the news but keep the students captive," Rhys explains, making my gut clench. After what I just revealed, that's never going to end well for me. I know it.

Burton scratches his head and turns to face me. Despite wanting nothing more to do with the man right now, I still can't help myself. "Are you okay?"

"I've been better," he admits. "I'm sure I'll get there, but you have a lot of explaining to do."

I feel Zane, Brax, and Eldon tense at his words, which ratchets up my own nerves. But before I can respond, Rhys beats me to it. "No, she doesn't."

He wraps his arm around Burton's shoulders and steers him toward the far corner of the room without a backward glance. My shoulders sag with relief.

"Seriously, let's leave. Now," Brax grunts, his hands flexing at my waist, and I nod.

"Surely there must be a way I can take you home with me," Eldon's mother states, appearing in front of us. "I can't leave, not if you can't," she insists, and my heart clenches. "Are you okay?" she asks, stepping around my parents to look at me.

How ironic that it's not my own parents asking me that, but someone else's. Despite the appreciation for her question, I don't have the ability to form an answer for her. There are so many concerns sitting on the tip of my tongue, but she doesn't need to hear them. So, instead, I settle on glossing over everything. "I'm okay."

"Mother, you need to leave. The sooner, the better. We'll be okay. We'll figure this out together," Eldon insists, releasing my hand to envelop his mother in his arms for a brief moment. I watch her almost go limp in his arms, worry getting the better of her, but the grip she has around him shows her strength through it all, clinging to him like her life depends on it. All while my parents stand and watch.

"Creed," Zane calls out, garnering his attention. He turns on the spot with his onyx eyes glossy and confused. "You need to say goodbye to your mother, help her get home, and then we can regroup back at the house."

He nods once, Zane's words kicking him into action as he strides toward the table where his mother is still sitting. I don't hear what he says to her, but she rises to her feet a moment later with a sniffle.

"We should do the same, Evangeline," Abel states, and

my mother's gaze cuts to mine.

"But, Raven."

"It's fine, you need to go. Hurry," I insist. If she tries to stick around, I won't be able to focus. It's almost like I'd be taking care of her and not the other way around, and I don't need the responsibility of someone else right now.

Abel places a hand on the small of her back and encourages her toward the door. He doesn't glance back at me or seek out Sebastian. He's just as focused on himself as he's ever been.

"Let's move," Eldon orders, squeezing his mother's arm one last time before he takes my hand again, and the five of us start moving, bypassing the students and families hovering in the hall who are wailing for help like they don't have magical abilities themselves. Not that anyone actually threw them around to defend our academy—or realm, for that matter—but I guess they must have known we didn't stand a chance. Not with the battalion waiting at the doors too.

We're so fucked.

"This is all your fault!" Genie appears in front of me, pointing her finger in my face as her own scrunches with ugly tear tracks down her cheeks. Her confidence wanes as her bottom lip wobbles, but I don't get a chance to push back at her outburst before she's turned into ice before my very eyes.

I blink at her a few times, making sure I'm actually seeing what I think I'm seeing, but it's not until a flash of blonde appears beside the ice sculpture that I realize it's Leila.

"I'm sorry, I just... fuck her."

"Yeah, fuck her," Zane repeats, pumping his fist in the air triumphantly, easing the tension around us. Just a little.

"Thanks," I murmur, sidestepping the icicles that hang from Genie's still-outstretched finger.

"It's no bother." She glances around as if searching for someone, maybe her father, but after a moment, her gaze falls back to mine. "I think you guys better get out of here. Who knows what tomorrow will look like after you just exposed yourself to him."

I nod numbly, my mind unwilling to consider anything past this very moment. I'm sure it will come alive later when I try to go to sleep, then it won't just be the shadows dancing in my vision. It'll be all of my thoughts and the worst possible outcomes that come with them.

The five of us move in sync once again, almost reaching the door before a breathless Burton appears in front of us. What is it with everyone wanting to get in my way?

"What now?" Brax snarls, clearly thinking the same as me, but Burton pays him no mind as he plants his hands on his hips and looks at me.

"Thank you. You didn't have to do that. But you saved

a lot of people."

I shake my head, not wanting to hear what else he might have to say. Stepping out from my guys, I move toward the professor. "The only reason I did it was for him." I point to where Creed stands a step behind me without looking. I need this man to know I mean exactly what I'm saying right now. "I'm not a hero, and I have no intention of becoming one, so don't expect me to start changing who I am."

Standing taller, my shoulders rolled back, I breeze past him without a backward glance. The only confirmation I have that the Bishops are still with me is when we make it outside and Zane sighs.

"Fuck, that was hot."

"Shut up, Zane," Eldon retorts quickly, but the snicker in his tone tells me he's not in complete disagreement with his friend.

All of the carriages have gone and, to our left, gateways are lined up. Those who can escape flee swiftly, while other students are left sobbing beside them, unable to follow their families home. Most of them don't even look back to console their children. They're just gone.

Spinning to face Brax, I part my lips, but Zane speaks first. "Get us home, Stoneman."

Brax rolls his eyes at the nickname thrown his way, but he still waves us to a quiet corner, hidden in an alcove of the academy building, where he creates his own gateway. I step through without hesitation, both relieved and worried at the familiar sight of our home that comes into view around me.

My feet hurt from not wearing shoes, but I feel too antsy to sit on the sofa and ease the discomfort. Creed steps past me, almost as though he's in a trance as he comes to a stop at the glass doors at the back of the house, looking out into the darkness.

"What now?" Eldon asks as Zane flops down on the sofa to my right, but I don't know how to answer him. My forehead crinkles with worry as I take the necessary steps toward Creed, desperate to pretend my own anxiety doesn't exist so I can focus on him.

"Are you okay?" I ask, knowing it's a pointless question, but I need to hear his voice in some way.

He tucks his hands into his pant pockets and continues to stare outside. "I don't know what I am."

Fuck. My heart clenches, threatening to take my last breath as helplessness claws at me, but I tamp it down, keeping my attention on him.

"I can't imagine what you're feeling right now." I reach up to tuck his hair behind his ear and he glances at me out of the corner of his eye as a heavy sigh rumbles from his chest.

"That's the issue, Raven. I don't feel anything. I'm just… numb."

"We don't have to just accept this, you know. We can demand answers, a war, whatever we want," Brax states, and Creed instantly shakes his head.

"We can't act rashly."

Fuck. Wouldn't we all like to, though? Direct all of the pain and anger we're feeling inside at those who deserve it.

"Tomorrow is a new dawn. You know we'll face everything together," Zane murmurs, his words empowering in comparison to his usual humor, making my chest puff out.

"Why does it feel like we're going to be waking up in the pits of Hell?" Brax asks, rubbing at the back of his neck, and I can't help but agree. The anticipation of what comes next, after being completely blindsided, is twisting me in knots.

"Maybe we should try and sleep. We're going to need all of our energy for whatever's next," Creed says, turning away from the window to place his hand on my back, and I immediately lean into his touch.

Everybody agrees with him as I nibble on my bottom lip. It's only when onyx eyes peer down at me that he notices I haven't responded. "What's wrong, Raven?"

I feel like a fool saying it, but damn…

"Can you guys stay with me? I don't want to be alone." Not when I exhibited the magic I'm capable of. Not to some people I trust either, but to everyone. Friends, family, and enemies alike. I just made myself their weapon whether I like it or not.

Without missing a beat, all four of them say the same word in sync with one another, confirming that, with them, I'll get through anything.

"Always."

THREE

Raven

Darkness seeps into my vision, painting everything black as the ground disappears beneath my feet, and a vortex swirls me around.

Disoriented, I don't know which way is up as shadows begin to spill from the vortex one at a time, getting larger and more prominent with every passing breath. I open my mouth to tell them to stop, but nothing comes out. They're uncontrolled, unrelenting, and manic.

My heart races faster and faster as I try to calm the impending doom that looms over me. It squeezes my chest so tight, I'm sure I'm about to pass out, but just as I expect to fall into nothingness, my magic comes alive in my veins. The purple orb inside of me grows until my hands whoosh out at my sides, palms up as if to stop the madness.

"Stop!" I yell, my vision clearing as an odd sense of

calmness washes over me. Finally, I take a deep breath, and the largest shadow of them all comes racing toward me. It reaches for my face, but before it can touch me, my eyes ping open and I startle awake.

My palm falls flat against my chest, my heart racing just as fast in real life as it was in my dream. Looking up at the ceiling, I try to loosen the constricting grip that the shadows have on me. The sheets shuffle beside me, startling me from my thoughts, and I tilt my head to find Zane's sleeping form.

The memory of last night comes rushing back. After everything that happened, we decided it was better to be together than in our separate rooms. Which is why I now have a new bed that's been adjusted to suit all of us in my room. On the other side of Zane lies Brax, and when I glance to my right, Eldon and Creed are spread out, too.

None of them raised any concerns when I asked for us to sleep together, fear clawing at me at the thought of being alone, and to my surprise, I managed to fall asleep quite easily. Staying asleep, however, seems to be another issue. A recurring one that clings to me whether I like it or not.

Taking a deep breath, I try to let my eyelids fall heavily again, but the fresh wave of adrenaline heating my body is making it nearly impossible. Movement on the far wall catches my attention and, a moment later, the room is drenched in shadows and dark silhouettes, just like my dreams.

They dance along the walls, over the bedsheets, and over the ceiling. There's no sound, there never is, but if there was, I can only imagine a murmur of giggles or snarls, both leaving me uneasy with the unpredictability this all brings.

It's strange watching them. It's like I can't breathe, but at this exact moment, I don't feel scared by their presence.

"Are you okay, Dove?"

I startle at Zane's question, glancing back at him with a tentative smile.

"Yeah, I just…" My words trail off as I wave my hand around the room, looking back at the outlines swooping across the ceiling.

"What?"

My eyebrows pinch in confusion and I turn to look back at him. Realization washes over me, and I gulp. "You can't see them, can you?"

His hand reaches for mine, squeezing in comfort as the puzzled look remains on his face.

"See what?" Two words, and it's all the confirmation I need. I clench my eyes closed, taking a deep breath. "Raven?" he pushes, still unsure of what has me all twisted inside.

"The shadows, the silhouettes, the darkness. You can't see any of it."

"Where?"

I pry my eyes back open to look at him in the darkness of the room. "Everywhere."

"Where is everywhere?" he asks, concern rich in his voice.

I wave my hand around the room. His eyes trace every inch of the space, but I know he doesn't see any of it.

"Do you feel like you're in any danger?" he finally questions when he's swept his gaze over the room enough times to know that he can't see what I see.

"No."

"Are we assuming it's connected to your magic? We know it's a struggle for necromancers, the darkness I mean, is this it?" My teeth sink into my bottom lip as I consider his question and, in reality, it's the only viable explanation. It all started after I saved Brax. It became less frequent in the past week or so, but having healed Burton last night, they're back in full force. I finally nod and his hand clenches tighter around mine. "Then we have to trust in it."

"After last night, I don't want to think what will happen with my magic, how dark and twisted my dreams and reality will become at the hands of Erikel," I admit, the words flowing from my mouth without pause. It's the first time I'm letting the truth ring in my ears, and I can't say I like it.

"After last night, Dove, I love you more than ever."

I gulp, his strong words stealing my breath until I manage a rasp. "Why?"

He shifts to his side, releasing my hand to cup my chin. I turn to face him, too, nestling my hands against his chest between us.

"Because you exposed yourself for one of us. No other reason than that. Not to be painted as a warrior goddess on some bullshit white horse riding in to save the day. But you laid yourself on the line for Creed, just like any of us would do for you, which is why it doesn't bother me that I mention love and you don't say it back."

Guilt twists my gut, disappointment in myself getting the better of me, but he has to understand. I've never uttered that word in my life. Not to my papa when I was small, not to my mama. No one. Plus, growing up in Shadowmoor, there was no desire to grow attached to anyone because death was waiting just around the corner. I guess that's the same here too, but the four of them left me no choice.

I feel it. I know I do. It warms my chest and makes my heart skip a beat, but saying it out loud? I don't know how.

"It doesn't bother you?" I ask, my voice heavy with clogged-up emotions, and I watch him shake his head as his thumb strokes across my cheek.

"I would love to hear those words slip from your lips, Raven, but your actions always speak louder. That's all I need. Now sleep, I've got you. I've always got you."

Exhaustion clings to me as my limbs unwind from the fetal position, stretching in every direction as a low groan bites past my lips.

Fuck, I'm tired.

The memory of Zane's words last night before I drifted back to sleep wrapped in the safety of his arms warms my heart as I blink awake, only to find the room empty. Not a single one of my men is filling the bed with me. Yet, despite its size, it feels snug and cozy with the remnants of their scents still clinging to the sheets.

Sighing, it feels strange to hear a hint of contentment in the noise in comparison to the usual frustration, and I curl deeper into the sheets. A beat passes when the bedroom door creaks open and Eldon appears in the open space.

"Good morning, Little Bird. How are you feeling? Zane mentioned you had a bit of a rough night, so we wanted to let you sleep as late as possible."

I smile at him, taking in his shirtless appearance, appreciating the way his shorts hang loose at his waist and the added ruffles to his hair that make me want to run my fingers through it.

"I'm good." And I am. Right now, at least.

"Good. Breakfast is ready, come and eat with us."

My stomach predictably chooses that moment to groan with hunger. Kicking the sheets off, I crawl to the end of the huge bed before sitting on my ass and swinging my legs over the side. "Fuck, Little Bird. Watching you crawl like that does things I can't even explain."

I grin at him while wagging my finger. "I'm in my badass independent era right now. If you ask me to crawl to you like a good girl, I will likely tell you to fuck off. Mention it again next week and I might just want to feel the bite of the floor against my knees." I wink and his head falls back with a groan as he readjusts his cock, the outline more than visible through his shorts.

"You're a fucking menace. Get out here. Now."

He gives me a pointed stare as he tilts his head and I stand, quickly cutting the distance between us so he can wrap me in his arms. I cling to his warmth, letting him fill my energy back up with a single touch before he leads me toward the dining table where the others are seated.

Brax is already digging into the eggs and bacon on his plate. Creed is shuffling it around with his fork, taking the occasional mouthful, while Zane seems to be talking away on some kind of device. Eldon pulls my chair out and I take my seat, the cool touch of the chair against my exposed thighs making me shiver.

I really need to start wearing more than just an oversized tee, especially since it seems to be getting cooler around here.

Eldon presses a kiss to my temple before dropping into his seat beside me and I take a bite of the bacon on my plate as I listen to Zane speak.

"Honestly, Pops, you did the right thing. We need to be looking at this situation from both angles. That involves someone being on the outside and someone being on the inside."

"I would rather it was me on the inside and you farther away from the danger."

Of course he would. Rhys has always seemed hands-on and loving with Zane, I can't imagine him wanting to leave his child in such a vulnerable position.

"I know, but we didn't get to pull the strings on this one. The enemy never gives us a choice. You know that."

"I know. That doesn't mean I have to like it, though."

"None of us do, Denver, but that doesn't stop us from fighting," Brax states before taking another forkful of egg.

"Morning, Brax. Is everyone else there too?"

"Yeah," Zane confirms with a nod, even though his father can't see him.

"And Raven?" Rhys asks.

"She's here too."

"Good. Let me talk with her."

Zane offers me the device without another word and I can't deny the slight tingle of anticipation as I take it from his grasp.

"Hi," I breathe, my voice quiet, and Eldon places his hand on my thigh, filling me with more confidence.

"How are you this morning, Raven?"

"I'm good."

"For now," Rhys states, completing the sentence based on his own conclusions, and I can't say that his assumption is wrong. "I've put some feelers out and ensured that Burton is prepared to go to the lengths I am while I'm not there. We want you as protected as possible, but we can't guarantee any outcome, so I need you to be completely alert and on guard at all times. None of us have any history with Erikel, so we don't know how he operates, but from what I've seen so far, he's unpredictable."

"I agree," I murmur, my chest tightening at the memory of last night again. "What did you mean about Burton? About him going to the lengths you would?" I feel stupid asking, but nothing makes sense to me right now, either.

"We protect you at all costs, Raven. All. Costs."

My heart races as my gaze locks on Zane's. Rhys's words sound just as solid as his son's did last night. It's clear where he gets his intensity from.

"Why?" I breathe, needing to hear from his lips that

he's not trying to protect me so that I can become a weapon for him instead. I know that's not the case with complete certainty, but I need to know his reasoning.

"Because my son says so."

CURSED SHADOWS

FOUR

Raven

"**A**re we supposed to continue classes as normal? Like yesterday didn't happen at all?" I ask, needing to hear Zane reconfirm for the hundredth time. I've never heard so much bullshit in my life, but if that's what Erikel declared yesterday, then that's what we'll all do now as his puppets.

Fuck.

"Dove, you know the answer to that. Now, we need to head out before we cause any more of a stir."

My eyebrows rise at his statement. "I wasn't aware I had caused a stir already." I drop my hands to my hips as I give him a pointed look, but my efforts are completely lost on him.

"So you don't think the fact that there's a necromancer on campus is going to cause mayhem?" He cocks his brow back at me, and I wave him off.

"He's right, Shadow. Genie had to be the first to try and knock you back last night, of course, but what is startlingly real to everyone at the academy now is that there is someone undoubtedly more powerful than them. And I don't mean Erikel before you try that crap," Brax states, making me pout.

I don't like feeling outnumbered. Especially when I'm not the one in the right.

Fuckers.

I look to Eldon and Creed, who are hovering at the front door, and when they choose to look anywhere around the room but at me, I know they're siding with Brax and Zane. Typical.

Sighing dramatically, I run my hands over my academy-issued blazer and skirt. "Fine." Before I can say another word, a knock sounds from the door, sending a shiver of uncertainty down my spine as the Bishops stiffen, their eyes sharpening as they become more alert.

Eldon nods for me to move out of sight from the door, only grabbing the handle once he's sure I'm out of eyesight.

"Hey, where's Raven?" My shoulders sag in relief at the sound of Leila's voice and I rush to Eldon's side. She smiles when she sees me, a sense of ease seemingly washing over her features.

"Sorry, I know we haven't really been doing this lately,

I just…" Her words trail off as she waves her hands at her sides.

"No, you're good," I reply as I step over the threshold to walk beside her.

"I'm surprised *Daddy* has let you out of his sight," Brax blurts, making my eyes widen in surprise as the Bishops swarm us. Leila doesn't miss a beat, though, she simply nods toward the end of our pathway to reveal Professor Fitch waiting. There's a deep scowl on his face, his arms are folded over his chest, and I'm sure there's an extra weapon at his waist that I've never seen before. "Well, then I'm surprised he let you steer from the path and come down here instead of playing it safe and heading straight to class," Brax relentlessly continues, but again, Leila brushes him off with a shrug.

"It was on Burton's orders."

Damn.

My chest clenches at the realization that they're definitely taking this as seriously as Rhys said they were. I don't even know what to say, so I opt to say nothing, falling into step with Professor Fitch as we take the pathway toward the academy.

The dark and muted sky continues to mask the usually pretty clouds and I can't help but wonder if this has something to do with Erikel. I don't recall it ever being like this until he got here.

No one speaks, not even Leila as she keeps close to my side. A few students move around us to get to class, too, each one side-eyeing me like I've either slapped them in the face or hurt their feelings somehow. I'm already desperate for today to be over. I think I would rather handle Erikel than this drama. I don't owe these people anything and I'm more than willing to aid them in fucking off out of my sight.

As we near the double-doored entrance into the academy building, the crowd thickens and our steps slow. Once we've integrated into the gathered student body, it doesn't take long to realize what the hold-up is.

Erikel.

Fuck. Fuck. Fuck.

He's blocking the entrance with the students he brought with him, making it impossible for anyone to get past. The students are wearing the same uniform as they've been in every day, a complete contrast to our blazers and pressed pants or skirts. Instead, they look ready for the Battalion with their black-on-black outfits and sheaths.

"Good morning, Basilica," Erikel projects, sending an overwhelming burst of fear across the crowd. He's not in Basilica, not now, and he knows it. This is just another part of his elaborate plan and I have no care for it.

Shouldering through the crowd, Creed grips my hand, trying to pull me back a step or two, but the man of the hour locks eyes with me and the fake smile on his face becomes more genuine.

"My little shadow dancer, I've been waiting for you."

"I'm not your anything," I bite, nostrils flaring with an instinctive bout of anger. My rage only seems to fuel his delight, which, in turn, makes me even more furious.

"We shall see," he murmurs, waving his hand for the sea of students between us to part. Without a word, they do, but once the pathway is clear between us, not one of us moves closer to the other. "You've seen little of this world, I assume."

I don't bother with a response as I continue to look at him with a neutral expression. The anticipation and worry kick up a notch around us with every passing second, but no one dares move. I'm quite sure there are a few people present who aren't even breathing at this moment.

The student to his right flexes his biceps, stretching out his back as he eyes me. I catch the movement out of the corner of my eye, but I still don't move. I've spent long enough being in uncomfortable positions. I'm more than happy to bask in awkward silence.

"Are we done here?" The student to Erikel's left asks, rolling his neck as he glances at his leader, and Erikel's mood sours. Not at his student, though, at me. His lip curls in anger as he takes a step toward me, a ring of gasps echoing around us as everyone watches him. Erikel doesn't inch any closer, though. That one step is all he's willing to take, but it's still one more than me.

"You'll do as I say. You're *my* little puppet," he grunts, pointing a slightly crooked finger in my direction. "I know exactly who to hurt if you don't follow my orders," he adds, his eyes glancing from one Bishop to another, and my gut clenches at the foolishness I displayed last night.

Fuck.

I never should have let him see my weaknesses, but I was caught up in the moment, in ultra-protective mode, and there's nothing I can do to change that now.

My teeth grind as my shoulders stiffen, but I keep my mouth shut, not giving him the taste of my anger that he so desperately seems to crave. He tugs at the ends of the cloak at his shoulders as he addresses the sea of people.

"Classes will continue as normal for now. You're dismissed. Until I call for you." His eyes find mine once more and the threat is clear. However, something tells me that the threat is going to become a promise quicker than I would like. "You may find the topics have shifted slightly," he adds, a knowing smirk on his face, irritating me even more.

"And Burton?" someone asks from the crowd, and Erikel smirks.

"Is still breathing. For now, at least."

I've never detested someone more than I do this man

right now, and that's saying something when there's Abel and Sebastian to consider. Thinking of Sebastian, I glance around the crowd, but he's noticeably absent. I can't decide if that's a good or bad thing. Genie, however, is leading the students into the academy as Erikel steps aside.

"I want to do is set him on fire and watch him burn until all that remains are a few embers flickering in the wind," Eldon snarls, and I nod eagerly in agreement. I could get down with that, but it's already clear that it's not going to be as simple as that. You don't come barreling into the Elevin Realm's most prestigious academy without pre-empting their magical abilities.

"Soon," I promise, eager to get the hell out of here. Instead, we fall into step with the other students filtering into the academy. We've barely reached the doors when the thunderous sound of metal hitting stone vibrates and echoes around us, and a moment later, Erikel's warrior appears before us. He's still dressed in his golden armor, stained with an array of red hues, and his gaze is fixed on Creed.

"Follow me," he rasps, turning to the right and walking around the outside of the academy building. The five of us instantly follow after him. I can see the uncertainty on Creed's face, but I'm sure there are a lot of questions he's got building up inside.

We don't make it two steps, though, before the warrior

glances back over his shoulder with a deathly stare that casts over each of us before settling on Creed.

"No. Just you."

CURSED SHADOWS

FIVE

Creed

I was eight years old when they stood on my doorstep and declared my father was gone.

Just gone.

Along with his squadron. Decimated, unidentifiable, that's what they told my mother. I remember hearing the words as though it had happened months ago. That's what I get for being a curious child with silent and stealthy footsteps that allowed me to go unheard so I could eavesdrop and observe anything and everything I wanted.

Seeing him yesterday was like an arrow to the heart; one of complete awe for five whole seconds. I'd recognize his presence anywhere. The way he dominated a room by simply breathing. It was like he had never left at all.

But he had. And with the enemy, no less.

Now, he's standing a few steps before me, demanding

I follow him alone, and as much as I want to cause a scene, demand this man explain everything to me in front of anyone willing to watch, the other part of me is that same eight-year-old boy that followed this man around like his shadow.

Glancing over my shoulder, my gaze falls to Raven first, watching as anger taints her cheeks pink and her fists clench at her sides. Fuck. She's everything. It was clear last night that I don't deserve her and what she did for me; how she willingly exposed herself to keep me out of harm's way.

I'll never deserve her. Ever. But that won't stop me from keeping her anyway. I'm just going to have to give her every piece of me and more in return.

"I'll be okay, Raven. I'll meet you guys in class."

Her eyebrows pinch at my words and she moves to take a step toward me, but Eldon swings an arm around her shoulders before she can get too far and guides her toward the double doors. I don't move an inch until she's in the academy building along with my brothers. Only then do I turn back to my father to find he's continued moving.

I don't rush to catch up with him. I've been unknowingly waiting for over ten years. He can wait an extra ten seconds.

He doesn't choose to slip inside anywhere. Instead, he stays out in the open, coming to a stop under a large oak tree.

My heart starts to race as I get closer, my chest tightening like a vice as I stand head-on with him. The awe I have cherished in my soul over the memory of this man is tainted by the realization of who and what he is now as I look up at him. I know I'm struggling to see the difference in him. Looking into deep onyx eyes that match my own, he's the man I loved deeply for as long as I can remember, but when my gaze travels down the length of him, taking in his crimson-stained gold armor, I know he's not the man who left.

He's always been a soldier of the Realm, a well-respected man among The Monarchy for the efforts he put into protecting Elevin. Yet he's here with the enemy, ready to take down the academy that proudly stands on the lands he once fought for. I don't understand. I don't think I ever will. But that could likely be because I'm still locked on to the fact that he's here. Breathing. Alive. Real.

When my eyes reach his once again, he grinds his jaw and the wrinkles around his eyes deepen for a brief moment. "Creed." My name is raspy on his tongue.

"So you do know who I am then," I state, a glimmer of Raven's sass rubbing off on me as I cock a brow at him.

"My loyalties may have changed but my knowledge of my family has not."

What the fuck is that supposed to mean? His loyalties changed? When? Why? How? Questions spin in my mind but I can't piece my thoughts and feelings into any semblance of a question that might help me understand.

"We were told you were dead," I grind out instead, still hearing my mother's sobs in my thoughts. From that fateful day ten years ago, and last night too. Her hurt and pain at this man's actions reverberate inside of me.

"I assumed as much."

I scoff. "You assumed, huh? And *that* makes it all okay?" Irritation claws at my insides, fury trickling down my spine as my magic zings through my veins.

"Unfortunately, Creed, there is more to this world than just our feelings."

"Have you always spoken so cryptically? Or is this a new thing you've picked up in the Basilica Realm?" I snap, desperate to reach out and shake some damn sense into this man.

"I didn't bring you aside to discuss emotions, Creed."

My nostrils flare as I try to take a calming breath, but it's futile. "I don't know what else you would expect from me. If you don't care about how you made everyone feel when you played dead for the past ten years, then please, enlighten me as to what it is you would like to say."

His arm creaks as he adjusts his stance, hands flexing at his sides as he looks off into the distance for a second before settling back on me. "My loyalty lies with Erikel and the Basilica Realm. Your presence here doesn't change any of that. You need to stay in line, follow orders, and not get in the way of what it is we're here to do."

"What *are* you here to do?" I ask, still desperately wanting something... more from him.

"That's irrelevant. Do as I say. Otherwise, your death could be demanded. At my hands."

His pupils shrink just a fraction, it's barely noticeable, but I see it. Despite all his big talk, he fucking cares. He must. Otherwise, why would we be having this conversation right now?

"Would that not hurt you at all? Killing your only child?" I want to spell it out to him, make him feel something, *anything*, more than this. I'm burning on the inside, he deserves to feel that too.

"Let's hope we don't have to find out," he retorts before taking a step away from me, dismissing the conversation before it can go any further. I don't move, watching as he leaves, but after he takes a few steps, he glances back to look at me. "You would be safer away from the necromancer too." He doesn't wait for my response. He continues to walk away just as easily as he seemed to last time.

Safer away from the necromancer? From Raven? Never. That's exactly where my loyalties lie. Fuck Basilica. Fuck Elevin. Fuck Silvercrest. My loyalty, my everything, it all rests with her and my brothers.

Swiping a hand down my face, I spin back to the main

building and notice Erikel in the far distance, watching me. He was obviously watching the interaction between my father and me. Why? I don't know. Maybe he is monitoring his trusty sword, but he doesn't have anything to worry about. That man is Basilica's mighty warrior more than he is my father.

Maybe it would be better if he really was dead. Then, my heart could still idolize my childhood hero instead of tearing it all to shreds in the form of the man standing before me.

Silence echoes in my ears as my pulse flickers harsh and fast. The company of just the air around me once brought solace and calmness, but today, it's turned the walk to the locker room into a war in my mind.

Chatter and murmurs quickly eliminate the silence claiming me as I head inside. A few of the guys glance in my direction but no one says a word. Zane spots me first as I stop beside him, pressing my thumb into the hanger as Eldon's eyes catch mine.

I can sense the worry and concern around them, but I don't have it in me to console them right now. Instead, I focus on getting changed. Thankfully, my brothers give me the space I need to do so, but I should have known it wouldn't last much longer. The second I'm ready to head out, Zane steps in front of me so I have to meet his stare.

"Is everything okay?"

"I'm fine," I grumble with a sigh, the irritation clear in my voice.

Zane's eyebrows furrow deeper as he plants his hand on my shoulder but I shake him off. "You know you can always—"

"I said I'm fine," I interrupt, in no mood for his pep talk.

"That's cool, man," Eldon says calmly, appearing beside Zane. "I get it, it's all a lot to take in and none of us can imagine what you're going through right now. It's going to take a minute for you to figure it out for yourself before you can even piece it together to share with us. So, you can be gruff and shit with us, that's all good." I don't respond but my shoulders relax ever so slightly. "But what you don't get to do is use that same tone with Raven. We all know she's going to be worried, as she's a protector. She's going to want to make everything okay for you."

"I wouldn't," I balk, my muscles bunching at the thought.

"I'm just being sure," Eldon states, patting my shoulder before taking a step back.

Fuck.

Turning for the door, I head out without a backward

glance. Using the smallest reprieve of silence to get my shit together before I see her. As if sensing herself in my thoughts, her gaze latches on to me the second I step outside. A ray of light peeks through the clouds for the first time in days and lands right on her.

It intensifies the worry in her blue irises as her eyes pinch. Leila is talking beside her but her words are completely lost on Raven, who is solely focused on me. I stride toward her, almost barreling her over as I come to a stop, cupping her cheek as I invade her space.

Eldon is right. No matter what I'm feeling, Raven doesn't deserve any of my wrath or misplaced anger.

"I'm okay," I breathe, attempting to calm her concern. "He just wanted to be clear where his loyalties lie," I admit, the words falling from my mouth without thought, but now that they're out there, swirling between us, I'm not upset about it.

"With them," she murmurs, a statement, not a question, and I nod in agreement.

Her hand finds mine at my side, squeezing tight as I stroke my thumb over her cheek. The rest of the students around us disappear. It's just me and her, basking in a little ray of sunshine for the smallest of moments, but it clenches my heart.

"We've got you, Creed. Always."

"I know."

She pushes up on her tiptoes and caresses my lips with her own. My soul settles, my body relaxes, and a different kind of need takes over me, but she's stepping back far too quickly for me to turn it into more.

I couldn't give a shit who is around us right now.

I just need her.

"Let's go," she murmurs, tugging at my hand, and we fall into step with my brothers and Leila.

Following the crowd, we head toward the patch of grass that is framed by the forest at the side of the lake. Murmurs fade to silence and a different kind of tension washes over the space.

"Where's your feather, Leila?" Brax asks, and we all turn to look at her. It's only then that I notice her eyes are a little red, but before she can open her mouth, a clap garners everyone's attention.

Five of the students from Basilica's institute stand in a line, dressed in their usual gear that almost seems like armor.

"Let's get this class started, shall we?" the guy in the middle calls out, a sneer tipping his lip up.

"Where's Professor Fitch?" Genie asks, more curious than anything, with a smile teasing her mouth.

"This is no longer his class," he states, and I quickly glance at Leila, who is staring down at the grass.

"Then whose is it?" Genie presses, making the guy in

the middle sneer even more, but the other student to his left smiles wide.

"Ours."

"And what does that entail?" Zane hollers, arms folded over his chest.

"You clearly need some more battle experience, and your poor excuse of a gauntlet isn't up to it."

"What do you have planned instead?" Zane pushes, eager for them to get to the point.

"A hunt."

"A hunt?" Genie echoes, uncertainty washing over each of us as we wait for a better explanation.

"Yeah. You need to survive one hour in the forest without being killed by one of us."

"You're going to kill us?" Genie screeches, hand flying to her chest as she takes a step back.

"Yeah." Gasps echo around us and Raven's hand clenches tighter around mine. "But don't worry, we've got a necromancer to bring you back to life again and again so we can continue the chase until your sixty minutes are up."

CURSED SHADOWS

SIX

Raven

If any of these fuckers die, I'll bring them back just to kill them myself. Erikel's men are just as crazy as he is if they think they can manipulate and control me at their will.

My chest clenches with a sense of panic nestling deep into my bones. I knew they would make a point of me being a necromancer, but not in this way. Not so stupidly and wastefully.

Before I can even consider giving the guy in the middle a piece of my mind, a siren blares, echoing around us and rustling the trees as birds take flight in every direction, trying to avoid the impending danger coming their way.

Every other student takes off as fast as they can, running full out into the forest, glancing over their shoulders every few seconds to see if they're being chased. The energy is practically static around us, anticipation running high as Erikel's men smirk with triumph. They know they've stoked the fears of the students, which gives them more control.

"I don't want to, but we should join them. We can think about this more when we're out of sight," Eldon states, and as much as I don't like the idea of it, I know there's no better alternative.

I nod, unable to use any words, before turning for the tree line like the others and taking off. Only, I don't glance back over my shoulder to check the enemy's proximity. Instead, I settle into my magic, hoping like hell I'll be able to sense any of their abilities coming my way.

Leila remains wordless at my side. I'm shocked that her father didn't pull her from this class. He's been so overprotective in other areas that it's surprising he would allow her to potentially die at their hands.

Rushing past the first line of trees, shrills of panic squeak from some of the students around us as they stumble over protruding tree roots, while others pant with every breath. We continue deeper into the forest until the deep-green leaves block out most of the sunlight, leaving it even darker than usual.

"Over there," Leila says, pointing toward a fallen tree with its roots sticking out in every direction. I follow after her, which, in turn, has the Bishops doing the same. She slows as we near the tree, bracing her hands on the bark as she catches her breath. "With the hole left in the ground, I can ice us in and create a protective barrier. There might only be space for two, though." She keeps her eyes fixed on me, making it clear who the second person is, but I shake my head.

"Not a chance in hell is she being separated from me," Zane grunts, grabbing my hand. Leila's eyebrows furrow with concern, but I offer her a reassuring smile.

"Do it for you. Do what you need to do to be safe and we'll find you when the time is up," I state, watching as she worries at her bottom lip. She nods nervously and I take a step back.

"Are you sure? I can stay with you guys," she offers, but Zane shakes his head.

"What you're going to do will work to protect you. Do it quickly before we continue on," he orders, and she nods with a sigh as she steps down into the exposed ground.

It takes her a few moments to get comfortable before a thick layer of ice forms over her, sealing her inside. Then another, and another, until she's built her own mini fortress. I give it an extra beat before I take a step back, and Brax takes off, guiding the way as we continue deeper into the forest.

A scream ripples through the air from behind us, making me pause as the telltale sound of flames whipping in the wind follows before a tree sets alight, flashing in an array of oranges and reds. Laughter sounds out a moment later and Erikel's men can be heard in the distance.

"One down, how many to follow?"

Fuckers.

Zane squeezes my hand, silently urging me to continue on, and we quickly fall into step again.

"If we can find somewhere less trodden and as quiet as possible, I may be able to focus my magic and try to hide us," he states, and my eyes widen as I glance up at him while continuing to hurry along. "Leila had a good idea, it just wasn't big enough, and there was no way I was trusting you in someone else's hands when I'm right here," he states, repeating his thoughts from earlier.

"Do you think you can expand your magic to make all of us invisible?" Creed asks, and I finally catch on to Zane's idea.

"I think so," he replies confidently, leaving me speechless.

"Over here," Brax calls out, waving us forward, and we move even quicker. Eldon gets to him first, with Creed a few steps behind him, leaving Zane and me bringing up the rear when I'm suddenly knocked off my feet and my hand slips from his.

I hit the ground with a thud, the wind completely knocked out of my sails as I stare up at the leaves blowing in the breeze in a daze. Pressing my palms into the earth beneath me, I take a stuttering breath and try to rise, but it's like I'm pushing against a vortex of wind that is pinning me in place.

"Raven!" I can hear the Bishops holler my name, but I can't see them, which spikes my worry and adrenaline all at once.

Surely it can't be Erikel's men. If there's one thing I took from their little speech, it's that I won't die at their hands because they need me. Unless they want to hold me in place so I can be their weapon, but why not do that sooner?

Attempting another, deeper breath, I try to push against the invisible force on top of me, but it's useless until I see the smallest string of magic dancing above me. Focusing on the small thread, I follow it all the way to a tree off to the left, where I find the culprit behind this.

"Sebastian," I holler, hoping to alert the Bishops as the pressure falls heavier on me. "It's Sebastian," I repeat, trying to lift my hand so I can touch the string of magic, but they're dead weight at my sides.

Fuck.

Why is he even here? This isn't his class.

Clenching my eyes shut, I channel all of my strength into my arms, desperate to grasp his magic in my hands. When I can't even move an inch, I snarl in frustration, blinking my eyes open to a grunt that echoes through the trees around me. I catch sight of Eldon flying through the air before he slams into the tree to my right with a *thud*, and my heart clenches.

What the fuck?

The move was too quick for me to catch the trail of magic, but my gut tells me it's still Sebastian I need to be concerned with. Anger at Eldon being hurt fuels me, vibrating through my veins as I try to move again.

Glaring at Sebastian, I notice another trail of magic lingering around his head and trailing off deeper into the forest where I can't see. What the fuck is that about? It doesn't matter. What matters is getting out of his hold.

His eyes cast back to me, a smirk on his lips as triumph flickers across his face.

I don't just hate this man, my blood, my supposed family. I fucking loathe him.

My nostrils flare as I fail to hide how he affects me when he topples forward with force, smashing into the ground face first as the weight holding me down suddenly disappears.

Scurrying to my feet, I don't bother trying to wipe the dirt from me as I take off in his direction. That's when Zane appears out of thin air, a step behind the motherfucker, with a smug grin of his own spreading across his face.

"Someone's helping him," Creed states, falling into

step with me. "I was trying to get into his mind, but it was impossible, like there was a wall there."

Fuck.

"That must have been the trail of magic I saw hovering around his head," I explain, almost tripping over a fallen branch in my hurry.

Zane remains in his stance and I catch a glimpse of Brax barreling toward Sebastian, but I freeze on the spot, remembering Eldon's slumped body against the tree. Spinning, I turn and instantly sag in relief when I see him racing toward me.

I slip on a damp patch of moss when I turn back to Sebastian in time to see Brax slam his fist into his face. I hear the crunch of his nose breaking beneath Brax's stone fist, but it's clear that's not enough for my gargoyle as he continues to pummel him with hit after hit.

Shit.

"Brax, no!" I shout, but I go unheard.

Rushing toward him, I go to grab his shoulder, but Creed quickly intercepts. "You'll get hurt."

"It will hurt me more if he kills the fucker and I have to bring him back."

The slamming stops, the groans from Sebastian garbled as Brax looks over his shoulder at me. His eyes are vivid. One brown. One green. Both wild with rage. "I warned this asshole if he attempted to come at you again, I'd kill him," he grunts, and I drop to my knees beside him.

"I know, you're as unhinged as this guy," I murmur, blindly pointing at Creed behind me.

"That guy got to kill that dick in Shadowmoor," Brax remarks, his jaw ticking as his thick stone fingers ball into fists again. He remains over Sebastian, desperate to have his blood staining his hands.

"If you do it now, it won't be permanent."

"How would they know he was here?" Eldon interjects, making Brax nod eagerly. Clearly, neither of them are thinking straight.

"Because we know he's with Erikel, just as his men are. How else would he know where to find us?" My heart races in my chest as a scream rings out in the distance. Sadness prickles its way to the surface and I know my magic is aware of another life gone.

Looking down at Sebastian, I push up to my feet. "He doesn't deserve the possibility of my magic helping him."

Zane grabs my hand, instantly dragging his thumb over my knuckles in a soothing gesture. "She's right. We need to get the hell out of here."

I wait with bated breath as Brax stares down at Sebastian squirming beneath him, blood splattered across his face and his nose completely out of place. With a heavy sigh, my gargoyle rises to his feet, returning his fists to flesh and bone once again before he stalks off.

Another yelp of pain rings out around us, hastening our pace. If I knew I could face these fuckers and not have to revive them, I would, without question, but I really don't want to give them the satisfaction. Although, they do deserve to be knocked down, and I would relish in the wonder of being the one to do it.

I can't help but peek back over my shoulder at Sebastian, only to find him rolling to his side. I scan the area, expecting the person who helped him avoid Creed's magic to come to his aid, but he's still all alone.

When you're toxic to the world, and the time comes, the world will be toxic to you too.

Zane squeezes my hand at the same time Eldon laces his fingers with mine on the other side. I don't know how they're expecting me to run like this, but thankfully, it's because Brax is heading into a small caved area. Slowing to a brisk walk, I falter at the opening to the slightly hidden structure among the trees and shrubbery.

"Doesn't it feel a little too good to be true that there's a cave here?" I ask, and Brax glances back at me with his brow cocked.

"I wasn't aimlessly walking through the woods, Shadow. I was getting us here."

Oh. Well. That makes sense then, I guess. I thought we were just blindly going with it like everyone else seemed to be.

I feel Creed right behind me, his lips by my ear. "Inside, Raven."

Nodding, I follow Brax's lead, and as we get deeper into the dark space, a flame appears in Eldon's palm, glowing bright enough to light the way. When we reach the end, I glance back at the entrance. It's still visible from here, barely, and with the way the shadows cascade around the stone walls, I don't think you would even be able to see the glow of light from out there.

"Zane, can you try to cover our tracks while we're in here as well?" Creed asks. "I'll sit somewhere and focus on trying to hear anyone coming."

"We're not going to hear footsteps from inside here," I state, and the smallest smile touches the corner of his lips as his onyx eyes shine.

"I'm going to be listening for thoughts, Raven. Not footsteps," he clarifies, and I nod dumbly. Apparently, adjusting to academy life is easier than remembering that we can use magic when life and death aren't on the line. I'm not used to thinking outside of the box like that, and that's where I need to adjust.

Zane brings my hand to his lips, softly kissing my knuckles before he moves a little more toward the opening. Eldon presses his lips against my temple. "I'll go and give him some light while he focuses, Little Bird."

The pair of them mumble between themselves about

how Zane is going to project his invisibility to cover us all while Creed gets comfortable against the rock wall that curves to my left.

Rubbing my lips together, I turn back to Brax to find him staring at me. I don't know whether it's because the light from Eldon's flame is farther away, making it dimmer over here, or if his facial features have darkened as he takes me in.

His feet are planted shoulder-width apart, his neck muscles bunched, and his fists are clenched at his side. "I want to go back there and rip his fucking throat out," he snaps, making me sigh.

"I know that, Brax. Believe me, I feel it too, but hear me when I say now isn't the time."

He takes a measured step toward me. "That doesn't change the fury burning in my soul."

"I'm sor—"

"I need him to know that you're mine, that when I threatened his life, I meant it. I need him to know that I will protect you, no matter what, that you will find safety in me, in us, like you never found in them."

Fuck.

My throat bobs, my breath lodged in my lungs.

"He doesn't deserve to know any of that," I rasp, unable to tame my racing heart.

His tongue peeks out, sweeping over his bottom lip as

his gaze somehow darkens further. "I fucking know that, but I want him to anyway. For me, for my selfishness, my stake on you," he states, taking another step toward me. "Now, since you stopped me from having that, you're going to have to give me something else."

Rolling my eyes, I wave him off. "Whatever, name it, and when we get back to the house, you can consider it done." If any man can go from beating someone bloody to killing me with sweet words that consume me, only to piss me off a split second later, it's him.

"No, Shadow. I want that pussy. Now."

My jaw drops as I gape at him, repeating his words in my head again and again, certain that I didn't hear him right, but in the next breath, he's tugging at the waistband of his shorts to reveal his hard, long length.

"We're being hunted, Brax. Hunted like fucking animals, now isn't the time."

He shrugs. "It's either this or I get to go back out there and kill him."

I shake my head as I gape at him. "That's extortion."

The corner of his mouth tips up as he takes another step toward me, using his magic to remove his shorts, discarding them to the side without care. "And yet you're still wet for me."

"I…"

Fuck, I can't even finish that sentence because it would

make me a liar. My thighs became slick with need as soon as he started rambling on about what he wanted his statement to Sebastian to represent. His words made my throat grow dry and my pussy drip. He knows he has a hold on me, pulling me deeper, bringing the darker side out of me to play at the most random of times.

"Tick-tock, Shadow. I don't mind the hunters finding us while I'm dick deep inside of you, but that's up to you because I sure as shit am not stopping until I fill you with my own desire. The clock's ticking."

Fuck just my pussy being wet, I'm a damn puddle.

Glancing over at the others, they're in their own little world protecting us, which should make me feel guilty for even considering this. But damn, his cock is on display and I want to chase away my demons on the end of it.

I sink to the ground in the next moment, the stone beneath me biting into my knees, driving exhilaration through my veins. But as I open my mouth, hinting for him to let me feel the weight of his cock on my tongue, he shakes his head.

"No, Shadow. I'm fucking feral right now and I won't hold back any longer. I want to feel the slickness of your pussy as I stretch you." Holy fucking shit. "On all fours, and get rid of your clothes."

"You get rid of them," I mutter, unable to soften the short sharp breaths making my chest rise and fall rapidly.

"No. Show me that you want this. Show me by following my orders."

Fuck. I would call him insane, but his words are like a siren call.

With my eyes locked on his, I use my magic to discard every piece of material clinging to me. At the same time, he pulls his t-shirt over his head, continuing to challenge me with his gaze.

I take my time turning, the stone sharp against my palms as I lean forward, bracing on all fours as he requested. I'm trembling, and it's not from the chill in the air. It's from the need thrumming through me. My hair cascades over my shoulder as I glance back at him, ghosting over my skin like a soft caress. His eyes rake over every inch of me, heating me on the spot. He drops to his knees with a *thud*, reaching for my hips a lot more delicately than I expect.

"You're taking your time after the big game you just talked," I tease, earning myself a glare as his grip on my skin tightens.

"The prey doesn't usually bait the hunter when it's vulnerable, Shadow," he murmurs, spreading my thighs a little more as he nudges the tip of his cock against my folds, and I gasp.

We really should be focusing on the enemy right now, but it's impossible when he's like this; all-consuming and unwavering.

"Get to the feasting, and we'll find—" My words are cut off, forced into a moan that rumbles my chest as he thrusts inside of me in one swift move. It almost burns, he's spreading me so wide, so fast, and I almost fall forward, but one of his hands comes around my stomach, holding me in place as he stills. I try to catch my breath as he gives us a moment to adjust, but it's not long enough.

He eases out until only the tip remains, making me gasp at the loss before he slams back into me harder and faster. His hand on my stomach shifts to my shoulder, holding me in place, and he doesn't stop this time, slamming into me again and again.

"Fuck." I can barely see with the sex haze fogging my vision combined with the frantic movement, but I spy Eldon's eyes across the space, watching us with awe.

It reminds me of the day he fucked me in the classroom to prove a point, just like Brax is now, but the main point it proves, time and time again, is that they're mine.

All. Mine.

Brax's fingers dig into my skin on the brink of pain, surely leaving bruises in their wake, but I crave it. His thrusts are on the verge of brutal as he takes and takes, my tits bouncing with every slam of his hips against my ass.

"Don't you fucking come, Shadow," Brax bites as my core clenches around him, pleasure rippling through my limbs as the tingle of my climax threatens to wreck my body.

"I'm not going to be able to hold it back even if I wanted to," I pant before his hand comes down on my ass cheek with enough force to have me crying out in a mixture of pain and pleasure.

"This isn't about you, Shadow. Don't. Fucking. Come."

This motherfucker. My hands ball into fists against the stone beneath me. I want to yell at him, give him a piece of my fucking mind, but it all falls short when Creed shouts, "People are near, very near, and time is almost up."

Fuck.

I'm so fucking close.

"Don't even think about it," Brax grunts, slamming into me more vigorously as his dick forces the cadence of my every breath. I feel the moment he hardens to stone inside of me, I sense the moment he pulses but doesn't spill his pleasure, but most of all, I feel his victory in getting what he wants.

I don't know whether I like him or hate him right now.

Which, deep down, is a lie because I know it's neither of those. It definitely starts with an *L* and still finishes with an *E*, but it leaves me way more choked up.

My orgasm still tingles at my nerve endings as he retreats from my core, making me moan with raw need. "You can't leave me like this," I plead, perspiration clinging to my skin.

He steps around me, grabbing my chin and pulling my

gaze to meet him head-on. "You get to come on my dick after I get to slay that fucker," he snarls, making me gasp.

"I don't know when that will be."

"Then neither do I."

Gaping at him, I take a second to focus once again and quickly rush to my feet. "I hate you," I bite.

He's in my face in an instant, his hold on my chin tighter than before as he crowds my space. "No, you don't. Just like I don't hate you, but we're not ready for that yet. So, for now, we'll have to settle on a little delayed gratification."

SEVEN

Raven

I can practically feel my heartbeat in my core, and this asshole is talking about delayed gratification. I can't decide whether throat-punching him or kneeing him in the balls will make me feel any better, but at this stage, it's worth a try.

His breath fans over my face, his closeness overwhelming my senses, and I'm desperate to forgo attacking him and fall into his embrace instead. But this is Brax. That's not how this works. And despite how pent up and electric my body feels, I know he means exactly what he says.

With my gaze fixed on his, falling under the usual spell of one brown, one green, I smile. "Zane," I call out, trying to keep quiet, but I have no idea where he is.

Brax sees the glint in my eyes and knows what I'm up

to. "He's too busy keeping us invisible, Raven. Try again."

Wetting my bottom lip, my tongue brushes against the tip of his thumb. "Eldon."

He's already shaking his head. "He's the one with the little flicker of fire, remember?"

I pout, narrowing my eyes at him as I call out to another of my men. "Creed."

"Is listening to nearby thoughts, Shadow. You're all out of luck and orgasms, it seems." The smirk that spreads across his face has the ability to somehow make him look even more rugged and gorgeous, and I fucking hate it.

A soft breeze along my back sends a shiver down my spine, followed swiftly by a warm presence. "Say the word, Dove, and I'll make us all visible and put my hands on you instead," Zane offers, making my core tighten even further.

That is oh-so-fucking tempting, but until the siren sounds to confirm the end of the class, I need to remember where we are and how vulnerable I already made us by stripping down to nothing at Brax's command.

"I would love nothing more," I breathe as Brax's grip on my chin tightens in warning. "But right now, I should probably get dressed and focus on what we're actually supposed to do. I can come all over your cock later."

Stepping to the side sharply, Brax's grip falls and I turn to see Zane raking his eyes over my naked body.

His eyes are darker, his teeth sinking into his bottom lip, and I'm about to go back on the very words I just said. Until his eyebrows suddenly furrow and he goes to reach out and touch me before remembering if he does, it will likely drop his magic. "You have two strands of black hair now, Dove," he murmurs, confusing me for a second as his words settle in.

Two black strands?

"One for me, and one for Burton," Brax states, and my chest clenches.

"What does it mean?" I breathe, but the look he gives me makes it clear he doesn't have the answer to that. Not yet, at least.

"I've got some people coming up fast. They might not catch us before the siren, which is due to go off at any moment, but we need to be prepared to fight," Creed announces, his voice somehow staying low yet traveling around the space clearly.

Springing into action, I quickly use my magic to dress, exponentially reducing the time of the mundane task. I resecure my hair in a ponytail and head toward where the others are gathered near the entrance of the cave.

A few beats pass before I hear footsteps among the trees, the snapping of twigs underfoot as murmured voices grow louder. My hands flex at my sides and I channel all of my energy into watching for any tendrils of magic drifting in the air.

I'm usually an act now and worry about the consequences later kind of girl, but my magic isn't outwardly aggressive until someone comes at me with their magic for me to turn on them, so I've got to bide my time.

"They had to have gone this way. I'm certain of it." Sebastian. I would know his voice anywhere. It's like a fork being dragged along porcelain, a groan from the pits of Hell and the sound of someone obnoxiously chewing with their mouth wide open all at once.

"I don't know if I've already mentioned it or not, but your brother is a cunt," Eldon grunts from beside me, the flame in his hand lowering to nothing more than an ember.

I fake gasp, placing my hand on my chest. "Sebastian? Never. He's the brother of my dreams."

"You mean nightmares," he quickly retorts with a grin, and that one little jolt of happiness from him eases the growing tension in my chest.

"He wishes." I wink at him playfully at the same time a siren blasts in the distance, signifying the end of the lesson.

"Do you want me to hold out or drop the magic now?" Zane asks, coming to stand on my other side.

"Drop it," Brax states. "We're not hiding from them. We're just playing along with their little game."

I can't explain why, but his words fill me with a boost of confidence, swirling more adrenaline through me as I roll my shoulders back. It's clear the moment Zane drops the magic because his arms are around me a moment later, draping me in his scent and peppering kisses at my neck.

"I said we weren't hiding, I didn't say we could relax," Brax grunts, whacking Zane in the arm, but he only chuckles in response.

"Let's get out of here," Creed murmurs, a tiredness flickering in his eyes as he nods for us to follow after him.

I slip out from between Zane and Eldon, rushing to keep up with him, but I skid to a stop when Sebastian appears through the trees with Erikel and two of his men.

Fuck.

He brought out the big guns. Why would Erikel waste his time being here?

His dark gaze falls on me instantly, the scar down his face crinkling as he smiles. "Come, you have work to do," he rasps, beckoning me forward with the tip of his finger.

"No." I widen my stance, solidifying my connection to the ground beneath me, like that will make a difference. If he wanted to lift me off my feet right now, I'm quite sure he could.

"It wasn't a question."

"I don't care what it was. I'm not going to clean up the bloodbath your men created."

At the mention of his men, the two that were present earlier when the class was announced step forward. They don't make it two steps before they drop to the floor, hands clutching their heads as they writhe in pain.

My eyes widen in surprise and I quickly assume it's Creed when I see the flicker of magical wisps coming from his direction, but I don't want to turn and draw attention to him.

"Nice work, Mr. Wylder. Why don't you take a shot at mine too," Erikel goads, smirking at Creed. Following his line of sight, I watch as Creed's magic redirects to Erikel himself, but before it can touch his target, the magic morphs in the air, and it's Creed on his knees in pain. His scream burns my soul, his cry forever fueling the darkness inside of me as I rush to his side. "I've trained much longer than you, Mr. Wylder. I recommend you work on blocking your own mind as well as strengthening your gift."

Sebastian chuckles at Erikel's statement and I turn to glare at both of them as Creed's cries soften but don't stop altogether.

I glance over my shoulder at Brax, Eldon, and Zane, the anger clear on their faces, and I know it's my fault they're dealing with all of this. I also know this isn't going to stop until I fall into line, just as he wants.

My nostrils flare as I take a step toward the enemy, my body hating every moment of giving in to this man. But maybe I have to see things differently. Maybe I need to be closer; maybe I need to bend to his will so I can take down his defenses and bleed him dry.

I don't fucking know.

I'm not thinking anything through. I'm running on my heart and emotions, something I've never done before, but now it's all I can do.

"Lead the way." The words burn my tongue but come out fiercer than I feel.

"Raven," Eldon warns, and a part of me wants to pretend like I didn't hear him, but I feel like that would only give Erikel and Sebastian another form of satisfaction, and I refuse for them to have that as well.

Looking back at him, I see the anger and worry clearly in his eyes. "We knew this was coming," I murmur, my gut twisting with the truth. So much has happened in such a short time, but there was no avoiding it. My gut twists even harsher with another thought, and a bout of worry stiffens my spine. "Please, don't worry about me. Find Ari."

I turn back to Erikel with that, snarling at the smug look on his face as I storm past him and Sebastian with no real clue where I'm going. It's not far into the tree line, though, where I see a gateway waiting, and I head in that direction.

My racing thoughts seem to keep circling back to one thing with every step I take.

Ari.

If anyone or anything could have potentially stopped

KC KEAN

Erikel's attack on the academy last night, it would have been him. Or he may have attempted to, at least. Where was he? That's not like him at all.

Coming to a stop at the gateway, I glance over my shoulder to check how far back Sebastian and Erikel are. I have a moment, a brief one, to focus elsewhere, and I close my eyes to try and sense the magic within me that connects me to my familiar.

It's weak, but it's there. I don't feel pain, just a slight tingle of rage and irritation, but it's not strong enough for me to be certain.

The memory of Ari mentioning that one day we would be able to talk into each other's minds flashes in my head and I wonder if I can project into his from this distance, but a blunt force from my left sends me tumbling forward and through the gateway before I can even think.

My hands and knees are greeted with sand as I land with a grunt on the other side. One day I might actually fucking walk through one of these, but at this point, it doesn't seem all that likely. Sebastian steps around me and I glare at the back of his head, hoping it might make him combust, but that doesn't seem to be the case today.

I rise to my feet, brushing off the sand as I look around. We're at the edge of the huge lake where Fitch had us do the water challenge, but it doesn't look like it did back then. Not with the row of dead bodies lined up beside each other.

Bile burns the back of my throat, the reality of what I'm here for making itself very clear.

Eight.

Eight students lined up with paling skin, lifeless eyes, and the pall of death clinging to them like a shroud. As much as I don't want to be Erikel's slave, none of these students deserved this. Does that make it my responsibility to save them, though? That's not what I signed up for. I can't carry the weight of that. I believed we didn't allow necromancy magic to keep the balance in the realm. That's what we were always taught. In Shadowmoor, no one would ever dream of harnessing such power. It was spoken of as almost a folklore myth at best. Now, I'm wondering what other facts I'm missing.

Erikel steps around me as the small group of his men move back from their huddle and look from their leader to me. "Bring them back," he states, waving a hand at the limp students.

"I can't right all of your wrongs." My chest aches already, my magic tugging at me to find a way to save them, which instantly has sadness creeping up my spine and through my limbs, consuming me.

I drop to my knees beside the first student on the end, darkness clinging to me as I become nothing more than a vessel for my magic. It's more than a tingle from my orb this time; it's consuming.

Shadows flicker across the back of my eyelids as whispers block out any other sound around me. I feel like I can't breathe as a sense of warmth takes over, just like it did with Burton. My hands blindly land on the first student and my body shakes with the sudden onslaught of power before I wind up cold and depleted. I sag, hearing the first beat of their heart.

"Another," Erikel orders, triumph in his voice, and I can't move or even open my eyes to see. Instead, the sadness intensifies, the darkness sweeping deeper into my mind.

I know the moment another body is thrust in front of me, and my body completes the same little ritual. Breathless. Warm. Icy. Empty.

Again, and again, and again, and again, and again, and again.

Breathless.

Warm.

Icy.

Empty.

I can't speak. I can't think. All I can do is feel anguish in every muscle, pain in every bone, and desperation in every breath I take.

Until the world shifts to complete darkness. Claiming me for itself.

CURSED SHADOWS

EIGHT

Eldon

nger coils in my veins as Raven is once again forced to use her powers in an attempt to protect one of us. That's not how this is supposed to go. We're supposed to protect *her*, and we're failing.

What she doesn't notice as she rushes off into the forest is that we're stuck in place, unable to move our feet a single step to stop her. Calling out her name a moment ago also granted me the punishment of my voice being lodged in my throat, so I couldn't yell out to her again. I can't turn to look at the others, but since none of them race after her, I can only assume they've been affected in the same way.

I keep my gaze fixed on Raven, watching as she comes to a stop by a shimmering gateway. Irritation winds tighter inside of me as Erikel takes his time to get to her, but just as he approaches, Sebastian ups his pace, knocking Raven off her feet and sending her tumbling through the gateway.

Motherfucker.

My head pounds, my heart aches, and my gut twists in agony.

The moment Erikel steps through the gateway, it vanishes and the magic keeping me in place relinquishes its hold. I fall to my knees as I lurch forward before quickly taking off for where the gateway once stood. Twigs snap and grunts follow and I can only assume it's my brothers, but I can't turn away from my target to confirm.

Not a single remnant of them remains and a snarl bursts from my lungs, rumbling in my throat as the ground shakes beneath my feet. Turning, I find the others just as feral as me. Brax has almost completely turned to stone, his magic uncontrollable when faced with the enormity of his fury. Creed's eyes are darker than ever, his power searching for their trail of its own accord, and Zane looks like he's wound so tight he's going to combust.

"Where the fuck did they go?" Zane bites, spinning on the spot, hoping and failing to find the answer we all seek.

I do the same, coming up just as empty, until my eyes catch movement back where we were a few moments ago. "I don't know, but those fuckers might," I grunt, pointing at Erikel's men, still on the ground after writhing in pain at the hands of Creed.

Without another word, the four of us charge at the two guys who are slowly climbing to their feet. Creed doesn't bother throwing his magic at them. Going for them mentally won't be enough. I want to feel their flesh break open beneath my fists as I pull the answer from them.

Just as they get steady on their feet, I charge, hitting the closest one in the gut with my shoulder, sending us both skidding through the mud.

"What the fuck?" he shouts before I grapple to pin him to the ground and smash my knuckles into his face. The grunt from his lips offers little gratification, so I do it again and again before I grab him by the throat and bring his bloodied face to mine.

"Where the fuck is she?" The fucker splutters and laughs through crimson-stained teeth, igniting further chaos inside of me. "Creed, you ready to fuck with his head?" I holler, channeling the heat of my magic into the palms of my hands. I smell the burning at his throat before he cries out in pain, matching the high pitch tone of the fucker Brax has in his hold, rattling him around like a ragdoll.

"Stop, please, make it stop," the asshole pleads in a hoarse voice, but I don't hear a location being tossed about, so I don't offer the sorry fucker anything more than an extra few degrees of heat.

"Enough." The boom comes from behind me, and I

turn with a scowl firmly etched into my features to find Professor Fitch standing with his arms folded over his chest.

"Fuck off," Zane says with a scoff, but Fitch just shakes his head.

"I know where she will be, and you're wasting your time here instead of going to help her."

Dropping my hold on the asshole beneath me, I'm on my feet and striding toward him before he's finished speaking, as are my brothers. He holds all of our attention. I swear I saw this man yesterday. He looks to have aged ten years overnight, but that isn't my concern at the moment. I need to get to Raven. Now.

"Where is she?" Zane demands, but I shake my head. We haven't got time to waste on doing this ourselves.

"Take us to her!" Fitch's gaze lands on mine as my hands clench at my sides, my demand hanging in the air for the longest second of my life.

With a single nod, he spins on his heels and takes off for the same spot Raven had been moments earlier. Despite being focused on getting to my girl, I can't help but notice that his usual uniform of choice has some new additions. He's wearing weapons and daggers around his waist like a woman would wear dainty rings on her fingers. Only, these accessories are far more deadly.

We shouldn't take his extra precautions lightly, not

when he's been thrown from his teaching position. It's on the tip of my tongue to ask what the deal is with that when a gateway appears and my thoughts are refocused on what's most important.

My little bird.

I don't offer the Professor another glance but trust in his gateway as I barrel through without care, stumbling slightly when my feet hit the uneven sandy ground. My heart races in my chest at the sight of Raven on her knees, her usual pink hair sporting far more strands of black than the two that had been present in the cave.

Two of Erikel's men drag a student to their feet from in front of her, and I watch in slow motion as she slumps to the ground, sand puffing around her from the force. Creed barges my shoulder as he kicks into action first, racing toward our girl as I hurry to catch up.

Brax snarls from a step behind me as Zane stumbles to his knees in the fine grains at our feet while Sebastian and Erikel watch with a glint of amusement.

"What the fuck have you done to her?" I bite, dropping down beside her as Creed rolls her onto her side.

"What she was made to do," Erikel replies with a hint of humor lacing his words. His shoulders rise, ready for the challenge he knows is coming, but I just snap my teeth. He looks deadly with his fur cloak draping down over his back, but I bet this fucker would lose a third of his bulk without the cloth covering him.

"She wasn't made to be your puppet," Zane grunts, ready to charge, but as much as I want to burn the world down around my pink-haired raven right now, I need to focus on her instead. She looks pale, her chest falling in short, sharp breaths, and I need to make sure she's okay.

"Maybe not to begin with, but she is now," Sebastian replies, earning a chuckle from Erikel, and I have to grind my teeth together to keep my mouth shut. Instead, I focus on Raven's features, dragging my thumb over her face as I add a little heat to my touch.

"That's enough. Take her home."

The order comes from Fitch with far more conviction than I would expect from a man in his current position.

"That might not be what I want," Erikel snarls, his humor vanishing as Fitch sighs, coming to a stop beside us.

He stands by Raven's feet, placing himself just between her and Erikel in an almost-defensive pose. "You have us all pliant enough. She needs to rest," Fitch states, folding his arms over his chest in the same stance he took with us earlier.

Keeping the temperature in my fingers low but present enough to hopefully have a warming impact, I glance across the short space to where Erikel and Sebastian stand. The latter sneers, like a feral dog waiting for its owner to let them go wild, and I'm beyond ready to put the fucker down.

"I'll send for a healer if Erikel feels one is necessary," Sebastian snarks.

"Like hell, you will," Brax bites, channeling his own crazed and untamed beast at the enemy. "We'll take care of her."

"No, you won't."

This is about to turn into a dick-measuring contest, and although I know we'll win, I can't waste any time with it. Glancing at Creed, who has his fingers rubbing at Raven's temples, I see the same thoughts flashing in his eyes.

A simple nod in agreement between us has us both rising to our feet, only I have Raven in my grasp. She's limp in my arms, which only adds to my worry as Creed spins to shield us from Sebastian and Erikel.

Fitch doesn't even bother to look over his shoulder at us as he speaks. "Boys, figure it out. Use Brax's gateway. No one else's."

I don't stand around and wait to be told twice. Running from a fight is not my usual choice, and I'm not likely to do it again, but I need to tuck my pride into my pocket and save it for later so I can save my girl.

Brax is at my side, a gateway appearing a moment later at his touch, and we're moving through the space as Sebastian starts to shout. Thankfully, his words disappear into nothing as we appear in our home. It feels like an eternity since we've been here, even though it's barely been two hours.

"Get her on the bed. Zane is going to bring a healer, Creed stayed with him so none of us are moving around alone," Brax explains as I move toward Raven's bedroom. I open the door with my magic, taking a moment to revel in the sight of the huge bed as I step inside before carefully lowering her to the freshly made sheets.

"Where the fuck was I when you guys were organizing who was going where?" I ask. "I don't recall the conversation," I add, and he shakes his head as he crawls up the bed on the other side of Raven.

"There wasn't one. It was a look."

A look.

Well, that explains it all, then.

Barely any time passes before the sound of the front door opening interrupts my anxious thoughts as I continue to stroke Raven's cheek in comfort. More for me than her at this stage. Zane and Creed step in a moment later, with Grave, another member of the Nightmare Guild. My brows rise in surprise, but I don't utter a word as he steps further into the room, his own eyes crinkling with concern.

"What happened?" he asks, dropping to his knees at the side of the bed as he runs his hands over the length of Raven without actually touching a single inch of her.

"Erikel," I mumble, unsure if we should trust this guy with anything, but it's going to be public knowledge, so what does it matter at this stage?

"So it's true then, everything that happened last night. She's a necromancer?" I purse my lips at his statement, unsure whether to just kill him now or torture him for any form of judgment aimed her way. But before I can express my concern to the others, he continues. "I'm sorry she's being used like this. That's not what anyone deserves, especially not with her level of power."

"Carry on," I breathe, focused on his hands as he runs them down her arms and over her chest again. His gaze flickers to mine for a brief moment before he swallows sharply.

"Sorry, it's just that my grandfather always told me stories of necromancers, how they danced with the light, made the world a beautiful place, and chased away sorrows by bringing balance to the realm. Until power became too corrupt, of course. That fucked everything up for everyone. As I'm sure Erikel plans to do." I'm not really sure what to say back to that, but he seems genuine enough so I decide to allow him to keep breathing for the time being. After a few more moments, he leans back, pushing up to his feet and brushing off his academy-issued pants. "There's nothing to heal. It seems to be magic exhaustion. She just needs to rest and she should rejuvenate on her own."

He doesn't hover, heading for the door with Creed right behind him while I remain helpless and useless at her side. A silence casts over the room as Creed re-enters, and we all stare at her with bated breath.

"We can't allow this to keep happening," Brax states after a while, and I immediately nod in agreement.

"What do we do?" I ask, eager to protect her by any means possible.

"I don't know, but we need a fucking plan, and now."

NINE

Raven

I blink my eyes open, confusion clouding my vision for a brief second as I figure out where I am... in my room. There's not a dead body in sight, and I heave a sigh of relief.

"Dove, you're awake," Zane murmurs, pulling my gaze to his where he lies beside me. A soft smile turns the corners of his mouth up as he rolls to his side, propping his cheek on his palm while he strokes a hand down the side of my face. "You were starting to make me worry."

"I'm getting pretty good at that," I reply with a smirk, and he shakes his head at me.

"I'm going to add it to the housemate handbook; no more making me worry." My heart warms and a sense of calmness washes over me. Although, it doesn't seem to ease the ache that has my limbs heavy and lethargic at my sides.

Refusing to let the tiredness get the better of me, I press my palms into the sheets beneath me and push up to a sitting position. I instantly feel lightheaded and my stomach clenches.

"Oh fuck," I groan, fighting harder against the ache in my muscles and bones to stagger to my feet and rush to the bathroom. I barely make it to the toilet before bile burns up the back of my throat, and I vomit.

Heave after heave; it's never-ending. Watery eyes distort my vision as I wretch, and I'm suddenly aware of a hand at my back. Small circles are drawn against my academy shirt as I cling to the porcelain. Only when I'm certain nothing else is going to come up do I take the towel that's at my side and wipe my mouth. Even then, I can't bring myself to look behind me.

"This is so embarrassing," I mumble, not wanting to open my eyes.

"Dove." The palm at my back continues to draw circles as another hand cups my cheek. "I can't, for the life of me, figure out what the fuck you have to be embarrassed about."

Of course he wouldn't.

"My insides just left me and you witnessed it. I need a minute to gather myself, brush my teeth, and get over the cringy feeling clawing at my chest," I admit, which somehow earns me a chuckle.

"Open your eyes, Dove." I shake my head, even as he taps his fingertip at my temple. "Open up."

"No."

"Come on, Raven. It's just me." Doesn't he understand that's my whole point? I don't need any of these guys seeing me like this. "Don't make me get the others in here and force us to pry your eyes open," he threatens, and my eyes ping open so I can glare at him, earning myself another chuckle.

Fucker.

"Now, can I have a minute?" I grumble, and he shakes his head.

"You're beautiful, Raven. When you're in your sexy dresses with your hair and makeup done. You're beautiful when you're bare-faced and sleeping. And you're beautiful when you're exhausted with magic strain and vomiting into the toilet." I roll my eyes, but he grips my chin, trying to cement the truth on his tongue. "You want me to kiss you right now to prove it?"

I balk, eyes wide as I try to lean back. "Don't you fucking dare."

"Don't hide from me, Dove, not even with this, because I'll continue to push until you see yourself the way I do. Your magic was depleted from reviving all of those students, your body is tired, and the fact that all you've done is vomit is impressive if you ask me."

He's insane. He has to be.

Pleased that he's pleaded his case, he releases his hold on me and rises to his feet with his hand extended for me to take. Relenting, I place my palm in his and let him tug me to my feet. Chest to chest, I breathe him in as he presses a gentle kiss to my forehead.

After a moment, I take a step back and turn to the vanity, catching sight of myself in the mirror. I've definitely seen better days. Speaking of…

"How long was I out?" I ask, curious if I've lost more time than I think.

"A few hours. We're still on the same day if that makes you feel any better," Zane answers with a soft smile.

Exhaling, I turn on the faucet and splash water on my face before brushing my teeth the mundane way. Even then, they don't feel clean enough, so I do it again. Once I'm satisfied, I take in my reflection again and notice more patches of black hair twisted in with the pink in my ponytail. Letting the ends down, the pink cascades over the darkness as I stare at myself.

Damn.

There are definitely more than two strands now. Channeling my magic, I try to turn them pink again, but just like last time, nothing happens. Zane offers me a reassuring smile in the mirror as I brace my hands on the vanity. I don't even need to ask what he thinks about the black strands. He'll probably declare black his new favorite color in honor of them.

The reality is, it's clearly not going anywhere, so I can either get mad about it or embrace the hell out of it. They're only noticeable when my hair is up; when it's down like this, the pink does a pretty good job of hiding it.

With my mind made up, I pull my hair back and secure a hair tie at the top of my head so the swirl of pink and black is fully on display.

"That's my girl," Zane murmurs, eliminating the space between us to wrap his arms around my waist. I bask in his hold, letting his warmth heat me too, until a knock sounds from my bedroom door, garnering our attention.

Stepping through the open bathroom door, I find Creed popping his head around the doorframe with a grim frown on his face. When his gaze lands on mine, the wrinkles ease a little and he attempts a smile. "Hey, Leila is outside. They've called a Nightmares Guild meeting. Are you up for it?"

My eyes widen in surprise. "They're going to attempt that, even now?"

"Seems so," he replies as Zane reaches for my hand.

"It's whatever you feel up to, Dove."

"Oh, we're going. I just need two minutes to change, then we can get the hell over there. Somebody needs to help make all of this make sense to me."

Fuck the Nightmares Guild's desire for black cloaks and golden masks. I'm over that fetish. If anything, the garish shit will only draw attention to us. Instead, I'm dressed in a pair of black pants, with a fitted, long-sleeved sweater tucked in and my combat boots laced up. My pink hair is pulled back into a low ponytail as I cling to Zane's arm, watching in awe and wonder as he masters his invisibility magic.

Just like earlier, he's projecting over more than just himself, and I can see the tendrils of magic drifting over us with every step we take as we all remain quiet so Zane can focus.

The paths are mostly clear, and any time we do hear footsteps or see a shadow approaching, we step off the well-trodden path and wait patiently for them to pass before we continue on. One thing that does remain the same is the suffocating air and feeling of impending doom that we've been dealing with since the day Erikel and his men from the Basilica Realm came into our lives.

I can't put a finger on exactly what it feels like, but it's coiling deep in my stomach, swallowing me with a sense of darkness and unwavering pain that I can't fully grasp.

As we near the academy building, we take to the grass

as we make our way around to the back in search of the steps down into the basement. Once we're halfway down, I watch as Zane's magic slowly dissolves around us until we're no longer protected from sight.

I reach for his hand, silently squeezing my appreciation, and manage to catch a glimpse of his smile in the dim, candlelit staircase.

Brax leads the way, as usual, and when we move into the wider corridor, Eldon steps up to my left, placing his hand on the small of my back while Creed protects us from behind.

The usual flicker of gold catches my attention as we step into the main room, the table standing prominently in the center while other members of the Nightmares Guild huddle in small groups, mumbling about everything and nothing. But the room goes silent when we approach, all eyes on us as my gaze shifts from one group to the next.

One guess at what has their attention… the necromancer in the room.

Me.

It's notable that no one's outwardly snarling at me, ready to hurt me, but their stiff shoulders and the way their eyebrows are raised makes it clear they're ready to act against me if necessary. I would have rather they all had those ugly as fuck gold masks on so I didn't have to see any of their expressions, but it seems everyone has forgone them tonight.

My men stand strong around me, ready to retaliate if needed, and I despise the standoffish vibe that's filling the room because of my presence.

"Is there a problem?" I ask, my words echoing off the walls as my heart thunders in my chest, waiting for a response. "If anyone has one, I think it would be a good idea to cut to the chase now so we don't waste any time," I add, continuing to scan my eyes around the room.

"It shouldn't be so hot when she just calls people out without even considering anything more than the answer she's waiting for," Zane murmurs to Eldon over my head like I'm not standing here, and my ball of inferno eagerly nods in agreement with his friend.

Assholes.

Now isn't the time.

"I believe, Miss Hendrix, that there are people present in this room who have never knowingly stood so closely to a necromancer until now. Some have spent all of their lives in fear of the dark magic they've heard stories about, and others may have family members who have died at the hands of such abilities. So you may have to forgive a few of them for their uncertainty, but luckily for you, they have seen you stand shoulder-to-shoulder with them in training already. They watched you come back from the wreckage at the Shadowmoor Outpost. They know you went back out into the wild in search of answers to that attack, but more so, rumors travel fast, and they know that you were magically drained today at the hands of Erikel and his men, bringing eight students back from the dead."

Burton steps into the light from his spot at the edge of the room, hiding in the shadows yet fully aware of everything going on around him. A few students nod in agreement as he comes to a stop beside the gold table, his eyes locked on mine.

"There's a lot of tension in here," I mumble, brushing over the praise that was clear in his little speech, and he nods his head knowingly. In my defense, everything he listed in the past doesn't affect the present for me, and that's exactly what we need to be focused on. Then, the future can become more of a consideration.

"You would be correct, but not because of you. Because of the situation we find ourselves in."

I nod, not wanting to argue and make this seem like it's all about me and the tension I'm feeling, because he's right, the situation we're now in is fucked all the way to Hell and back and we need to find a way out.

Taking a step toward the table, the Bishops follow, but I don't speak until I'm standing directly across from Burton. "So what are we going to do about our current situation?"

"I'm glad you asked," he remarks with a small smile,

like he wasn't bleeding to death yesterday. "Sebastian was just—"

"Sebastian?" I interject, my spine stiffening at the mere mention of my brother, but if Burton notices, he doesn't let on.

"Yes, he—"

"No. No. Backup. Sebastian is here?" I snarl, anger burning through my veins as Burton waves and throws his arm out to where he was moments ago to reveal the asshole that, unfortunately, shares the same DNA as me.

"Little sis," he says with a smirk, stepping closer, but Brax quickly cuts him off from getting too close.

"Sebastian can't be trusted," I state, watching Brax closely because I know he wants to slay my brother where he stands, and as much as I don't want to stop him, I also don't want to lose the potential allies within the Guild for rash behavior.

Burton shakes his head. "Sebastian is our ally, Raven. You may see him at Erikel's side, but that's because we placed him there."

No. I refuse to believe it.

"But he's the reason Erikel is here to begin with."

I can feel everyone staring at me like I'm foolish, but I know I'm right. Whatever Sebastian has twisted in his favor is working on them, and I need to prove him wrong.

"Have you got any proof of that?" Sebastian smarts,

smirking wider as Genie moves closer to him. I can't deal with this bitch today. But none of that matters because I don't have any proof. All I have is the conversations I've overheard. Conversations that I'm certain Sebastian will be able to twist to his advantage.

"I heard you talking to Erikel the other day where Erikel said, 'I told you; get me in here, and there will be endless power at your feet. I'm a man of my word.' Was that right? Or was I a word or two off?" I challenge, knowing I'm right, and even though I can see the anger brimming in Sebatian's eyes, I can also see the cogs turning in his head to paint this in a better light for him.

"Sebastian?" The question comes from Professor Fitch this time, who takes a step forward but makes sure Leila stays exactly where she is.

"I've never had a conversation like that with Erikel, or anyone else for that matter, but if you would rather believe a newer member over me, then go for it." Sebastian takes a step back as Burton's gaze flickers between the two of us before he sighs and settles his attention on my brother.

"Sebastian, come, of course, we take your word. Let's discuss today's events, shall we?"

Without a backward glance, the two of them leave while I stand helplessly gaping at them. "Someone's got to be fucking with me. This can't be happening, surely," I mutter under my breath, and before any of my men can even attempt to reassure me, it's Fitch who steps up close to me.

"Nightmares are as cliché as nightmares are dreams themselves. We keep our friends close and our enemies even closer."

TEN

Raven

One day swirls into another as the week goes on, and the grueling new atmosphere at the academy takes hold. Each lesson seems to be turned up a notch, becoming more ruthless than it was before.

Darker, harder, more sinful.

The Basilica Realm is certainly making its impact and it seems no one higher up in the Elevin Realm is really sure how to react so we've been left to deal with it. On the other hand, I also haven't had to revive anyone since the beach, and I'm taking that as a win.

Staring up at the ceiling, I notice the emptiness around me. I'm alone, tangled in the sheets, and a little warmth still remains from where the guys were lying. It may be the weekend now, but I know without even looking that they'll be outside training. They slowed down their training when we joined the Nightmares Guild, but they're right back at it harder than ever now that Erikel and his men are in control.

Burton has remained out of sight, Fitch along with him, while the other professors quiver in Erikel's presence and scurry to follow his every order. Everything is upside down, and I don't know where to aim my anger for the most effective result, but the one thing that has been working me up the most is prominent in my mind this morning.

Ari.

Something isn't right. I know it.

There's no use in me lying here worrying about it when I could be on my feet figuring it out. With a heavy sigh, I kick the sheets off and crawl to the end of the huge bed that now fills my room. My oversized tee falls to mid-thigh as I stretch out at the foot of the bed before heading for the backyard.

Stepping into the lounge, it's not hard to spot them, spread across the lawn, their muscles bulging, hair damp, and skin glistening in the morning air.

Hot.

Hot. Hot. Hot.

I take my time, admiring the view before me as I make my way to the patio doors. Goosebumps swoop over my skin as I watch them, just like they did the first time I walked into the house to find my new housemates. I'm more obsessed with them now, though, and more willing to admit how they make me feel.

The moment I open the door separating us, each of them looks up at me. Creed is the closest, arms folded over his chest as he sits on the floor, ready to continue his workout while offering me a soft smile. Zane is a step behind him, hands on his hips as he pants, his chest rising and falling with every breath. Eldon and Brax drop the weights in their hands to the ground with a thud as they both take an instinctive step toward me.

"What's wrong?" Eldon asks, leaving me to gape at him for a second as I process his question.

"What?" I finally manage, folding my arms over my chest as my eyebrows furrow.

"It's written all over your face," Brax grunts, pointing at me like that will help clue me in on what my face looks like. If it's clear, though, I may as well get straight to the worry on my mind.

"Something is wrong with Ari. I don't know what, but the fact that I haven't seen him since Erikel's attack at the ball is concerning. He's usually quick to react when he senses my panic."

"He's your familiar, Raven. You know him better than any of us," Creed states, rising to his feet.

"He did appear at the outpost when she was in danger. Fuck, he saved us all at the time," Zane confirms. "And when she went to Haven Court, he was here almost instantly once she returned. So distance can't be the issue."

I nod along with everything he says as Eldon cuts the remaining distance between us. His hands grab my waist, squeezing in comfort as I tip my face up to meet his gaze.

"What are you thinking?"

"Honestly, I think he's either back in with the other creatures, trapped in the forest, or worse," I mutter, scared of the words I know are on the tip of my tongue.

"What could be worse?" Brax asks, and a shiver runs down my spine.

"That he doesn't think we're in danger with Erikel."

"Yeah, that's definitely worse," Creed agrees, standing beside Eldon in front of me. "Which means we're going to the forest to check, aren't we." It's not a question; he already knows the answer. I can see it in his eyes, but I still nod in confirmation.

"Fine," Zane declares with a sigh. "But I want it to be known that I was two sets away from sneaking back inside and plowing you into the mattress, Dove." He appears on Eldon's other side with a pout on his lips, and I laugh.

"That can be my reward later," I say with a smirk, my core clenching at the promise as Zane presses a kiss to my cheek.

"I like the sound of that."

Eldon holds on to my hand tightly as we step through Brax's gateway. I'm sure Zane isn't the only one who would happily stay back at the house, tangled in the sheets for the entire weekend. As much as I would like that too— fuck, I would like it a lot—my fear for Ari comes first.

Ever since we met, he's put me first; I owe him that.

Nothing else seems out of the ordinary as the rest of the Bishops join us, so we silently make our way toward the tree line like last time.

"Does anybody else find it crazy that, from here, the forest looks completely empty, but we've been in there. We know what lies beyond the trees and shrubs; you just can't see them," Zane rambles, his eyebrows rising as wonder lifts the tone of his voice.

"It's crazy that we thought the academy keeping them locked up here was the worst of our worries," Creed retorts, making me scoff as Eldon's hand flexes around mine.

"Can you hear him?" Brax asks, and we all refocus on the reason why we're here.

Shaking my head, I sigh. "No, I've tried to reach out to him, but he said that would only be possible when my magic strengthened. I was hoping since I was aware of the mirror magic that it would be possible, but apparently not," I admit, defeat clinging to me like a second skin.

"Why don't you try again now? Just in case it was a proximity thing," Eldon suggests, and we come to a stop.

Nibbling at my bottom lip, I nod slowly, trying to find the strength to try again.

"Ari?" I close my eyes, trying to hear anything at all, but nothing comes. *"Ari?"* I attempt again, hoping and praying, but only silence greets me. Heaving a heavy sigh, I turn to the others with a shake of my head.

"It's okay, Dove. If Ari said it would happen, it will. It's just going to take time." Zane smiles, attempting to reassure me, and I take it, trying not to let myself get too down about it.

Turning to face the tree line, I call out his name again, only this time, I say it out loud. "Ari?"

A breeze flutters out of nowhere, rustling the leaves on the trees.

"It's not safe."

"Ari?"

"It's. Not. Safe."

I frown, glancing around in search of him, but I can't see him anywhere. It sounds like him, only darker, and I don't like the way it makes me feel.

"Can you hear him?" Creed asks, and I nod in acknowledgment, repeating Ari's words to them as I continue to search for him.

"What isn't safe?" Eldon presses himself against my side at my question, taking up a protective stance.

"You being here. You need to leave. Now."

"Ari, I'm not going anywhere until you tell me what's going on. I'm worried."

Silence greets me for so long that I'm sure he's gone, but if he thinks I'm going to just let him walk away, he's in for a surprise. Taking another step toward the forest, I'm halted when he shouts in my mind.

"No." My heart races as his silhouette appears in the distance, his telltale feathers peeking out. Instinctively, I go to take another step toward him, but he barks his disapproval in my mind again. *"Don't."*

"Ari, you need to explain to me what's going on," I insist, swiping a hand down my face.

His head dips, a pang of sadness swirling in my gut, the feeling coming from him before he mutters, *"I'm trapped in here."*

"I assumed that might be the case. But that doesn't mean I can't come and see you. Then I can go and find Professor Figgins. She'll let you out."

"No, it's not safe for Gia. I chose to be in here."

"Why isn't it safe for Gia?" My chest tightens, my own fear combining with his and swirling like a destructive tornado inside of me. I can just make out that he's shaking his head, but that's not good enough. "Ari, tell me now, or I'm coming in."

"It's not safe in here for you. I'm not sure if the magic has been shifted in the ward, so you could be trapped

here too."

"Fuck."

"What's going on?" Eldon asks, releasing my hand to caress my arm, and I quickly reiterate Ari's concern. "Shit."

"Tell me what isn't safe, Ari. I can't help if I don't understand."

"Erikel didn't come alone. He brought his own creatures with him."

The tremor in Ari's voice makes me gulp. "And I'm guessing the creatures aren't just misunderstood like you guys."

"Creatures far worse than you can imagine. So you have to go, and I have to protect Gia while trusting in these fuckers to protect you," he grunts, nodding toward the Bishops.

"I'm safer in their hands than anyone else's," I state, believing every single syllable. I may have gone through life alone, never trusting anyone else to keep me safe, but I trust in them. I believe in us.

For Ari to believe that, too, he needs to know I believe in him and trust in his knowledge of these creatures that I'm unaware of. "I'll find a way to get you all out, Ari. I promise it. You, Gia, everyone. I won't allow Erikel to get you guys as well."

CURSED SHADOWS

ELEVEN

Brax

I can see her pain, feel her anguish, and if I lean in close, run my nose up the column of her throat, I'm certain I'll catch the scent of rage at the world crumbling around us. It has me twisted up inside. Everything is going to complete shit, but that's my life, it's always been a downward spiral. Raven, though, she doesn't deserve this and I don't know how to fix it.

Wordlessly, we step through my gateway and into our lounge, misery clinging to the air around us. Raven takes a seat on the sofa, a sigh parting her lips as her head falls into her hands. I hate her feeling like this, but even more so, I hate her wallowing in it. She might not be, but the knot forming in my chest tells me otherwise and I can't shake the feeling. Which can only mean one thing.

I need to do something about it.

She needs a distraction. Fuck, we all do. Ari isn't going anywhere anytime soon, and our first point of contact needs to be Professor Figgins, who isn't going to be so easily accessible over the weekend, so we're at a standstill.

Creed flops down onto the opposite sofa, directly facing Raven with his own quiet look, which I know will be linked to his father on top of all this. I don't know how I would feel if I found out my father was a weapon for the enemy after believing him to be dead, and I'm not going to try to, but I know he needs us right now. Eldon slumps down beside Raven, his hand stroking up and down her spine comfortingly, while Zane paces back and forth, running his hands through his hair. He's a solver, too, but the puzzle laid out before us isn't easy.

Feelings and emotions are all tangled and I sure as shit don't know how to handle my own, nevermind anyone else's.

My hands clench at my sides, irritation creeping through my bones at the unsolvable situation placed before me. We've spent all week running on adrenaline under Erikel's new rule and I want to forget about it all. I want all of us to.

"We can't just sit here worrying all weekend," Zane blurts, and I cock a brow and fold my arms over my chest as I stare at him, waiting for him to continue. This fucker is going to think out loud and I'm intrigued to hear what he has to say. He paces back and forth a few more times before raking his fingers through his hair as he spins to a stop. "I can reach out to my Pops and see what he knows on his end with regards to... all of this," he rambles, throwing his arms out to the side. "But I don't think our lives are going to magically go back to how they were over the weekend." He sighs, his mind going a mile a minute as his brows furrow.

"Or..." The encouragement comes from Raven, who looks at him with a hopeful glint in her blue eyes.

"Or we forget all of this bullshit, like literally, and just fucking be us without worrying for the rest of the weekend, or until the end of today at least."

We all stare at him in surprise as he nods lightly, as if his own words are fueling his decision to push for the latter. Which actually does sound appealing. But even I know that I can't be selfish with the decision-making here; really, it has to come down to Raven and Creed. Raven *more* than Creed from my standpoint, but only because she does things to my fucking soul, and I'm a sucker for her mere existence.

"When you say forget..." she breathes, staring at Zane with a hint of wonder mixed with uncertainty drifting in her eyes.

"I mean, make Creed work his magic," he explains, tapping at his temple. "I know it's not as simple as that, and we wouldn't want to leave ourselves exposed, but I like the thought of having nothing to worry about when we're so helpless right now."

Pursing my lips, I consider the bigger picture. What would we need in order to do this?

The house would need to be on lockdown. We wouldn't be able to go outside, not even into the yard, that's vulnerable. The memory of the Guild taking us only a few weeks ago is a stark reminder.

"What does everyone else think?" Raven asks, pulling me from my thoughts, and that's an instant tell that she wants to do this.

"I think we could make it work for the day," Creed answers, and a shimmer of excitement seems to spread across her face.

"What do we need to do?" she continues, bracing her elbows on her knees as she looks at each of us, making sure she has all of our attention.

"Brax," Eldon calls, nodding at me like he knows damn well I've already started to go over all of the aspects.

"We can't leave the house, not even to the back yard," I state, pointing to the full glass wall. "I would also tint them for the entire time, just to be safe, and I would place two gateways at both entry points so if someone did manage to get in, they would be transported somewhere else the moment they crossed the threshold."

"What else?" Zane asks, a grin spreading over his face at the fact that his plan is coming together.

"One of us will have to remember, because I don't think Creed's magic comes with a timer." I look to Creed and he nods in agreement. "But otherwise, I think we're covered. We'll still have our magic if anything becomes a problem." I shrug, failing to downplay the hint of excitement flowing through my veins. "I'll also be the one to remember."

Zane claps his hands before rushing across the room and slapping me on the back. "You're awesome, man."

I roll my eyes at him. I don't care if anyone thinks I'm awesome.

That's a lie. I care if she does. I just don't like leaving myself exposed.

"So we're doing it," Raven murmurs, lacing her fingers together in her lap.

"If that's what you want, Shadow."

Her eyes meet mine, a slow smile trailing over her lips as she nods. "Just for today, I want to forget all of our problems."

"And what are we going to do instead, Little Bird?" Eldon asks, tucking a loose tendril of hair behind her ear.

"Eat, laugh, and fuck."

Raven's head falls back against the sofa as she laughs wholeheartedly from her belly. It's so intoxicating I'm close to grinning along with her, but I catch myself at the last second. I'm happy to admire her from afar right now.

My cock doesn't like that decision, though. Nor does it like the fact that I declared delayed gratification on her sweet pussy until Sebastian is dead. Even now, I'm wondering if I overshot my mouth, but fuck, I won't go back on my word.

Lacing my fingers together, I brace my elbows on my knees and keep my gaze fixed on her. None of them are aware of the troubles swirling around us, none of them seem to know anything else exists except the five of us in here, and it's almost… serene.

I've done security checks on all the entry points and triple-checked my gateways as discreetly as possible, so I don't burst their bubble. They were occupied with baking cakes and eating pizza earlier, but now they're relaxing on the sofa like we're normal. This is probably the hardest I've ever had to blend in before in my life, but it's still amusing to watch.

"I bet you've never embarrassed yourself with your magic," Raven says with a soft chuckle, pointing at Eldon, who just recalled the time she made food with her magic and forgot to create the plate for it.

"Please, I've embarrassed myself more times than I

care to admit," he retorts, his gaze drifting to mine, and I shake my head, fighting off another grin. "Tell her, Brax. Tell her it's true."

Raven's bright blue eyes swoop my way, eager to hear the story to back up Eldon's words, and I'm a sucker to deny her, even if it embarrasses me too. "There was the time he wanted to go swimming and he was adamant he could figure out our swimwear," I state, making Zane chuckle as he sits on the floor by Raven's feet.

"Please tell me you flashed everyone, because that would be priceless and I would need to see a reenactment," Raven giggles, and I shake my head, wishing that's what it was.

"We wish," Creed says with a smirk as Eldon swipes a hand down his face to try and hide his pink cheeks. "Instead, Eldon had been fixated on the popular girl at school in her little pink two-piece, and the next thing we know, we're all fucking wearing them as well."

Raven claps a hand over her mouth, attempting to smother the burst of laughter on her tongue, but it's impossible. Amusement swirls around the room, intoxicating each of us as she laughs at our expense.

"Wait, how old were you guys?" Raven asks, looking specifically at Eldon.

"How old? Dove, it was less than twelve months ago. None of us get our powers until we're eighteen," Zane explains, and I watch as Raven's lips purse.

"Do I know her?"

The four of us look at Raven in confusion. "Know who?" Eldon asks, his hands no longer hiding his face.

"The girl."

It takes me a second to understand where she's going with this, and I decide to keep my mouth shut and enjoy the front-row seat to Eldon fucking it all up for himself.

"Dotty Bramwell."

"Does Dotty go here too?" I can practically taste Raven's jealousy, and the strength it takes to bite back my smile gets harder and harder with every passing second.

"Does it matter?" I ask, earning a deathly glare from my pink-haired shadow as I stoke the fire brewing before me. But before she can answer, Zane cuts in.

"Dotty died the first week of having her powers," he admits, and Raven's eyebrows shoot up to her hairline. I watch the slight cringe as she looks down at her lap, likely feeling foolish for being so green with jealousy just moments earlier.

"Now I feel bad." Raven pinches the bridge of her nose, instantly flustered, and I'm just as quickly irritated by the fact that it's completely uprooted the lighthearted vibe that was rocking the room.

Maybe I should have stepped in earlier and redirected the conversation before her jealousy got so potent, but it's too late to change that now. What I can do is redirect everything from now on so it doesn't continue to gut my good mood.

I cut the distance between us in three strides, eating up the space just as hungrily as I want to feast on her.

"I didn't think green was your color, Shadow," I breathe, crouching in front of her.

She rolls her eyes, knowing exactly what I'm talking about. "It isn't."

"Are you sure about that? It's shimmering in your eyes, and I'm certain the ends of your hair are changing too," I tease. Her pout and forced glare send a jolt of desire to my cock, fueling the embers already burning with need for her.

I haven't been able to stop thinking about her splayed pussy ever since she agreed to forget all of her troubles while demanding food, fun, and fucking. My three new favorite words that all begin with an f.

"You're an ass, Brax."

I smirk at her poor attempt to snap at me, which only irritates her more. I think I like driving her crazy just as much as I enjoy hearing her scream. I want to hear the latter. It just can't be at my touch. That's not going to make this any less fun at all.

Planting my hands on both of her thighs, I squeeze, making her glare narrow even further. "Do you want me to spank your *ass* and see if you want to call me that again?"

She leans forward, jutting her chin up as a flicker of defiance shines in her eyes. "I said, you're an ass, *Brax*."

"Ohh, someone's feisty today," Zane says with a snicker as I swoop my hands to her hips and flip her over, earning me a yelp.

Her ass is up in the air, her face smushed into the back of the sofa, and my cock is hard as hell. Before she can come at me with that tongue of hers again, I slap my palm against the globe of her ass. The sweet sound of her muffled groan has me shaking my head in disbelief.

She's an enigma. A teasing, wanton little brat who wants me to fucking spank her just as much as I want to do it.

"That sound is from the soundtrack of my dreams, man," Eldon states, a moan lilting his voice as Raven pushes off the cushions to smirk over her shoulder at us.

She's our undoing. There are no truer words than that. But if she thinks I'm going to play her game where she acts like a brat and gets what she wants, then she's in for a surprise. Squeezing her thighs, I lean forward and sink my teeth into her ass cheek, just deep enough to force a squeak of surprise from her before I rush to my feet and take a step back.

The pout is right back on her lips and I smirk. "What do you want, Raven?"

"To come." Her response is immediate, along with the

shake of her hips.

"Do you want everyone all at once or one after the other?"

Her eyes widen, her jaw going slack as she drags her gaze from Creed to Eldon, then Zane, before settling back on me. "Two at a time," she finally answers, cocking her brow.

Of course, she had to throw another scenario at me. The challenge is clear in her crystal blues, but that will work in my favor too. With a sweep of my hand, her clothes are gone, along with my own, and her eyes quickly drift to my cock that stands prominent and eagerly pointing in her direction.

"If you don't let me join in on this one, I'm going to come before I get a chance," Zane states, stepping forward with his clothes completely gone too, and protection secured around his dick.

Nodding, I turn my attention back to Raven. "On the coffee table," I order as I step toward the wooden furniture. It's the perfect height.

I expect another bout of defiance from her, but to my surprise, she rises to her feet, swooping her hair into a hair tie as she sways her hips with every step. Without any further commands, she climbs onto the table on all fours, looking up through her lashes at me with need shining in her eyes.

Taking two steps, I stand right in front of her, the curve of her lips perfectly in line with my dick as I wrap my fingers around my length. Her eyes track every move as I notice both Creed and Eldon silently move to get a better view. Their time will come and they know it. She's so willing, so eager, so needy, it's addictive.

"No prep, guys. I want to stretch our Raven and leave her aching in the morning."

No one argues with my demand and Raven's teeth sink into her bottom lip hungrily.

"Use me," Raven pants, and I groan, my head falling back as my eyes drift closed. She hasn't even touched me yet and my toes are already tingling with desire.

"If you say so, Shadow," I breathe, glancing down at her through hooded eyes as I nudge my cock against her lips.

"I do, but I want to hear you," she whispers, her breath floating over my sensitive head before I push past her lips and feel the warmth of her mouth around my dick.

"Fuck," I hiss as she takes me to the back of her throat. She swallows around my length as she cups my balls, and any question of who is in control here is gone.

Raking my fingers through her hair, she hums around my cock as I tighten my grip. When she leans back to take a breath, I give her two short pants before I thrust into her mouth, grappling for control between us as ecstasy ripples through my bones.

"That's it, Shadow. Fuck," I groan, giving in to what she wants as she swallows around my cock again. Her hums around my length shift to garbled moans as she pauses, and I look down the length of her to see Zane balls deep in her pussy. "That's it, stretch your sweet pussy around his cock, Raven. Fit him perfectly," I rasp, watching her skin start to blotch in pink patches.

Hot. As. Fuck.

"Damn, Dove," Zane groans, giving her a moment to adjust around his length.

"Don't pause. Fuck her."

Zane's eyes flash to mine, a reply likely on the tip of his tongue, but it's quickly shut down when Raven shakes her hips ever so slightly. I know I'm rougher on her than the others, but she fucking loves it. She may like their softer approach too, but right now, she wants to be claimed, and who are we to deny her?

He moves so fast I'm not sure he's moved at all until she jolts around my cock, gagging at how deep I am briefly before he pulls out and does it again. Her hand drops from my balls as she braces herself on all fours, letting Zane thrust into her pussy as I claim her mouth.

Back and forth she takes it, takes everything we give her as our moans mingle in the air and turn up the heat.

"Fuck, I'm going to come," Zane groans. His breath

coming in short pants.

"Take her over the edge with you," I demand, tightening my hold on her hair as I relentlessly fuck her mouth.

Zane changes his angle slightly so he can reach around to swirl at her clit, but Creed beats him to it, teasing her folds, and a moment later, she's screaming around my cock, eyes rolling to the back of her head as she comes apart at the seams.

"That's it, Dove. Fuck, fuck, fuck," he chants, embedding himself in her core as she sags between us. Only my hold on her hair keeps her up as her arms give out and Zane's head lulls forward as he catches his breath, but I'm not done with her.

"Switch out. Now," I bite, nodding at Eldon. I like Creed playing with her clit right now, and I want Eldon to chase her over the edge too.

Without a word, he slips protection over the end of his cock and fills the space Zane stumbles from a second later.

Raven moans around my length as she adjusts to the new dick between her folds. "How quickly can we make her come again, El?" I ask, my gaze on my shadow as she peers up at me through half-mast eyes. "I want her choking on my orgasm as she feels her own. Can you make that happen?" I ask, challenging my friend, who nods eagerly. He has no idea how close I've been since we began, but I can hold on a little longer.

"I want her creaming all over my cock in the next sixty seconds," he retorts, gripping Raven's hips tight as he slams into her, making her jolt on my dick again. Fuck, sixty seconds could be more than I can handle at this stage.

"Make it happen." I keep my gaze fixed on Raven's as I fist her hair and take control of her mouth, no longer keeping in tandem with Eldon.

She wants to be used. I can do that.

Creed at her clit, Eldon at her core, and Zane gaping from the sidelines; it all fades into the background as I focus on her and her alone. My balls tingle, the warmth of her mouth bringing me to the edge time and time again as she becomes pliant.

"Fuck. Fuck, Shadow," I rasp, my chest tightening as pleasure floods my veins.

The words on my tongue have her eyes drifting closed as she moans around my length, and I shatter into an abyss as rope after rope of my release paints the back of her throat. Her entire body tightens, coiling like a spring until she explodes along with me.

A pleased smile tips the corner of my mouth as I try to catch my breath, my cock still twitching at the back of her throat as I drag out every ounce of my release.

"That's it, Little Bird, squeeze my dick," Eldon groans as I take my cock from Raven's mouth but keep my hands fisted in her hair to hold her in place.

"Take over, Creed. She needs two to hold her up," I grunt as Raven stares up at me in a sex-fueled daze.

The moment Creed's cock is against her lips and his hands are in her hair, I take a step back and appreciate the wonder that we're all addicted to. I want to drop to my knees and take Eldon's place at her pussy, but my gut tells me that goes against my word.

That doesn't mean I don't want her to be drenched in euphoria, though.

"Fuck, I can't last, Raven. I'm so close," Eldon moans, breaking my thoughts, and I glare at him.

"You'll hold the fuck out until she comes one more time," I growl, not waiting for a response as I spin to Zane. "You. I want her clit fucking raw in the morning. Make her detonate."

Crouching down beside Creed, I'm acutely aware of how close I am to his dick, but I don't care. I want to be staring into her eyes when she falls apart again. Zane falls to his knees by her waist and does as I demand, finding her little pink nub as she groans with every thrust from Eldon and Creed.

She's the center of my world, consuming my vision as I see her and only her. A second, a minute, an hour, I don't fucking know how much time passes. But I know the softness in her eyes, despite the force of my brothers, I know the tremble in her shoulders when she's close, and I know the smallest, sweetest moan that slips from her lips as she climaxes. All while her eyes remain fixed on mine.

For one moment, she got to forget.

For one moment, I'll remember everything.

TWELVE

Raven

My limbs ache in the most delicious way as I stir, stretching my arms over my head as a yawn parts my lips. My eyes are heavy, my breathing still labored, and my temperature is high with the body heat coming from the guys I know are lying beside me. If they're still beneath the sheets with me then it's too early to be waking up.

My mind begs for me to settle back down again and drift back into an unmemorable dream, but my eyes have a different idea as they blink through the fog involuntarily, and the second I'm able to focus, I see why.

Shadows.

Everywhere.

Silhouettes dancing across the walls, along the bed sheets, and over my men as they sleep beside me none the wiser. My heart rate accelerates, but the fear doesn't come like it usually does. Once again, I'm left speechless, watching them in their all-consuming ways, wondering what the fuck is actually going on.

I try to focus on just one, following it around the window, over the far wall, and down the bedroom door, but it quickly disappears among the others before I can track it any further. Pursing my lips, I consider rolling to my side, but it's as if I'm held in a trance with my arms still above my head. However, the stretch is long forgotten.

My chest tightens as a tingle of apprehension creeps through me. What do they want from me? A sudden onslaught of memories perilously cascade over me as I fall victim to the reminder of yesterday and the days that came before it.

The memories we ignored, the despair we hid, the truth we clouded, all for a moment of tranquility. Fuck was it worth it. The ache between my thighs and the tightness of my jaw is a lasting recollection of our antics, but the dismay at all of the pain and anguish rushing through me once again hurts like a bitch.

Brax must have had Creed lift the magic when I fell asleep, which I'm grateful for because the way the thoughts run through my mind now, fast and unrelenting, I can't help but wonder how I ever managed to fall asleep before. My chances of falling back asleep with these shadows dancing along my walls are extremely low, leaving me to wallow in thoughts of Erikel and Ari.

A bad situation always has the ability to get worse here, and it's embarrassing that I sometimes think otherwise.

Groaning from my left distracts me, but all I can do is peer out of the corner of my eye, unable to turn my head as the sound becomes more panicked. By the third husky moan that melds into a snarl, the shadows disappear as if startled.

My body becomes my own once again and I scramble to see what's going on. Rolling to my side, I prop my face on my palm as I stare at Eldon writhing beneath the sheets. His brows are furrowed, his jaw tense, and the muscles in his neck are bunched. Yet he's asleep. His head thrashes from side to side, making the cord in his neck protrude with anger, and I tentatively place my palm against his cheek.

I have no idea if waking him is a good idea or not, but I can't stand to leave him in distress like this. No matter the consequences.

"Eldon?" I whisper, unsure of what I'm actually doing, as I try not to alarm the others. "Eldon?" I stroke my thumb across his cheek and the thrashing stops, but the way his face continues to scrunch up tells me he's still deep in his dream. His name is on the tip of my tongue, but before I can murmur it, his eyes ping open and his body stills.

He frowns up at me, disoriented, as he tilts his face. "Raven?"

"Hey, you were having a dream of some kind, I think," I explain, avoiding the word nightmare for some reason, but he knows what I'm referring to.

"Come lay down. I'm sorry for disturbing you," he breathes, pulling me against his chest and draping his arm around my shoulders.

I nestle into him, relieved he's okay, as I melt against his body. "Is everything okay?" I ask, tipping my head up to meet his gaze as he swipes a hand down his face with a sigh.

"I'm not so sure it was a dream. I think it was more of a vision."

"A vision?"

He nods, taking another deep breath before he turns to face me head on. "Yeah. I'm trying to think how to best explain it." He looks up at the ceiling, his eyes scrunching closed every so often, and I try to give him the space he needs to think. "It's dark, cave-like, and cold. So fucking cold." A shiver seems to ripple through him as he speaks, making me tense a little. "There's a platform in the distance, something shimmering gold, and my gut feels relieved to see it."

"Can you make out what it is?"

"No." The disappointment is clear in his tone as he tightens his hold on me in comfort, more for him than for me.

"It's okay; I'm sure it will come to you. It always does." My attempt to reassure him earns me a tired smile. "Maybe we should start a mood board for all of your visions so we can try to solve them and piece them together as a team," I add, and his smile grows before he presses a kiss to my temple.

"That sounds like the perfect plan, Little Bird. Thank you. But for now, snuggle with me. You need the rest."

His calmness and ease seems to seep into me. My earlier thoughts are nonexistent as I focus on him instead. Feeling his heartbeat beneath my palm, the world becomes dark once more.

Sleep may have claimed me again, but not for long enough. Out in the crisp morning air, I'm wishing I'd stayed beneath the sheets. The only thing keeping me out here is the joy of watching the Bishops workout.

It's not something I usually get to see. I'm either hiding in bed or working out with them, whereas this morning, I get to enjoy the view.

So good. So, *so* good.

Brax's muscles flex with every breath as he uses the weights, likely oblivious to my watchful gaze. I didn't think I could be so attracted to a back, but here we are. Eldon works out beside him, but he's facing me, his pecs bunching together every few moments, accompanied by a wink everytime he catches me looking. Creed is the closest to me, doing what I'm sure is his two-hundredth sit-up, with only the smallest beads of sweat gathering at his temple. Zane, however, has a thin layer of perspiration clinging to every inch of his skin as he runs short sprints back and forth across the lawn.

I never knew sweat could be so appealing. Watching all of the deliciousness is exhausting on it's own, I can't imagine how draining it is to simply exist and be that fucking hot.

With my legs crossed, I run my fingers through the blades of grass, and other than enjoying the view, I can't stop thinking about my magic. Not the necromancy, but the magic that comes with it. As if sensing my thoughts brimming back to the surface, Creed sits up and shuffles closer to me so his legs frame either side of me.

"What are you thinking about?" he asks, tucking a loose tendril of hair behind my ear as his onyx eyes pierce mine.

"I'm thinking it might be a good idea for me to start

working on my mirror magic," I admit. "I don't want to end the week with my whole head covered in black hair as I bring people back from the dead again and again, while ignoring the importance of the abilities that also come with it."

"You don't want to be defenseless, Raven. I understand that. We've got a bit of time now if you want to dive into it before we leave."

I gape at him, speechless for a moment as I bask in the awe I feel for these men. I mention my thoughts, and not even a second passes before they're willing to put everything on hold. For me.

It's not because of my new-found magic either. They were like this before all of that. They were like this when I thought I was a Void. I scoff at the word that tainted my life before coming here.

Void.

It's weird to look at me now. In such a short space of time, everything has changed.

"Raven?"

I blink, focusing on Creed again as I nod eagerly. "Please, that would be great."

"Perfect." He stands, offering me his hand to pull me to my feet, and my toes curl into the grass, keeping me grounded as I nervously glance around.

I don't know what it is, but whenever I'm practicing

my magic, I get this nervous butterfly feeling in my stomach and it never seems to wane.

"Want to start with me, Shadow?" Brax asks, discarding the weights as he turns and gives me his full attention.

"Uh, yeah?" I'm aware it comes out as more of a question than the confident answer I was going for, but a moment ago this was just a thought, and now we're digging deep into it. I just want to magically have the hang of it without facing failure. I feel like I'm sinking in enough of that already.

His big hand engulfs mine, pulling me away from the others as the two of us stand closer to the cliff's edge. The breeze picks up a little, ruffling the hem of my oversized tee as I nervously cling to him.

"Do you want to try mind magic again or do you want to see if you can go full gargoyle?" he offers, cocking a brow at me as I consider my options.

The mind magic was natural last time, I'm sure it would be easy enough again, but really, Creed was right. This is about feeling defenseless, and the thought of turning my fist to stone is exactly what I'm in need of.

"Gargoyle," I breathe, and Brax's grin spreads wide.

"Good answer, Shadow." He releases my hand and takes a step back.

Without a word of warning, he turns to stone. Not just his arm; but head to toe. His shoulders somehow manage to widen, his fists clench at his sides, and he slowly cracks his neck from side to side. The last time I saw him in full gargoyle mode, a blade pierced his back at the hands of the Amayans. There was never a moment to appreciate his true beauty.

His eyes, one brown, one green, darken yet glitter under the morning light.

"Take your time, Raven. Focus on the magic," he rasps, his stone lips moving and making me gape more.

Clearing my throat, I shake out my arms in hopes that it will help me focus on what I'm supposed to be doing instead of ogling him. I close my eyes as I take one final breath before settling my gaze on the wisps of magic dancing over his skin. It almost looks like electricity zapping around him since the magic is coming from every inch of him instead of just one single strand.

I take a tentative step toward him, my fingers extended in his direction, excitement dancing over my skin as I touch the strand of magic. My arms go heavy at my side, dropping me to my knees with a grunt as I hear the guys behind me call out my name, but I shake my head.

Fuck.

I just need a second.

My eyes squeeze shut as my fingers plead to release the tendrils of magic, but I'm not falling at the first hurdle. I refuse. Exhaling, my nostrils flare as I take another deep breath, working my way through each inhale as I slowly wiggle my fingers.

It's strange. They're thicker, heavier, slower... but stronger.

Blinking my eyes open, I glance up at Brax, who is standing patiently before me. There's a softness in his eyes, a silent understanding, and it fills me with the strength I need to push on.

I nod, more in confirmation to myself than anything else, but he tilts his head at me in response, encouraging me on.

Curling my hands into fists, I press my stone knuckles into the ground and push up onto my feet before taking a big breath and standing tall. Everything begs me to slump back to the floor again, my head light and my vision slightly blurred with disorientation, but I breathe through it, gulp after gulp. Brax and the others remain silent, giving me the time I need to learn and adjust.

Slowly, oh-so-fucking-slowly, my shoulders relax and my arms sway slightly from side to side as I clench my fingers tighter around the strand of magic transforming me. Taking my time, the magic drifts over me, the initial weight that knocked me off balance slackens, and I can manage a little better.

"Just high-five me for today, Shadow," Brax murmurs, lifting his stone hand for me.

Two minutes ago, I would have laughed in his face, but as the magic tingles up past my elbows, it doesn't seem so unachievable. Wetting my bottom lip, I take what feels like my one-thousandth deep breath before I raise my right hand. It feels good until I get three-quarters of the way up to his and I start to falter, my body straining in the strangest way, but I grit my teeth and push through it until I feel his palm against mine.

It's the briefest moment before I drop my hand back to my side, releasing the tendrils of magic in my grasp.

"Fuck, Dove. You smashed it," Zane hollers as I hear someone clapping behind me too, but my gaze is fixed on Brax. I don't know why I'm seeking his approval, but he is the gargoyle, after all.

"You did good, Shadow. I can't deny that I'm impressed with the fact that you even managed a high-five too." My body tingles at his approval on top of Zane's. "But I think you might need to save any more mirror magic until later because classes start in thirty minutes."

My eyes widen in surprise and I nod in agreement.

That clearly took me a lot longer than I realized.

Lips press against my temple as I'm pulled in against a firm chest and I look up straight into Eldon's eyes.

"You are a badass, Little Bird. A. Bad. Ass," he says with a smirk as he pulls me toward the patio door, and I shake my head at him.

I honestly don't know what the fuck I am, but I'm starting to like it.

THIRTEEN

Creed

Watching Raven adapt to Brax's magic was unbelievable. When she asked to try the mirror magic with us again, I thought we would be taking much smaller steps than we already were. I could see the challenge in Brax's eyes when he said to high-five her. Even that was pushing it, yet I should have known she'd smash it.

She's incredible. Awe-inspiring. She's Raven.

I can't wait to see her weave my magic and control people's minds like me. I want to see her do it all. To just be in the vicinity of her greatness is a gift; to watch her not even realize just how special she is makes it that much more memorable.

Glancing toward her, she's already looking in my direction, a hint of concern on her face as we continue down the pathway to the main academy building. Our knuckles brush and I engulf her small hand in mine, squeezing with what I hope feels like reassurance to her. A soft smile spreads across her lips, and I grin back at her for a moment before focusing on the path ahead.

Students move around us, heading in the same direction, but the somber air is far more noticeable today. We're pawns at the hands of the enemy, strung along like puppets and helpless to do anything other than what they say.

What causes me more stress is being in the presence of my father. My *not* so dead father. Even now, I can remember all the nights I would cry myself to sleep, desperate to dream about my father returning to us. I can say with absolute certainty that I never dreamt it like this.

He was never the enemy, and I was always filled with a sense of relief and love at his reappearance. The two things that are impossible to feel in his presence now. Now, I'm riddled with anger, deeper than what rooted me mere days ago, and it's all raging at his existence.

I don't know why it disappoints me, but there's no avoiding it. Instead of letting him see how he turns my insides, I'm going with the more volatile approach and swallowing it all down.

Fuck him. Fuck Erikel. Fuck all of it.

"Are you okay?"

I glance down at Raven as she pulls me from my

thoughts and nod. The way she quirks her eyebrow at me makes it very clear that my response isn't quite up to par with what she's looking for.

"I'll be okay, Raven. With you by my side and the others here with us, nothing else matters."

She nods as she purses her lips, aiming those bright blue eyes at me. "I don't want you to bottle everything up, though. If you need to talk, please, just... don't get trapped in your head with it all."

Fuck.

She's too damn sweet once you get the luxury of digging beneath her tough exterior.

"I won't, I swear."

The words slip from my lips before I can stop them, solidifying my trust in her, because there is no way in Hell I would make a promise to her and break it.

Never.

"Creed."

My spine stiffens at the sound of my name and my steps falter. Only for a split second, but I feel it enough to worry that it is noticeable to others. I consider continuing on, letting him go unheard, but the child in me can't help but seek out those familiar onyx eyes.

My father.

He stands off to the left side of the double doors that lead into the academy building. His gold armor glares at everyone who passes, making the unspoken statement I assume it's intended to.

"It's your choice, man," Eldon murmurs, coming to a stop behind Raven as Brax glances back over his shoulder at me. Zane remains plastered to Raven's other side as I try to find the words.

It's *not* my choice. That's the point. Making a big deal out of speaking to him will only bring Erikel amusement, revealing the sore spot my father now leaves on my soul, and they don't deserve to see my weakness.

"I won't be a minute," I murmur, squeezing Raven's hand one last time before I head off to the side. My father turns before I reach him, heading toward the same tree he lured me to last time.

When he comes to a stop, I make sure to keep a few inches between us as I glance around, surprised not to see Erikel and his men watching us like last time. It's hard to decipher what is and isn't a test right now, and I don't want to be blindsided by my father's proximity.

"I thought I said to keep your distance from the necromancer."

"Hi, Father, how are you? I'm good, despite the circumstances. What circumstances, son? Oh, you know, it's just the academy that I'm trapped in is now being ruled by the leader of the Basilica Realm, who is basically the enemy. To top it all off, he seems to have brought a blood relative back from the dead, but shock, they're the enemy too." My chest tightens, my anger getting the better of me.

My father gives me a pointed look, making it clear that my snark doesn't impress him, but I don't give a fuck. He acts like he can express his thoughts and I will take them as law, and it's laughable.

"You're putting yourself in danger," he states, opting to ignore my outburst, and I shake my head in disbelief.

"No, *you're* putting me in danger. You and the rest of the Basilica Realm you brought with you. I have no interest in your bullshit. If you would like to fuck off back to where you came from with your fearless leader and his lackeys, then please, be my guest. I'm sure you will see how much danger I would no longer be in."

His tongue runs over his teeth as he assesses me, coiling my muscles even tighter. "What are your magical abilities, Creed?"

My head rears back, my eyebrows rising in surprise at his question. Is he fucking joking right now? "You should have been around a few months ago when I turned eighteen. Then you would have been able to see for yourself. Otherwise, you can look at the academy records; I'm sure the details are written down there."

"Don't waste my time, Creed." His hands flex at his sides, his irritation clear, but his annoyance isn't greater than mine at the sound of my name repeatedly on his tongue.

"I won't." I turn, taking a step toward Raven and the others, who are watching inquisitively from the doors, but I don't make it two whole feet before a hand clamps down on my shoulder, stilling me in place.

"Why the fuck do you even care?" I snarl, unable to contain my fury at his gall.

"I don't," he snaps back, his fingers flexing on my shoulder, and I feel completely overwhelmed with the mixed signals floating around me. It can't be right, though; he's nothing more than the enemy now.

"Then my magic shouldn't matter to you any more than everyone else's," I state, glancing back over my shoulder at him with a cocked brow, and his eyes narrow at me. "If we're done here, I'm leaving."

A beat passes, followed by another, as our matching onyx eyes battle with one another until his hand drops from my shoulder. His chin dips ever so slightly and I take that as my cue to leave. I don't bother to look back, not wanting to give him any satisfaction that he's gotten under my skin.

When I reach Raven, she wordlessly takes my hand as Brax leads the way inside. The five of us move as one, and thankfully, no one tries to pepper me with questions about whatever that bullshit was back there.

I haven't heard anything from my mother since she

left. I've never had to reach out to her through the academy before, or her to me. We tend to keep to ourselves really, but it surprises me that she hasn't attempted to since my father is here.

It's no shock as we arrive at our first class of the day to find Erikel's men standing at the door. They're not letting anyone inside, which stirs my gut with uncertainty.

"I wonder what fun they have planned for us today," Zane murmurs, nodding at the assholes, and I hum in agreement.

"Hey, can we get in there?" Genie asks, pointing over their shoulder, and they just smirk at her in amusement.

"We won't be needing the classroom today. Once everyone is here, we can head out."

"And your name is?" Genie plants her hand on her hip, raking her eyes over him from head to toe as she waits expectantly for a response.

"Roma, now get the fuck over there and wait for us to call the next orders," Erikel's man grunts in response.

"Genie might be a hardcore bitch, but at least she got the name of one of these fuckers," Raven murmurs under her breath, and I nod in agreement.

A few minutes pass as more and more students gather, and I spot Leila at the other end of the corridor, her father murmuring something into her ear before he nods and disappears again. She looks our way a few moments later but doesn't approach us, which would mean crossing paths with Roma and his men. Instead, she offers Raven a subtle wave, which my girl returns.

"Something tells me today is going to be… interesting," she states, a heavy sigh quickly following, and I have no words with which to respond because she's right. Today already feels like a fucked up day, and it hasn't even begun.

"Okay, we're heading to the Gauntlet. Let's go." Roma and the two men flanking him turn toward us, parting the students as they head our way. I don't move like the other students, and one of Roma's muscle men shoulders past me, but I don't falter.

It doesn't stop Raven from getting angry, though. "That motherfucker," she snaps, moving to step around me, but I squeeze her hand, keeping her at my side.

"Don't give them what they want, Raven. This is all about power plays, remember? You show them that they're successfully getting under your skin, and they'll only do it more. They already know we're a soft spot for you. Let's not give them anything more to go on." I lift my other hand to cup her cheek and her gaze settles on mine.

She searches my eyes, for what I don't know, but she must find whatever she's looking for because a moment later, she nods, and I drop my hand from her face.

Brax signals that he'll go first, but he doesn't take a single step until the rest of the students are gone and only Leila remains. I don't release Raven's hand and Zane keeps close to our girl's other side, silently confirming that she can fall into step with us, but neither of us is moving from Raven's side.

"Do you have any idea what this is about?" Raven asks, looking at Leila, who nods softly, twiddling her fingers nervously.

"Yeah. My father overheard them discussing that they wanted to get a visual of our magic. I don't know in what capacity, but the fact that we're going to the Gauntlet doesn't bode well," Leila admits, and the adrenaline that started pumping through my veins when my father called my name reignites.

"I won't hurt a single creature in the Gauntlet. I swear it," Raven states, her voice solid like steel as she grits her teeth.

"Let's see what they have in store for us before we start getting too worked up, Dove," Zane says, attempting to calm the worry and anger already radiating from Raven, and she nods reluctantly as we head outside and take the path to the arena.

Concern is thick in the air as the other students mumble among themselves. The second we step into the arena, all noise ceases, though the memories of the last time we were here register in my brain.

"The last time we were here, you met Ari."

Raven looks at me with a softness in her eyes which only appears at the mention of her familiar.

"The time before that, however, was shit," Brax grunts, recalling when we had to face the Gauntlet and Raven's magic hadn't come to fruition yet.

"At least I don't have to keep my magic a secret. Those fuckers know what I can do. If I'm bringing someone back, it will be for the right reasons, I hope," Raven says with another heavy sigh.

As the domed area at the center of the arena comes into view, I notice there's nothing filling the space. It's just Erikel standing front and center with my father a few steps behind him.

Excellent.

If what Leila said was right, and my father is here, why would he bother to ask when he's going to get a front-row seat anyway?

"Please, everyone, take your seats. Where, I don't care. When your name is called out, I expect you to come forward," Erikel announces, flinging his hands out wide as his usual fur cloak drapes over his shoulders and down his back.

I can't see any other year groups in here, so he's either fixated on the first years or he will put us through our paces one year at a time. Either way, we're about to be on display for him in some way. I fucking hate this. More than seeing my father. When you give men like this a glimpse of your magic, they then believe it's theirs to wield, and we're not his weapons.

Brax leads us down to the fourth row of seats, pointing at Zane to take the end seat. Raven drops into the spot beside him, and I take the space to her left while Brax forces his way into the row in front, and Eldon climbs back a row, just like we did last time; she's covered.

Leila tentatively takes the spot beside me, nibbling on her lip nervously, and I sigh. Lifting Raven's hand to my lips, I press a kiss to her knuckles before letting go and standing. I signal for Leila to move up, and she smiles appreciatively at me as I trade places with her.

Getting comfortable, I'm acutely aware of where everyone and everything is. Roma and one of the other guys remain at the top of the stairs at the entry point. My father and Erikel remain in the center of the room while four more of Erikel's men hover on another set of stairs.

"Fuck, let's just get this over with, shall we?" Brax grumbles, rubbing his palms over his thighs.

As if hearing his words, Erikel lifts his hands in the air again, garnering everyone's attention. "We will begin with Miss Leila Fitch."

A noticeable gasp sounds from beside me, followed by a lodged gulp as I turn to see the worry in Leila's eyes. She rushes to her feet quickly, tucking a loose tendril of hair behind her ear as she moves to the end of the row and descends the stairs toward the center.

"Miss Fitch, your magic," Erikel says as she comes to a stop a few meters away from him.

"What do you want me to aim at?" she asks, her voice barely audible from here, but the tremor is clear enough.

"At my golden warrior," he declares, taking a step back as he waves at my father.

He's the target? Why?

"What the hell is going on? Did your father mention any of this?" Eldon asks, leaning closer to murmur, and I shake my head.

"Nothing. He just warned me off Raven again and asked what my abilities are, but since I didn't share, he didn't explain why," I answer, my hands clenched in my lap.

Would he have spoken openly with me if I had asked? Do I need to swallow my pride and heartache and get close to him to gain answers for all of the things we don't actually know?

Fuck.

Turning my attention back to Leila, she takes a few extra steps back before lifting her hands in my father's direction, aiming her icy magic his way. Ice blasts at him, but the second it touches his armor it crumbles to the floor.

"That's enough, Miss Fitch. Take a seat in the green

section," Erikel orders, making everyone frown as they glance around the room.

"Green section?" she asks, staring at the otherwise gray space.

Erikel rolls his eyes with irritation before snapping his fingers. One by one, colors drape across the back wall and down each section of seating.

Red. Orange. Yellow. Green. Blue. Purple. Black.

Leila tucks her chin against her chest and rushes from the center platform, taking a seat on one of the green rows with her arms folded over her chest.

One by one, we're called out, and one by one, we're assigned a color.

Eldon creates a ball of fire in the palm of his hand and is assigned a seat with Leila in the green section. Brax reluctantly goes to the center of the platform, turns half gargoyle, and is directed to the blue section, while Zane is placed in the yellow seats. When my name is called, I hate leaving Raven, but I know it will cause more of a scene than is necessary to stay, so I head to the center and face my father.

"Creed Wylder, your magic," Erikel orders, waving a hand toward my father with a grin on his face.

Nodding, I contemplate what to do, as I have the entire time I've been watching. Everybody else who has mind-based magic has frowned at him in concentration before advising Erikel of their abilities not working, which means I'm unlikely to be able to bring him to his knees screaming in pain. Which leaves me with few options.

I focus on him still, his dark eyes boring into mine as I stare him down. You can always feel the blockers and defensive techniques someone may be using as if they're untouchable, and as I thread my magic in his direction, I feel the walls instantly.

His eyes furrow at the first tap against his walls, and I let my magic dance along the blocker between us for a few moments, knowing I won't be able to get inside, but I want to be sure. As I'm ready to retreat and declare my abilities like the others, the barrier cracks, the smallest slither opening for me to pry inside.

Instead of infiltrating his mind with anger and pain, a small whisper lures me closer. Searching his eyes, I try to piece together the murmur, but it's too difficult, so I close my eyes, hoping to focus a little more.

"I love you, son. I love you, son. I love you, son."

I stumble back, my heart racing in my chest as the chant continues to echo in my mind.

"Well?" Erikel grunts, tearing my gaze from my father's, who remains as placid as ever before me, like those words aren't swirling around in his mind.

"Uh, I control mind magic," I ramble, sure my chest is going to shatter as the words in his mind continue to consume me.

"Join the purple section," Erikel orders, turning away from me without a backward glance, and it takes me a second to gather myself enough to take a steady step.

I join the purple section, and search out Raven the second I take my seat. I can see the concern on her face as she stares at me, but I don't even know what to say. Not that she can hear me from here.

Maybe now I might have a few moments to get my shit together so I can explain, but it seems Erikel has other ideas.

"That seems to be everyone except Raven. Who gets to fill the only seat in the black section," he announces, waving a hand for her to move to the black section.

She purses her lips but does as he says, and I notice that he's organized us into the seven categories of magic. Nature-based, divination, conjuring, psychic, medics, shifters, and necromancy.

Surely, our groups were already listed down somewhere since we've been divided like this before, but again, this is another power play on his behalf.

"Now, if your name is called out, you are to follow Roma," Erikel states, not missing a single beat before he starts calling out names. None of it matters to me, I'm locked on my father's words until the next words from his lips makes me pause. "Creed Wylder."

FOURTEEN

Raven

My breath lodges in my throat and I gape in horror as Creed rises from his seat, following after the others who have been called out. I thought my name was going to be called instead of the others, so the fact that Creed is walking away has me panicked.

"The rest of you are dismissed," Erikel declares before moving to follow after them.

The rest of the students murmur inquisitively among themselves, but I'm up on my feet and rushing toward the end of my row to get to Creed.

"What the fuck is going on?" Zane asks as he suddenly appears at my side, but I don't slow down.

"I don't know, but we're going to find out," I state, turning up the stairs. "Creed," I holler, but he doesn't stop. Erikel, on the other hand, turns to me with a glare.

"Did I call your name, Raven?" he sneers, the scar down his face looking redder than ever.

"No, but I want to know where you're taking him," I demand, coming to a stop in front of him, but he shakes his head dismissively and looks over my head.

"Warrior, follow after them. I'll be along in a moment." The telltale sound of the golden warrior's armor clanging echoes in my ears, getting louder as he gets closer, but I keep my gaze focused on Erikel instead of turning to look at him approaching.

Erikel watches his every move, though, not glancing back at me until Creed's father walks by us. "You're dismissed," Erikel repeats, but that's sure as shit not good enough for me.

"You can't just take him," I retort, my voice getting louder. Glancing over my shoulder, I find Zane is now joined by Eldon, Brax, and even Leila. Surely he has to listen to us. I turn back to him, but he's already waving his hand dismissively.

"I can do as I please, Raven. But continue to push me, and you'll see what I'm capable of. Just because he's a motivator for you to do as I want doesn't mean I won't kill him to teach you a lesson. You have plenty of other motivators around you," he snaps, stunning me as the creak of the golden armor pauses for a beat. I look toward the golden warrior, noting the tension in his jaw and neck from his side profile, but after the longest second, he continues on his way. "I won't warn you again," Erikel adds for good measure, before turning up the stairs again, swooping his fur cloak dramatically as he goes while I stare at him, speechless.

"What the fuck do we do now?" Eldon asks, wiping a hand down his face, and I snatch it, pulling him along with me as I take off up the stairs when Erikel disappears through the entryway.

"We follow them."

"But, Raven, he said—" I turn around to look at Leila while blindly trying to race up the stairs.

"I couldn't give a fuck what he said. It's Creed. He needs us."

Nobody else argues as I turn back to face the direction I'm walking, hearing the footsteps of my men and my friend right behind me as Eldon squeezes my hand tightly in his. The second we make it to the top, my pace quickens as I spy the students who were called out being ushered through a gateway.

Fuck. There is no way he is going through there.

We're too late, though. Creed steps through without a backward glance, with his father and Erikel right behind him, and as I near the spot where the gateway is, it disappears before my very eyes.

No. No. No.

Spinning on the spot, my hand falls from Eldon's hold as my heart races wildly in my chest.

"What do we do now?" Zane asks, looking between Brax and me.

I don't have an answer. Not even a hint of one. All I can feel is terror seeping into my bones as I turn back to where the gateway was. How can this be happening?

Fuck.

"I'd rather he had taken me," I bite, hands on my hips as I heave every breath into my lungs.

"Don't say stupid shit like that, Shadow. Besides, you don't know what's going on," Brax states, gripping my chin and forcing me to look up at him. His chest rises and falls heavily like mine, proving that he's as stressed as I am, but it doesn't matter how worked up we are. That's not going to make a difference right now.

"I don't know where he is, Brax. I can't breathe," I admit, my voice raspy as my eyes sting. I'm not a crier, I'm not usually so damn emotional, but this truly feels like the rug has been pulled out from under me.

I'm not in control. I'm powerless, and this just proves it.

"I know, Shadow. I know. But I'm here, we're here. All we can do is wait. We'll wait for him," he murmurs, his voice softer than I've ever heard it before, and I find myself nodding along in agreement.

If this was a power move from Erikel, it's working. He knows he has total control over all of us. I'm just another soldier in his grand plan. We all are. But fuck him if he thinks he can hurt any of my men.

If all I can do is wait, I will, but I won't fucking forget. Even if it's a fucking day trip to the seaside, I don't give a shit.

Erikel will pay for this.

I think I'm going to be sick. I'm certain of it. The way my stomach muscles keep tightening violently as worry continues to cement itself in my soul is unbearable.

"Is this what it was like for you guys when I disappeared because of my parents?" I ask, nibbling on my fingernails.

"Yeah," Eldon answers, his voice as solemn as mine as he sits on the sofa across from me.

It's been hours and he's still not back. My skin feels itchy, my heart aches, and the antsy feeling burning through my veins is unrelenting.

"Fuck," I grunt, making Zane scoff from his spot on the floor. "It's too much."

"You need to keep busy," Brax states, and I immediately shake my head.

"I can't focus on anything else." Pretending that it's

possible is just wasting time.

"You need to," he grunts back, standing before me a moment later.

"Why don't we play with your mirror magic again?" Zane offers, trying to be the voice of reason. It just might be the only thing that could hold my attention in short bursts, but it still feels pointless.

"I don't know," I mumble when he reaches for my hand.

"Let's try," he encourages, pressing a kiss to my knuckles before Brax grabs my other hand and yanks me to my feet. I slam against his chest, my breath lodged in my throat as I look up at his towering frame.

"We're doing it." He doesn't leave any room for argument as he uses his magic to push the sofas back to create a bigger space for us to try.

"Then when Creed gets back, you can show him what you've done," Eldon adds, his smile wide as he tries to fill me with reassurance, but I'm feeling sassy.

"I'm not a child seeking praise for doing well, you know."

Brax smirks, or at least I think he does. It's over too quickly for me to be certain. "We're very aware you rule the castle, Shadow."

"Or that's what you let me think sometimes. Other times you ignore me altogether and force me to practice magic even when I don't agree to it," I snap, and he cocks a brow at me as Zane's chuckle rings out around us.

Brax leans in close, his lips against my ear as he speaks. "You love it. Now, save your bite for later. You're making my dick hard, and right now, we need to focus on your magic."

I gape at him as he releases his hold on me and takes a step back.

Fucker.

I almost consider pushing for him to fuck me, but I can't keep hiding my emotions and using sex as a distraction. Besides, he won't get me off. Not yet. Not when my brother is still breathing.

Sighing, I turn my attention to Eldon and Zane, considering what I would like to try and mirror first.

"Calm your enthusiasm, Little Bird," Eldon says with a smirk, and I roll my eyes at him, but it still eases a little of the tension consuming me. "Why don't you decide which of our abilities you feel comfortable trying? Then we can start there," he offers, and I nod.

Do I start with Eldon's magic or Zane's telekenesis? Do I want to understand their other abilities? Hell yeah, but just like it was with Brax, I want to be able to use the abilities to defend myself and attack my enemies if necessary. Once I don't feel so defenseless, the rest will be good to wield too. I know I won't have control over what skills my opponent might have, but I just need to focus on honing what tools I have the best I can.

"Can we start with fire?" I ask, opting to feel heat in the palm of my hand before I start launching things around the room.

Zane smiles, Brax nods, and Eldon steps forward with a new kind of heat in his eyes.

"I can't lie, I'm excited to share my magic with you."

A shiver runs down my spine at his words. He knows exactly what he's doing to me and I'm a sucker falling under his spell.

Thankfully, he doesn't wait for a response, and a moment later, he produces a ball of fire in his palm. Flickers of pale red magic thread around his hand, centered on where his abilities are, and I take a deep breath before I cut the remaining distance between us.

My fingertips are a magnet to his skills, inching closer and closer like a moth to a flame, and the second I touch the strand of magic, I feel the burn.

Hissing, I snatch my hand back, staring at him with wide eyes as I hold my palm to my chest.

"Did you just fucking hurt her?" Brax snarls, shoving Eldon back a step, and his eyebrows almost reach his hairline as he gapes at me.

"No. Shit. Raven, I'm—"

"Stop." I hold my other hand out to make him pause,

and thankfully he listens. "Please don't apologize. You did nothing wrong. I just didn't actually consider that you felt so much of the heat," I admit, and he drops the fire in an instant as he approaches.

My gaze shifts quickly to Brax, who I can sense wants to push him again, but I'm hoping my eyes tell him to stay the hell back. Whether they do or not, he doesn't charge his friend again.

"Can I look?" Eldon asks, pointing at my hand still clenched against my chest, and I slowly pry it open.

There's nothing there, not a single mark. It's more shock than anything, and now I feel dumb.

"Does it feel like that all of the time?" I ask, hoping to distract him from my embarrassment, but he still takes my hand and blows gently on the skin, which is somehow more soothing than I expect.

"In the beginning, it hurt like a bitch, but the more I practiced, the more my body adjusted to the heat. So now, it's just a dull warmth. I'm sorry, I didn't think to warn you of that."

"It's all good. I didn't consider the weight of the stone effect of Brax's magic either. You guys all do it so effortlessly that I forget that it can take its toll on you."

"You've got this, Dove. Just take your time. We're here with you every step of the way." My heart swells as Zane smiles softly at me.

I'm a goner for these guys and those gentle words that crop up from time to time.

"Thank you," I breathe. Inhaling deeply, I let the warmth from my chest ripple through my body before turning my attention back to Eldon.

"Are you ready to try again, or do you want to save it for another day?"

I shake my head. "Let's go again."

"That's my girl," he replies with a grin, producing another fireball in his hands.

Feeling a little more prepared this time, I relax my shoulders and reach out my hand again. The second I connect with the rising inferno, I gasp, but I focus on the heat first, letting it simmer through my veins. I have no idea how much time passes while I stand and simply feel the magic, but when I'm comfortable, I hold out my other hand and try to direct the magic to my palm.

A few flickers of added heat dance over my skin as I fixate on the spot, but it takes a few tries for me to get the right balance of pulling from both my magic and his to create the smallest ember in my hand.

"That's it, Raven. Envision it growing. You're doing amazing," Eldon murmurs. Wetting my dry lips, I close my eyes and imagine the small ember growing into a ball similar to Eldon's. "Open your eyes, Little Bird."

Blinking, my gaze settles on my hand where the ball of

fire replicates Eldon's, and I grin.

"Fuck yeah," Zane cheers, and I drop my hand from Eldon's magic, watching as the fire burns out.

Eldon's crowding my space in the next breath, his mouth capturing mine like a man starved as I feel the remains of his magic warming his lips. All too quickly, he's retreating, leaving me desperate for more of his heat, but before I can complain, Zane is filling the empty spot with a wicked grin on his face.

"You're phenomenal, do you know that?" He cups my cheek and I can feel my face heat, but this time it's not from the magic.

"Stop," I grumble, trying to brush him off, but his hold tightens.

"One day, you will see yourself how we do, and it's going to be magnificent." His words leave me breathless as I peer up at him, unable to fathom a response. "For now, I'm adding it to the housemate handbook that you have to accept praise with a smile, possibly even a blowjob, but no more doubting." He raises an eyebrow at me, but I still don't offer a response as he takes a step back. "Ready?"

Just like that, he's all business again. I can't keep up with them, and I secretly love how they leave me swirling in a vortex while keeping me grounded all at once.

Three words pierce my mind, desperate to part my lips, but my head refuses. My heart burns, my soul aching just to release those words from my mouth, but I can't.

Shaking my head, I take a deep breath and focus on his question instead. "Yes."

I can see it in his eyes that he knows I'm in my head a little, but instead of pushing, he offers me a wink before using his magic to bring a chair from the dining table closer.

"I'm guessing you would prefer to learn how to move things first, invisibility another time?" I nod, and he places the chair in front of me before doing the same with another. Once they're both in place, he smiles at me. "Try to remain calm. It's not going to burn you or weigh you down, but it's very sensitive, so tension or stress can make it erratic," he explains.

"Okay."

Slowly, Zane uses his magic to simply lift the chair off the ground this time, and I watch the strands dance from his hand to the chair, swirling in the air before me. Taking a tentative step toward the threads, I try to take a deep breath before I latch on to his magic, settling my attention on the second chair. The moment I do, it fires into the air without warning, clattering against the ceiling before falling around us.

I brace for impact, but nothing comes and I quickly realize that Zane's controlling how they fall with his magic, slowly drifting them down to the floor.

"Are you okay?" he asks, and I nod.

"It seems our girl doesn't know the meaning of the word calm," Eldon says with a chuckle, winking at me, and I roll my eyes again.

"I think it's going to be hard to ask her to be calm when she's worrying about Creed," Brax states, and my heart clenches at the reminder.

Dropping my hands to my sides, I let go of Zane's magic and sigh. The stress over Creed quickly comes gnawing at me once again, leaving me helpless to feel the pain.

"It's alright, Dove. He's going to be—"

His words are cut off by the slam of a door and the four of us whirl around to the source of the sound to see the man himself before us. Relief floods through me as his onyx eyes find mine, but it's short-lived when I notice his hands clench at his sides and the way he pants with every breath.

"Creed," I breathe, worry consuming me for an entirely different reason now as I gape helplessly at my man.

"What the fuck happened?" Eldon asks, the first to take a step toward him, but he shakes his head. Tension ripples from him in thick waves, rooting me to the spot.

It's almost like he's a ticking time bomb, ready to go off at any moment, and we're going to feel the backlash, no matter the distance.

Wordlessly, he storms right past us, heading to his room and, a second later, another slam booms through the house as his bedroom door shuts behind him.

FIFTEEN

Raven

My gaze moves from the closed door, to Brax, to Zane, then to Eldon. All of us have the same bewilderment scrunching our eyebrows as we stress over Creed.

"What are we supposed to do?" I ask, feeling helpless, but I can't just sit here any longer and wait for him to come out of his room. He might not be ready to explain what the fuck just happened, but selfishly, my heart is tearing up inside and nothing makes sense.

"I don't know. Creed is usually the level-headed one," Zane admits, swiping a hand down his face.

Fuck this. I need to know he's okay. I just need... something.

Rushing to his door, I knock. "Creed?" My pulse pounds in my ears, but no response comes. *Please, answer me.* It feels like the distance between us now that he's

195

home is greater than it was when he wasn't here and it's suffocating. "Creed?" I repeat, tapping against the wood once more.

"Fuck. Off."

My heart aches at the snarl on his tongue, but I know deep down it's not aimed at me. I'm just the closest one to him to feel his wrath.

"Don't speak to her like that," Brax snarls, pounding his fist against the door. Silence greets him in response, which does nothing to ease the rapid rise and fall of my gargoyle's chest.

"What the fuck happened?" Eldon mutters as I place my palm flat against the door, separating me from my onyx-eyed man.

"I don't know," I whisper, powerless to the pain consuming the room.

"Well, we can't help until we know. Come and sit back down with me, Little Bird." Eldon takes my other hand, but I don't want to move. My fingers splay against the wood, praying for Creed to just appear, but nothing happens. "Come on, Raven," Eldon encourages, sensing my anguish as I reluctantly take a step back.

My hand falls with a slap on my thigh as Eldon pulls me in close and guides me to the sofas, which have now been returned to their usual spots.

Dropping down into a seat, Eldon's arm drapes around

my shoulders, keeping me close as Zane sits on my other side while Brax paces back and forth in front of us. It's not easy when the one we would usually turn to in moments like this is on the opposite side of the door. Both physically and mentally.

The constant help he's given me, the reassurances, I want to give it all back to him, but how?

As if sensing my inner turmoil, the click of a door sounds and, a moment later, Creed appears in his doorway. His head is down, his dark hair flopping over his face as his fingers flex at his sides. He knows he's putting a wall up between us, something he wouldn't want us to do to him. He's fighting himself, for us, for *me*, proving he's far stronger than I'll ever be.

With a heavy sigh, he takes a step, then another, and another, until he's standing right before me. His eyes lock on mine and he drops to his knees while my heart gallops in my chest. His lips part, but whatever he's about to say doesn't come as Brax slams his fist into his face, knocking him backward.

"Brax!" I slip out of Eldon's hold and drop to my knees beside Creed. Blood trickles from his nose and he wipes at it without a single ounce of anger.

"Don't ever speak to her like that again," Brax growls, the floor practically vibrating with his anger.

"Brax," I repeat, lifting my hand in his direction for

him to stop.

His eyes widen innocently as he shrugs. "What? He's lucky I didn't shift my fist before hitting him."

Rolling my eyes at him, I shake my head and turn back to Creed, who is sitting up again.

"Creed?" I murmur, tentatively reaching my hand out, and when he doesn't inch away, I place my palm on his shoulder.

"I'm sorry, Raven." The pain in his eyes is clear. But I don't give a shit if he told me to fuck off or not. This is his safe place. I want to be his safe place. Two inconsequential words are nothing.

"None of that matters, Creed. What's going on? What did they have you do?" I ask, hoping to redirect the conversation.

He sighs, grabbing my hand from his shoulder and running his thumb over my knuckles.

"Nothing."

"Nothing?" I repeat, eyebrows pinching in confusion.

"You're going to have to give us a bit more than that, Creed," Zane states, leaning forward to brace his elbows on his knees as he stares at the pair of us on the floor.

"There's not much else to say," he mumbles, but it's clear he's in his head a little, replaying whatever went down. "There were fifteen of us in total. Two nature-based students, three divination, two from conjuring, two medics, four shifters, and two psychics, including me."

"And?" Brax encourages when he drifts off.

"And they took us to Pinebrook."

"Pinebrook," I repeat with a frown. "Why did you go there?" Despite asking, my gut already knows the answer and nausea starts to swirl in my stomach.

Jet-black onyx eyes find mine, pain written all over his face. From the pull of his brows to the tic of his jaw. Fuck.

"To attack them."

His words echo around us, holding us captive for what feels like an eternity until Zane finally clears his throat, breaking the silence.

"Attack?"

Creed nods. "The news is spreading that the Basilica Realm has taken over the academy. People want to fight back, especially those with children who attend here. They're trying to fight, demanding more from The Monarchy, who still haven't issued a statement."

"How do you know all of this?" Eldon asks, and Creed taps at his temple in response.

"I wasn't there for my good looks, Eldon. But even if I was doing Erikel's dirty work, I questioned the citizens of Pinebrook too." I didn't think it was possible, but it's almost as though his eyes got darker.

"Erikel's dirty work?" I'm like a damn echo, but I need to say the words out loud to register them above my pounding heart and swirling emotions.

Creed nods again but doesn't respond right away, which only amplifies the tension in the room.

"Creed?" Zane murmurs, trying to nudge him along, and Creed's hold on my hand tightens.

"Erikel wanted to set a precedent."

"What does that mean?" Brax quizzes, arms folded over his chest as he looks down at Creed.

"He wants to make it clear The Monarchy is nothing against him and the power he wields."

Fuck.

"What did he do?" I ask, my eyes drifting closed as I brace for his response.

"He killed them."

"Alone, with his men, or did he rope you all into it?" Eldon mutters, rubbing the back of his neck.

"Honestly, I don't know." He gulps, looking down at the ground. "I just know it happened, I know what the aftermath looked like, but everything else... it's just not in my mind."

"Has someone used magic on you?" Brax asks, sounding just as angry as he did when Creed told me to fuck off.

"I don't know for sure, but it feels like it."

Fuck.

"It's not your fault, Creed." I mean every word. None

of this is his fault. Not a single ounce, but the way he shakes his head tells me he thinks differently.

"How many are dead?" Brax sits on the coffee table as he looks at his friend, waiting for an answer.

"Too many, but in the mass were three Monarchs, and I think they were his targets."

A knock sounds from the door, making my muscles lock up in surprise as I glare at the front door. "Why is someone knocking on our door?" I ask like anyone else here would have the answer.

Creed squeezes my hand again, defeat shining in his eyes as he stands, tucking his hands into his pockets.

"Because on top of all of that, I then got another unfortunate job," he explains, and I remain frozen in place on the floor, staring up at him.

"What job?" Zane asks, but my heart already knows the answer. My magic can feel it beneath my skin and I'm already rising to my feet.

Creed's eyes find mine, desperation consuming him, and despite the anger and frustration raging through my limbs, I smile. I stand by what I said. This isn't his fault.

"It's okay, Creed," I breathe, and he shakes his head, fury blazing in his eyes.

"No, it's not." His voice cracks as emotion gets the better of him. I reach for his hand, squeezing, just like he does to me, but it doesn't calm the storm in his eyes.

"What are you talking about?" Eldon asks, slightly agitated, and I sigh.

"He was sent to get me."

Brax walks up front, Eldon a step behind, and I'm flanked by Creed and Zane on either side of me. My fingers crave the touch of them, to hold their hands or feel the weight of their arms around my shoulders, but I don't want Erikel's men to see me vulnerable.

Three of them guide us along the paths of the academy grounds. It's not lost on me that they don't opt to use a gateway, but I take the silence as a moment to gather myself and tamp down the fury raging inside of me.

It's all bullshit.

All of it.

For them to have put Creed in such a position. To use him as a weapon against me... fuck. That will be worse on him than me because I see right through it.

None of us say a word as we're led through the double doors heading into the main academy building. There's no one around. No one to give me a hint of the kind of situation I'll be walking into. I almost think that's purposeful, but I don't believe Erikel's that smart, either.

Our footsteps thump along the marble floor are the

only sound around us until we near the ballroom where all of this began. My heart stutters, the memory of that night fresh in my mind as the doors open to reveal what can only be described as Hell.

I keep moving, despite the horror drenching my veins in darkness, as a gasp falls from my lips.

Bodies. Bodies everywhere. *Dead* bodies.

They're lined up, one by one, and I can't help but count them.

Thirty-six.

Fuck. It's not a complete massacre, but that's still thirty-six innocent lives taken at the hands of Erikel's order, and for what? Realm dominance?

It's a mess, that's for certain.

"Ah, please welcome the lovely Raven Hendrix." Erikel's voice is like poison, trying to bring me to my knees, but I would never let this fucker know. I don't think anyone has ever described me as lovely before, and hearing it from him sounds so condescending. I want to correct him, but I manage to keep my mouth shut as I look at where he's standing.

He's on the small platform at the front of the hall, with two men seated facing him. I would have assumed they were actually here in person, but a slight flicker around their feet makes it clear they're projections.

Blood stains Erikel's fur coat. A fact I'm sure he'll

enjoy if pointed out to him, so I keep my lips tightly locked as we walk up the line of lifeless bodies.

"Raven is quite special. I'm not sure if you're aware of her abilities or not," he states, waving his hand toward me, and the projections turn my way. Two men dressed in Monarchy-issued suits, similar to what my father wears, but he's not one of the men before me tonight.

The man closest to me fixes the glasses on the bridge of his nose as he assesses me while the other gulps, his Adam's apple bobbing quite noticeably.

"I'm going to assume she's the necromancer," the man with the glasses states, turning back to Erikel, who gleams at his response.

"She is, and she's going to bring everyone back from the dead if you agree to my terms, but there isn't much time, so delaying will only increase the true death rate," he explains, as if noting a trip to the grocery store, and my stomach turns.

This man is completely void of any feelings or emotions other than his desire for domination over everyone and everything. A part of me wonders what his trauma is, what caused him to be this way, but I quickly tamp it down. Seeking answers to those questions would only make him a person, relatable, and he doesn't deserve that.

"Who are they?" I whisper, glancing at Zane.

"Monarchy."

I had assumed as much, but I don't recognize them. Although, I haven't really seen anyone from the Monarchy, other than Rhys, to confirm. A thought does make my lips purse, though. "Why didn't he go for your father while he was here? Why do this?"

Zane looks at the men on the platform, talking among themselves like we're not here. I'm surprised he's not complaining that Brax, Eldon, and Zane are present too. His order to Creed was to come alone, but none of us agreed to that, so it was the five of us or none at all.

"I don't know. I don't think anyone but him truly understands his game plan," Zane mutters, and I nod in agreement. The enigma that is Erikel from the Basilica Realm has us all confused.

"What are your terms, Erikel?" The gulping Monarch asks, his nerves still getting the better of him, and Erikel shakes his head before cocking his brow expectantly at the Monarch. "Erikel, leader of the Basilica Realm," the guy corrects, making Erikel grin from ear to ear, and I want to puke.

"Surrender the realm."

The Monarch with the glasses splutters with a shake of his head. "No." It's more confident than I expected and it impresses me a little.

"Are you sure you want to play with the lives of these men and women?" Erikel asks, sweeping his hand in the direction of the dead bodies, but neither of them turns to look.

"I believe it's you that is attempting to play God among men, Erikel, and that's not how the Elevin Realm works, nor will it ever."

Erikel doesn't falter under the intense stare of the guy with the glasses. If anything, he stands taller, smiles wider, looks deeper. "Oh, you need me to start smaller. We can waste precious minutes and take this one step at a time if you like. Let me see…" He taps at his chin, pacing ever so slightly back and forth before the members of The Monarchy, until he nods, almost to himself. "Agree to leave us alone here at Silvercrest Academy."

"Why would we do that?" Mr. Nervous asks, and I glance over my shoulder at the lifeless civilians. It's not my place to heal everyone, nor is it my place to be a damn hero, but it's hurting my chest to see them like this.

"I'll have Raven bring back one person. Monarch Dutton."

Both of the Monarchs lean back in their seats, murmuring between themselves as we just idly stand around. Turning to Zane, he must sense my question because I don't even part my lips before he speaks. "Monarch Dutton is the head of Elevin Realm's soldiers."

Fuck.

So that's his reasoning behind all of this? To gain

control of the realm's fighters? Maybe he's smarter than I gave him credit for.

"We can agree to this," Mr. Glasses states, pulling me from my thoughts, and I gape at them. Are they serious? "On the terms that he is returned to us immediately," he adds, and I stifle a scoff.

He can't seriously believe that Erikel would agree to this, can he?

"Excellent. Raven, heal this man," Erikel declares, not actually responding to the audience he's holding as his attention turns my way.

"No," I blurt, staring at him as I prepare for the fight that's about to come my way.

"It wasn't a question." The smile on his face doesn't falter.

"And I'm not a puppet," I retort, rolling my shoulders back as I glare.

"Do you need me to hurt one of your men?" The smile slips just a little and I shake my head.

"You already did when you took him with you to Pinebrook. Explain to me what happened there, and I'll consider your request." I'm not going to just roll over and do as this man asks. I can't. *If that's the life I'm going to be expected to live, then kill me now because I refuse.*

Erikel tsks, his smile slowly transforming into a snarl as the Monarchs turn their heads in our direction. "It's not a request," he repeats, and I shrug.

"And, like I said, I'm not a puppet."

"Warrior," Erikel bellows, and a second later, the door to his right opens and the golden warrior steps into the room. His eyes slip to Creed for the briefest of moments before turning to Erikel. His leader doesn't even speak a word, he simply nods in our direction, and the sound of his sword sliding against the sheath at his waist echoes around the room.

"Don't you fucking dare," I snap, wagging my finger at the pair of them. "I'm not going to bend every time you threaten to set this guy on someone important to me. Especially his own son."

"But I think you will," he taunts, his eyes darkening as he takes a step my way, but he's not moving quicker than the warrior.

I can't let him do this to me. I can't let him treat me as a weapon again and again. I can't have him use Creed's father as a weapon against us too.

No. No. No.

I can't breathe as rage clogs my throat, and my hands clench at my sides.

"Don't let him see your magic, Raven."

I stiffen, glancing around the room, but nothing signals that he's here.

"Ari?"

"Don't let them see what else you can do. Not when I can't get to you. You have to think logically."

"How are you in my head right now, and how can you hear me?" I should be focusing on how close the warrior is getting, but I'm too stunned.

"Because you're getting stronger, Raven. But right now, what matters is doing what you have to do to stay safe."

"And you're saying that's to give in to him?"

"Yes."

"Fuck, why?"

The warrior's sword drags along the floor, taunting, as adrenaline trickles down my spine.

"Because mirror magic is a rare attachment to being a necromancer. Letting him see that will only make you more useful to him."

"I can't keep jumping every time he tells me to," I retort, clutching at straws when I know deep in my soul that he's right.

"For now, you have to. Bide your time. His is running out."

"How?"

"You're more powerful than him. Once you realize that and hone your skills, you'll see it too."

Impossible. I'm not made for this. I'm not made for any of it.

The golden warrior's heavy footsteps vibrate beneath my feet as he lifts the sword toward his son. I glance at Creed, but he doesn't move, staring his father down without a single ounce of fear in his eyes.

Fuck.

"Fine," I bite. "Tell me who."

Erikel claps slowly before pointing to the man I hadn't realized was lying on the platform.

"Raven," Zane warns, but I shake my head, looking deep into his eyes, hoping that I can convey enough emotion to show that I know what I'm doing, or I think I do. I'm trusting in Ari, he's the one thing that makes sense among the rest of this madness.

I drop to my knees beside the clean-cut, suited man on the floor. To look at, you wouldn't assume he was the leader of the soldiers. You would expect someone more rugged, bigger, muscular, but he's none of those things.

My magic takes over, sensing its calling as my hands hover over the man's chest. Darkness creeps in, hanging on for what feels like an eternity, to the point I'm sure there's no light at the end of the tunnel. I feel light-headed, my body uncontrollably swaying from side to side as I try to keep my balance. It's cold. So fucking cold.

"Raven," Brax calls out, but I can't respond. My magic is taking every ounce of energy from me, and I'm sure I'm on my way to certain death when the smallest flicker of light appears in my mind. Warmth slowly touches my fingertips, working its way up my arms and down my spine, and I manage a deep breath before I can no longer hold myself up, and I fall to the floor beside the body I can only hope is no longer dead.

"You should be proud of yourself, Raven," Ari murmurs into my mind, barely audible above the pounding in my ears, and I sigh as my world turns completely black, with only one thought on my mind.

It doesn't feel like there's anything to be proud of at all.

SIXTEEN

Creed

Sleep hasn't claimed me. Not even for a second. I've laid beneath these sheets for what feels like an eternity, staring at the back of my eyelids as time passes me by. Raven hasn't woken since she dropped to the floor at Erikel's feet; another factor adding to the anger burning through me, keeping me awake.

I'm left suffering in the unknown, drowning with worry and choked up with disbelief at yesterday's events. Events I don't truly know or understand. I've never experienced memory loss, nevermind to this capacity, and it's leaving me reeling.

One minute, I was stepping through the gateway with the other students, and the next, I was hovering beside a pile of dead bodies. An actual pile. I can still smell the stench of death. It lingers on my skin.

There was actual blood on my hands and I had to get it off as soon as I stepped into the house. I couldn't let Raven see that, see the state of me. She didn't need to deal with my mess on top of her own, but Erikel was making it impossible for me to separate it.

Raven deserves the best from all of us at all times, but that's getting harder and harder to deliver, and now I'm hurting her in the process with bursts of anger, which are in no way actually aimed at her.

Fuck no, but the words had parted my lips before I could realize that. I deserved the punch from Brax, and the fact that I had to be the one to bring her to Erikel earned me another. I don't deserve to be lying beside her in this bed. She needs men who will protect her, not lead her to danger like a good little puppet.

When did this all go to shit? There was no warning, no time to get the hell out of here before the shit hit the fan. In the blink of an eye, our entire world was rocked. Erikel played the perfect guest until it was too late, and now we're dealing with the repercussions.

How can a man like Erikel walk in here and control us all so easily?

Where the fuck are Burton and the rest of the professors?

Somebody somewhere higher up needs to start helping us out since it seems The Monarchy is willing to sacrifice our safety for the return of one man. *One* man. I don't even know if Erikel did as agreed. I wouldn't be surprised if he had Raven save him, only to keep him for himself. I don't know. The second Raven dropped to the floor, we scooped her up and carried her the fuck out of there.

He didn't protest either. Fucker clearly knew he went too far, but I'm sure it won't stop him from doing it again. With my father still by his side. Another fucking conundrum that plagues my mind. The soft whisper of his voice plays on repeat in my head, reminding me that he allowed me through the walls of magic protecting him.

Why? What did that mean? I don't even know if I can trust him.

Fuck.

This is exactly why I haven't slept. Once I've exhausted myself on one subject, my brain moves on to another, and the process starts again.

Movement pulls me from my thoughts, and I know it's Raven. The guys shuffled out of the giant bed as quietly as possible almost an hour ago while I laid as still as possible with my eyelids closed. My arms are straight at my sides, fighting against the urge to reach out and snuggle her. She needs to rest, not to wake up and instantly have to deal with my mess.

Hopefully, if I lay still enough, she'll slip from the sheets, too, and join the others.

It's almost as if she hears my thoughts because, in the

next breath, I feel the sheets shift, but instead of clambering from the bed, she inches closer. All at once, her hair is on my shoulder, her breath on my chest, and her palm gently pressed against my abs. Her heat consumes me, her proximity setting me alight.

"I know you're awake," she whispers groggily, and I pry my eyes open. The light coming from the window burns, but not as much as her brightness does. Fuck. She's beautiful. "Did you sleep at all?" she asks like she didn't go through her own ordeal last night.

She leaves me breathless and it's impossible to speak, so I shake my head. Her eyebrows gather with concern.

"Is it everything that happened yesterday that has you worried?" I shrug. Kind of, but I don't care what Erikel puts me through. It's the impact it has on her that has me torn up. "Cat got your tongue?" she adds with a smirk, so I offer the best smile I've got, which is weak as shit, and nod.

It fucking seems that way, and I can't explain why.

"What kept you awake?" She props her head on her hand as she strokes my chest and I cock a brow. Surely, she knows everything I worry about revolves around her... right? "Me?" she clarifies when she sees my expression, and I nod, still lacking the skills to talk.

Fuck. Stupid brain. Work.

"Why?" she asks, staring at me in disbelief, and I shrug

like a fool. "You're not making this easy," she retorts with a smile, swirling her fingertip over my abs.

I'm really not doing it on purpose, but it's like my throat has tightened up and there's nothing I can do about it.

"What about me has you worried?" My eyes drift closed, stuck on where to even begin, and as the thoughts drift through my mind, my throat only tightens further. That doesn't stop Raven, though. When she's a woman on a mission for information, she's on it. "Are you worried about what I think about what happened yesterday?"

Ding. Ding. Ding.

This woman can effortlessly see right through me.

I force my eyes open, but I can't bring them to reach hers. I'm embarrassed.

Her hand cups my cheek, warming my skin and burning my soul, and I finally find the strength to look into her eyes.

"Are you for real, Creed?" Her voice is low, with no harshness or frustration, but there's a hint of desperation and helplessness that twists my gut, and I exhale. "Creed," she breathes, and I realize I dipped my gaze. Fixating on her baby blues, she holds me captive. "Whatever happened yesterday, that was not your fault, and I don't hold you accountable for any of it."

My lips twist. I can tell by the steel in her voice that

she means what she says, but it still doesn't ring true in my mind and I hate it.

This time, it's her turn to sigh as she runs her thumb across my cheek. "It doesn't really matter what I say right now, does it? You've had all night to get lost in that head of yours." Again, her voice remains soft, revealing more of my vulnerability, yet exposing hers too, and I offer her a weak smile. "Fuck, Creed. All I want to do is tell you three little words. I do, but my mouth doesn't know how to form them and my head is still refusing. I want to utter them to you so badly, make you see how much I care for you, how little everything else matters."

She's definitely trying to send me to the land of the dead and back. If anyone can do it, it's her. Her strength, her softness, her mere fucking presence... it's all more than I deserve. I know those exact three words she speaks of. They plague me. Desperate to be screamed in her face with uncontrollable excitement and adoration, but I was so scared that it would push her away, so I kept my lips locked. Now, I finally have the opportunity, and I've lost my voice.

My heart races as I lift my hand to her face, mirroring her hold on me as I try to convey with my eyes just how I feel for her. She leans forward, pressing the tip of her nose against mine, and I sigh with comfort at her touch.

"Maybe I could show you," she whispers, her breath

dancing over my lips, and I cock a brow at her in confusion, but she's already moving.

Her usual oversized tee that falls to mid-thigh disappears, revealing her breasts and pretty pink pussy as she swings her leg over my hips, getting comfortable in my lap. My boxers are the only thing sitting between us and my fingers itch to reach for her, but this is her show and I'm helpless to do anything other than follow her lead.

She pulls the hair tie from her wrist, sweeping all of the loose tendrils back before securing it on top of her head. The movement arches her back, elongating her neck and making my dick stiffen even more between her thighs. I know she can feel it with the way she wiggles slightly back and forth, her baby-blue eyes darkening with desire as she looks down at me.

"Nod if you want this." Her tongue peeks out, sweeping over her bottom lip before disappearing back into her mouth as if there's a hint of nerves there. I nod eagerly, needing to put any uncertainty out of her head.

I might have lost my tongue, but my desire for her only grows with every second that I breathe.

Sweeping the palms of my hands over her thighs, I feel the goosebumps rise along her skin. I don't stop until my hands wrap around her waist, making her tense and gasp at the same time.

What neither of us can say with words, we can say with

our bodies instead.

I continue to glide my hands up her sides, loving the way she shivers as I ghost over the side of her breasts. Her hands reach for mine, and in a flash, she has them pinned beside me. She's closer now. So fucking close. With her nipples dragging across my chest as her nose nudges at mine again.

Her heat is palpable at my cock, and I gulp as I eradicate the final layer between us.

"Fuck," she groans, making my cock thrust of its own accord toward her.

Gripping her hands tight, I tilt my head and crush my lips to hers.

It's messy. It's filled with desire. It's us.

Angling my hips, I tease her core with my cock, eager to get inside, and she doesn't let me down as she adjusts her hips, enveloping my dick with her sweet, sweet haven.

She looks deep into my eyes as she sinks farther and farther down my length, making me hiss. The noise only encourages her desires.

She's intoxicating, claiming every inch of me as she looks into my eyes, caressing my soul. Nothing else matters. Nothing at all. My heart beats for her. Only her.

Her nose brushes against mine again as she continues to claim me, perspiration clinging to my skin as I fight the urge to flip us over and fuck her into the mattress.

"All that matters to me is the four of you," she murmurs, gaze still fixed on mine as she bounces slowly on my dick. "I want to be here for you. Just like you're here for me." I groan, my body tensing at her words in that sultry voice of hers as she melts all of my worries away. "I want you to trust that I'm not going anywhere, just like I trust in you. I want you to find comfort in me; whether that's grunting swear words, crying in anger, or taking what you need, however you need it. But most of all, I want you to feel safe enough to be yourself with me."

I see nothing but her big blue eyes.

I hear nothing but the promise in her voice.

I feel nothing but her core, uniting us in every way possible.

"You're it for me, Creed. I'll take the ups, the downs, and the mundane in between. I want it all with you."

Fuck.

Fuck. Fuck. Fuck.

"Ah," I moan, the block in my throat moving ever so slightly as I try to find the strength to say it all back to her.

"You set me on fire. You make me feel safe. You make me want to see tomorrow. You make me want to fight for more," she continues, her hips slamming down on my cock harder and faster.

"Fuck, Raven," I rasp, and her eyes blow wide at the sound of my voice.

"Fuck. I love hearing my name from your lips," she admits, and I cling to her hands like my life depends on it.

"Raven," I repeat. My throat is sore, but the words are there as I give her what she wants. Her head tilts back, her eyes falling closed as she takes from me and fills me up all at once.

"Creed."

I drag my lips up her throat at the sound of my name, loving it on her tongue just as much as she loves hers from my mouth.

"I love you, Raven," I bite, my throat bobbing as I let the words spill out, and they're the trigger.

I explode inside of her, wave after wave of raw emotion and pleasure taking over me as she squeezes my cock tight with her pussy, finding her own release. I capture her mouth with mine, claiming her cries of pleasure along with her orgasm as we come apart and meld back together as one.

Whatever it takes to protect her, to fight at her side, to face the world, I'll do it all.

SEVENTEEN

Raven

I can't stay bundled up in Creed's arms any longer. The need for the bathroom after being so royally fucked is unavoidable. Not even magic can make it go away. The second I step back into the room, I spot Creed perched at the bottom of the bed with my night tee in his hands.

He waves me closer, a lazy and relaxed smile on his face as he watches me approach. Wordlessly, he slips the material over my head and I silently appreciate the way he performs the actual task of it instead of just using magic to do it. His fingers drag down my sides delicately, reconnecting us once more as he plays with the hem of the top.

"No lessons today," he states. It's not a question, and I can't think of a single reason to push back.

"It sounds like the perfect plan to me. I don't give a

fuck what trouble we might get into. That man was on the brink of no return yesterday and it wiped the floor with me to bring him back," I admit, and a darkness attempts to fall over his features again. "Don't do that," I murmur.

"I'm not. I swear it." He smiles, pressing a kiss to my stomach as his hands wrap around the back of my thighs, drawing patterns over my skin. "Is there anything I can do to help you?" he offers, and I shake my head.

"I'm good. I'm just tired. Is there anything I should know about after I passed out? We didn't really talk much when I first woke."

He shakes his head, a hint of disappointment flashing in his eyes. "No, I wish I had something to give you. But the second you hit the ground, we got you the fuck out of there. You've been sleeping ever since."

"That would probably explain why I'm so hungry then."

He's on his feet in the next breath, pulling me toward the door before I can utter another word. Heading into the lounge, I expect to see the others outside of the patio doors in full workout mode, but to my surprise, they're sitting around the dining table.

"Oh good, the fuck bunnies are here," Zane says with a smirk, making my cheeks heat as Creed throws his arm around my shoulder.

"What time is it?" I ask, hoping to distract them from

the fact that there's definitely the scent of sex clinging to Creed and me.

Brax shovels a forkful of eggs into his mouth before replying. "Almost ten."

My eyes widen in surprise. "It's a good thing we're not doing classes today then," I state as Creed guides me to my seat between Zane and Eldon before taking his own across from me beside Brax.

"You'll return to classes when you're fucking ready. Not when anyone else tries to tell you so," he quickly retorts, waving his fork in my direction, and Creed knocks it away even though I'm completely aware that it's not me he's aiming it at.

Hopefully, what he's saying doesn't cause more of a stir, but truthfully, I still feel drained, and he's right. I need to take a minute to heal myself. Otherwise, I'll be no use to anyone.

I've located the new bunch of black strands in my hair, right at my crown, and I'm silently dreading the day that my entire head is black. So today, I don't have to worry about anything going on past these four walls. It'll be like the weekend again, only this time, I don't have the luxury of forgetting all of the bullshit that's happening.

"What do you want to spend the day doing?" I ask, and Zane grabs my thigh, drawing my attention to the fact that he's wagging his eyebrows. Before he can speak a word of what's going through his mind, Eldon beats him to it.

"I was thinking we could eat then figure out what the fuck is actually going on around us—what Erikel is *actually* planning. We need to try to piece everything together the best we can. Then we can try to figure out what our next step is. It feels like we're sitting ducks and I'm done with that shit. We're not here at Erikel's will. *You're* not. We need out. Now."

Damn.

That's just as hot as Zane's fingers digging into my skin hard enough to leave bruises.

"Count me in," I breathe, eager to get ahead of the game. Eldon is right. It may not have even been two whole weeks since Erikel stabbed Burton and exposed my magic, but it's been long enough. I'm done sitting idly by.

That's not who I am. That's not who *we* are.

"Eat first, Dove. Then maybe, if you do good with the jigsaw puzzle that is our lives, I might eat you," Zane murmurs against my ear, and my thighs clench in excitement.

"Deal."

I can't knock the smile off my face as I stuff my mouth with bacon, avocado, eggs, and toast. It's clear I'm not only exhausted from the strain on my magic, but I'm starving, too, as I refill my plate and keep going.

Once I'm done, I fall back in my seat with a sigh,

my stomach full as I consider whether a nap would be worthwhile before we dive straight into everything. But it seems Brax has other ideas.

"Let's go, Shadow. Before you have everyone else at the table tugging at their dicks over the noises you make when you eat," he grunts, pushing up from the table as the others snicker at him.

Eldon adjusts himself through his shorts beside me and I nip at my bottom lip.

"But I think that would be hot as hell to watch," I state, quirking a brow at Brax as he glances back over his shoulder at me.

"I'm sure it will be. Once we get through all of the bullshit. It can be your prize, along with Zane snacking on your pussy, I promise."

Damn.

That's a promise I'm going to hold him to.

I tug the hem of my tee down as I stand, following him over to the sofas without another word, and as my ass hits the cushions, he produces a random whiteboard out of nowhere. It stands dead center between the two sofas so everyone can see.

"Where do we begin?" Creed asks, taking the seat to my right, and I lean into his side. After earlier, I feel closer to him, now more than ever, and I'm happy to keep riding that high.

"I think the issue is there's so much at play. So maybe we categorize what we do know, and then we can break down whether it connects to any of the other chess pieces," Eldon offers, sitting across from me, and I nod in agreement.

"Okay, what is there?" Brax asks, making a red marker appear in his hand a second later before he raises it, ready to scrawl on the board.

"If we're talking categories, we have Erikel, his men, Burton, The Monarchy, and the Monarch they were keen on saving yesterday," Zane reels off rapidly.

"I think Sebastian needs to be up there too, and the unknown creatures that Ari mentioned," I add, watching as Brax scatters the words around the board.

"Anything else?"

"My father... me," Creed states, his voice wavering slightly as I glance at him. I want to tell him he's wrong, that they don't belong up there, especially not him, but the reality is, he has no idea what happened yesterday and that just leaves gaping holes in everything.

Brax adds the golden warrior and Creed's name to the board, and I don't miss the fact that he didn't actually write 'Creed's father.'

"If we think of anything else, we can add it, but for now, let's break down the points on the board," Brax states, and that's exactly what we do.

We note the fact that Erikel managed to get past the guards and wards that protect the perimeter of the academy, along with his men, and that it likely links to Sebastian, who is a total dick. We discuss the fact that Erikel has never actually shown his magic, and that becomes a big question mark. We point out that his men are feral, but we still know very little about them.

Burton hasn't shown his face since the Guild meeting last week and he is supposed to be our leader. But more importantly, why is Erikel happy for him to remain alive and in hiding among us?

Sebastian is a total dick.

The Monarchy is giving us major red flags, Rhys currently included since we haven't heard anything from him or anyone else in over a week, except when the two men yesterday agreed to leave Erikel here to save that guy's life.

Sebastian is a total dick.

The creatures in the forest with Ari are definitely a new addition, but why has no one actually mentioned them? Yet they're here, lurking in the shadows on campus.

Then there's Creed.

And Sebastian is still a total dick.

"What feels off the most to you about yesterday, Creed?" Brax asks, and my hand tightens around Creed's in silent comfort. He put his own name up on that board, which means he has to open up to us the best he can.

"Honestly, it all started in the arena," he admits, making my chest clench with worry.

"What do you mean?" I ask, turning to face him head-on.

"My father practically deflected every single flicker of magic that was thrown his way. From ice to random items, shifters, and even psychic abilities." Each of the Bishops nod in agreement. I recall watching everyone's magic practically hit a wall around the warrior before dispelling, but I never got to go up there myself to understand properly. "When I got up there, whatever defense he had around him fractured, just for a second, almost like he let me in."

Holy shit.

"What did he want you to see, Creed?" Eldon asks, interlocking his hands as he stares at his friend.

"He just kept chanting the same thing," he admits, swiping a hand down his face before he looks up to meet my eyes. "He just kept saying, 'I love you, son. I love you, son. I love you, son,' and it's thrown me for a fucking loop."

Fuck.

My knuckles turn white as I tighten my hold on his hand.

"Do you think—"

"I don't know what I think, honestly. I just… shit. Is he hidden away? Is he doing everything demanded of him to protect me? My mother? Does he know what he's doing? I don't fucking know, but hope is a fickle thing, and I don't know if it's something I can entertain right now."

My heart aches for him. That's shit. That's shitter than shit. That's shitter than my father murmuring some crap about loving me no matter how much I hate him.

"Parents are fucked up, man. Who knows why they do anything?" Zane grumbles, his lips pursing, and I know he's thinking about his own father. Rhys was a guiding light before all of this, and now he's non-existent, and that must be even worse because it's not hope Zane has in him; it's undying trust.

Brax clears his throat as Creed glances down at the floor. "What's on the top of our to-do list?" he asks, circling back to the board.

"We need to figure out a way to get more information on Erikel's men, understand more about the creatures in the forest, demand that Burton explain what *his* fucking game plan is, and understand the golden warrior's motive," I list off, and Creed's gaze snaps to mine at the mention of his father. He shakes his head as he tries to dismiss my last point, but I cut him off before he can speak. "You're probably going to tell me that everything with him doesn't matter among everything else, but it does, Creed. It matters a lot, and I'm not going to enable you to hide from that fact."

I immediately worry I've overstepped the mark and my pulse pounds in my ears, but, to my relief, he offers me the smallest of smiles.

"Thank you, Raven."

I'm beaming inside, happiness and that fickle thing called hope blossoming inside of me, when a knock sounds from the front door.

"Fuck," I grunt, staring at it like whoever is on the other side will be revealed to me without me getting up to answer it. Zane is already moving, though. Swinging the door open wide without a backward glance.

His shoulders relax as he nudges the door open further to reveal Leila, who doesn't attempt to take a step inside as she smiles at me. "Hey, there's a meeting tonight. I know you weren't in classes today, but I wanted to stop by and see if you guys were in."

"Was there an issue with our absence today?" Zane asks, glaring down at her, and she shakes her head.

"Not that I'm aware of."

"What time is the meeting?" he presses, giving her a pointed look.

"In an hour," she answers, her tone a little snappier as she matches his energy, and it's almost amusing.

"An hour? What time is it?" I ask, glancing at each of my men as I frown in confusion.

"A little after six," Brax states and my eyeballs almost fall out of my head.

"We have not been sitting here talking for that long," I insist, but we clearly have.

"What's that?" Leila asks, distracting me, and I find her pointing at the board.

"Uhhh…"

"We're trying to piece together everything we know about all of the bullshit we're drowning in," Eldon states, leaning back in his seat as he waves her in. "Anything to add?"

Leila steps into the lounge, taking small, measured steps toward us as she fixates on the red scribble on the board. She's wearing a long black coat that she wraps tighter around herself as she assesses everything. Her eyes scan from left to right again and again, and my nerves start to spike when she gets to the bottom of the board and seemingly goes to the top and starts again.

"Is this a collection of facts?" she asks, looking to Brax, who remains beside the board with his marker in hand, and he nods. "Then you should add my father to it," she states, her tone not wavering or seeming uncertain.

"Why's that?" Brax asks, folding his arms over his chest as he looks down at her.

"Because he's holed up with Barton and I haven't really seen him since the last meeting myself, either."

I frown. "How do you know there's a meeting if your father hasn't told you?" I always assumed he was the one to tell her, so if she hasn't seen him, I'm intrigued to know where she got her information from.

"Grave."

"You mean the guy you say fucked you and made you hot gossip? Because I'm going to be real with you right now, Leila, that's not the story he's telling me," Creed interjects, and my head whips to him. Since when?

"One and the same. He called me out after you questioned him at training, and it seems Genie has a talent for taking pictures of quite a lot of people against their will." Her gaze drops to the floor and my jaw tightens with anger for her.

Genie is a total dick too.

"Okay, we'll be there." Creed stands, pulling me along with him. "Is there anything with your father we should be more focused on?"

Leila shakes her head. "I don't know."

It seems that we don't know much at all between us. Let's hope the Nightmares Guild can offer us something.

Stepping down into the meeting room, I half expect to see Sebastian pop up out of nowhere, but to my surprise, as I scan around the gathered crowd, he's not here. With Leila on my left and Eldon on my right, we come to a stop by the golden table where Burton and Fitch stand side by side, murmuring among themselves.

"It's good to finally see you both. How is the plan to save the academy and the realm looking?" I ask, folding my arms over my chest as I glance between the pair of them. Fitch frowns as Burton purses his lips, and I'm left wondering why the hell I saved this guy if he's not going to do something useful.

"There's a lot at play right now, Raven. Patience is key," Burton states, and I shake my head.

"Patience would be key if there was time for that. Instead, the students are feeling the wrath of the enemy while you two hide away and, when questioned, reveal nothing. I exposed myself and my abilities for two reasons. One, to protect Creed, and two, because I believed in you to be the leader we needed to survive, but I'm not seeing it."

Apparently, I'm madder than I initially thought and now I'm on a roll with no inclination to stop.

"She does have a point." The interruption comes from Dalton, one of the fourth years, and hearing his agreement makes me stand a little taller. He's not saying it to appease me. He has no need, he clearly thinks the same as me and my men, and it's reassuring. His comment also quiets the other members of the Guild and everyone settles their attention on the two men who are supposed to be our leaders.

Burton clears his throat, adjusting the tie at his neck as he looks around the room. "We won't be battling tonight. Our focus needs to be on us collectively coming up with a plan of action," he states, piquing my interest, but it's still odd to me that this is suddenly now a group effort. It certainly wasn't that way before Erikel.

"You need to start telling us where the fuck we stand because, from our perspective, you're just leaving us to rot under Erikel's reign," Brax grunts, moving slightly so he's standing protectively in front of me without blocking me completely.

"I'm not," Burton attempts to reassure us, but it doesn't seem like anyone is taking the bait.

"Do you know what happened at Pinebrook?" Creed asks, cocking a brow at Burton and Fitch before turning his attention to the rest of the members. "Was anybody else forced to go?" he adds, and nobody makes themselves known, which makes him scoff in disappointment. At whom, I'm not entirely sure, but that clearly doesn't make his whole ordeal any easier.

"What happened there, Creed?" Fitch asks, giving him

his full attention, and Creed sighs, likely trying to figure out where to begin. I keep my eyes locked on the pair of them as Creed gives them a clipped overview, and when he confirms that I was forced to bring back Monarch Dutton, Burton curses under his breath.

"What?" I ask, wanting to know exactly what he's thinking. A look passes between Burton and Fitch and it only irritates me further. "How can you lead us if you don't know any of this and don't share what you do know?"

"Because I know I have something they want. Something only one other person knows of," Burton explains, pinching at the bridge of his nose.

"Monarch Dutton," Zane states, piecing it together, and Burton nods, sighing heavily as he drops his hands to his sides.

"What could you possibly have that they don't?" Leila asks, her eyebrows pinched in confusion as she stares her father down, but it's Burton who answers.

"The location of the stone."

The stone?

"What stone?" I ask, close to needing to sit down as the stilted information comes through. "What does a stone have to do with anything?" I push when Burton starts to shake his head. It's like pulling teeth. It really shouldn't be this hard.

"I'm assuming the stone is what he wants to help in

his big plan to dominate the realm and merge us with the Basilica Realm," Fitch states, nostrils flaring with anger as he addresses the entire room. "That's where we've been, hiding it."

"Hiding what?" another member hollers, the frustration in their voice matching exactly what I'm feeling. But also, they've been able to get off campus? How? We're fucking trapped here, and they can do as they please? Bullshit.

"The Poten's Ruby." It's on the tip of my tongue to demand why the Poten's Ruby is so important, but Fitch seems to understand that we've already worked hard enough to draw this information from them. "You never truly own the Poten's Ruby. If anything, you're its vessel if you allow it to control you, and in return, it gives you the power to take powers from others. To leave other supernaturals defenseless, or to take their abilities for yourself."

EIGHTEEN

Raven

One thing I love about my magic is the ability to set the water in the shower to the perfect temperature. Back in Shadowmoor, you were crossing your fingers in hopes of it being tepid, and you were showering as fast as possible before the cold stream returned.

It was a luxury showing up here, to have water that ran at a hot temperature consistently, but to have it so perfect it feels like a gift that will warm my fucking bones until the end of time.

I have to find some positives about being here, other than the Bishops and my magic, of course, and water temperature seems to be one of them. The negatives keep stacking up against me, firmly led by Erikel at this stage, and last night's revelations at the Nightmares Guild meeting only confirm it.

Who the fuck created the Poten's Ruby? Surely, it wasn't just naturally found like that, harvesting such abilities when power-hungry fools like Erikel exist. It's ridiculous. Of course there's something this powerful out there that we now have to contend with. I understand why it wouldn't be common knowledge, but it's clear Burton knew this was of importance to Erikel and he chose to keep it to himself until it was impossible not to.

He swears the location of the ruby has changed over the past few days, confirming that Monarch Dutton won't know its whereabouts, but that only leaves me worrying over his well being. The pain of the other thirty-five dead people from Pinebrook hurts, and adding another feels like I'm going to pass out.

My magic doesn't like it.

It's as if it has its own conscience living inside of me. Selfishly, I want to fight to protect myself and the others while my magic wants to save everyone. I *think* it's to save them, anyway. I've heard folklore about necromancers before me and their need to heal everyone to create an army of the dead. That's what I read about in the books at Shadowmoor, but that doesn't feel like this… I don't think.

Running my hands over my drenched hair, I tilt my face up to the downpour, trying to calm my racing thoughts, until a soft, cool breeze dances over my skin. My eyes startle open to find Eldon closing the bathroom door behind him.

The grin on his lips as he grazes his eyes over me from head to toe makes me shiver. With a flick of his hand, his clothes are gone and he's prowling toward me.

Fuck.

"Good morning, Little Bird," he says huskily, stepping into the shower beside me, and all I can do is gape at him for a moment as I try to remember how to fucking speak.

"Morning," I manage to breathe, and his grin widens. He's so aware of the effect he has on me. It should be embarrassing.

"I missed my little spectator while I worked out," he states, explaining the sweat beading at his temples.

"I'm disappointed I missed the visual."

He grabs my waist, turning me to face him as he towers above me. He doesn't bat an eyelid at the water now pouring over him, which somehow makes him look hotter.

Skimming my hands over his chest, I settle them on his shoulders as I eliminate the remaining distance between our lips, but if I had any hopes of claiming him, I'm mistaken.

He's in control.

My back is plastered against the cool tiles behind the shower head a moment later, my back arching as he sinks his teeth into my bottom lip, and I groan.

Good morning to me.

I rake my fingers through his hair, clinging to him as

tingles ripple through my body.

"I want to taste you."

I nod eagerly at his words as he trails his lips down my chin, over my neck, and across my collarbone.

"Fuck. Please," I moan, desperate to feel him between my thighs.

His lips curve up into a devilish smile against my skin before he runs his tongue down the valley between my breasts. His heated gaze as he looks up at me makes my core burn with need. A need that grows fiercer when his knees hit the floor and his breath ghosts over the apex of my thighs.

"Say it again, Little Bird."

I frown, unsure what he's talking about, but the quirk of his brow tells me he's not going to give me a hint. Recalling what I last said, I rub my lips together as understanding washes over me.

"Please, Eldon. Taste me."

The last word has barely passed my lips when he drags his tongue through my folds, turning my plea into a garbled moan as my palms slap against the tiles behind me.

Fuck.

He hoists my left thigh over his shoulder, offering him better access to my pussy as he draws circles around my clit with the tip of his tongue.

"Use your magic to hold you steady against the wall,"

he orders, but I shake my head.

"No. I like the way it feels when my muscles clench, holding on for dear life," I mutter, looking down at him through hooded eyes, and his own darken with desire at my words.

"Have it your way."

My lips part, but the words don't come when he thrusts two fingers deep into my core at the same time as he nips at my clit.

Holy shit.

A deep moan rumbles from my mouth, burning my tongue as my eyelids fall closed and my head knocks back against the tiles. He knows how to play my body perfectly. Every flick of his tongue, every sweep of his fingers at my pussy, every graze of his teeth, it's perfection.

"Eyes on me, Little Bird. I want to watch you when you come," he orders before sucking my clit into his mouth, teetering on the line between pain and pleasure.

Gulping, I try to focus on him. His blue eyes hold me captive as he feasts on me, finger-fucking me into oblivion. Seeing the enjoyment on his face, the pleased glint in his eyes, is all too much and the orgasm that crashes over me is chaotic in the sweetest way possible.

I scream, my lungs vibrating with the power behind it, my hips jerking against him as I ride out my climax to the very end. Sagging against the tiles, he slowly lowers my foot to the floor, making me groan when his fingers retreat from my core.

I'm spent and I don't want the feeling to end.

Eldon stands, stroking his thumb over my cheek as he grins down at me, and I push up off the wall and start to sink to my knees, eager for my turn, but he stops me before my knees can touch the ground.

"There's no time for me," he breathes, crowding my space once again as he peppers soft kisses over my lips.

"But—"

He places his finger over my lips, shaking his head.

"It was never about me, Raven. This was for you. I get the pleasure of your taste on my tongue for the rest of the day."

Well, fuck.

I want to argue back and demand we take another day off from classes so I can taste him too, but the bang of the bathroom door opening interrupts the moment and we both turn to find Zane in the doorway.

"Oh, you motherfucker," he grunts, wagging a finger at Eldon, who laughs into my neck.

"What's going on?" I ask, nudging my shoulder so I can see Eldon's face as I glance between them.

"He knows what he did," Zane growls, but there's no true anger there. Jealousy, maybe, but nothing more.

"What did you do?" I ask, confused as fuck as I come

down from my waves of pleasure.

"I finished my last set and said I'm going to go and find my Dove." He wiggles his eyebrows suggestively, making it clear what he had in mind. "But this asshole created a ring of fire around me so I couldn't move and he could have you all to himself."

"You've got to be quicker, man. It's not my fault you announced it to the group. Maybe you just need to be a little stealthier. That's all I'm saying," Eldon says with a chuckle, and I smush my lips together as I try to hide my grin, but Zane sees right through me.

"You're an encouraging menace, Dove," he says, aiming his finger in my direction this time, and I beam.

"One of my four favorite people in the world made me come before class. I'm not complaining. If that makes me a menace, I'll take it," I remark, and Zane grins at me as Eldon kisses my shoulder.

"If it puts my Dove in a good mood, maybe morning orgasms need adding to the handbook."

Maybe they do.

Zane wraps his arms around my waist, lifting me off the ground with a squeal as we step out of the house. He's been handsy the entire time I was getting ready. Apparently, post-orgasm Raven is even hotter than regular Raven, and in his words, that's a hard feat.

Either way, if he carries on like this, I may just self-combust before we get to our first class.

He continues to carry me to the end of our pathway, my back to his chest as he presses sloppy kisses against my neck with every step.

"Wait up," Brax hollers, likely wanting his usual spot of leading us all, and Zane takes the moment to stop and lower me to the ground.

"You're fucking beautiful, Dove," he whispers against my ear, squeezing my sides and making my body clench.

"If you're hinting at getting me back in the house, I'm in," I reply, turning to face him, and he smirks at me.

"Don't even think about it," Creed interjects. "We're supposed to be starting phase one of our plan today. That means no fucking until later."

I roll my eyes dramatically at him as he approaches us. A retort is ready on my tongue when a blast from behind me forcibly pushes me into Zane and we tumble to the ground.

Zane grunts but bands his arms around my body and rolls us over so he's protecting me from whatever the fuck that was. My heart races in my chest, my pulse rings in my ears, and my body falters as I scramble to get over the hit I just took.

"What the fuck, Genie?" Eldon snaps, a glimmer of something orange in his hand as he storms past me, but I can't see everything that's happening with Zane on top of me.

Attempting to take a deep breath, I manage to ease the pain in my chest enough to speak. "Let me up."

Thankfully, he does, pushing up to his feet before offering me his hand. Turning to look for Genie, I find her standing in front of Eldon and Brax, hovering an inch off the ground as she glares at the pair of them.

Creed appears at my side, trying to take my hand, but I shake him off as I approach the crazy bitch that keeps appearing in my life when I'm trying to have a good time.

Her eyes meet mine as I step to the side of Eldon. "You!" she bellows, her hair standing on end as energy seems to swarm around her.

"What did I do now, Genie?" I ask, bored at this stage.

"You fucked up everything," she snaps back, and I cock an eyebrow at her.

"Please, enlighten me," I push, folding my arms over my chest.

I haven't seen her in days. I was hoping she had fucked off for good, but unfortunately, I don't seem to be that blessed.

"I've been kicked out of the Guild." She bares her teeth as her feet touch the ground, her hands fisting at her sides.

"And that's my fault because…"

"Because you got Sebastian kicked out, and now, apparently, I'm a liability because I love him and I can't be trusted." She goes to take a step toward me, but Eldon lifts his hand, and I notice it's a ball of fire in his palm that must have been the flash of orange from earlier. The warning is clear. Take another step toward me, and she's going up in flames.

"I'm sorry to break it to you, but this all seems like a you problem, Genie." I force a smile to my lips, but it doesn't seem to have the desired effect I was going for. If anything, it makes her angrier.

"Listen here, you little bitch," she snarls, swinging her arms around, and Eldon completely fills the space between us so she can't get to me, but too little too late, I realize she wasn't trying anyway.

A knock to the head, the wind taken from my sails once more, and I'm flat out on the ground.

Fuck.

Disoriented, I can hear the Bishops going insane as I lazily blink up at the dull sky. For a split second, I consider getting the Poten's Ruby for myself so I can be done with this bitch's magic attacking me, but I quickly shut it down.

She needs to be put in her place, but I would rather use my powers and do it myself than rely on a tool. She's not worthy of an artifact. She's not worthy of my effort either, but I'm so done with her fucking presence.

I just need a second to nap first because it hurts everywhere.

"Raven? Dove?" Squinting, I focus on Zane as he hovers above me, concern etched into his features as I try to focus. "I'm here. It's okay. Can you sit up for me?" he asks, delicately cupping my cheek, and I nod even though I know for certain that I definitely can't. His fingers intertwine with mine, poised and ready to help me, but when I make no attempt to move after a few moments, he lowers them back down. "Take your time."

Inhaling, I try to hold it in for a second before I exhale. I repeat the motion a few more times before I feel a little more stable. "What hit me?" I rasp, my head still pounding from the impact.

Zane glances over his shoulder briefly before turning back to me, but the wince drawing his eyebrows together tells me he's not sure what to say. Tilting my head, I try to follow his line of sight to see a fucking full-sized tree lying across the pathway.

"That bitch threw a tree at me?" I clarify with a gasp, and he nods, swiping a hand down his face.

"Roots and all," he adds, a soft smile on his face as he tries to make light of the situation. It feels too surreal to actually be my life.

"I'm going to knock her the fuck out," I grunt,

tightening my hold on his hands and lifting up to a sitting position.

"I'm sure you will, Dove. But unfortunately for you, someone beat you to it," he explains, nodding to where I was standing a few minutes ago.

Frowning, I glance at the backs of Brax and Eldon. Did one of them beat me to it? I'm not about men hitting women in general, but I'm quite sure this is an acceptable circumstance. When I find Creed crouched down over Genie's unconscious body, I quickly realize it was none of my men.

Blonde hair floats in the light breeze as icicles hang from Genie's nose.

Leila.

Her eyes find mine as if sensing her name in my mind and her chin quickly dips, her cheeks heating as she tucks a loose tendril of hair behind her ear.

Zane helps me to my feet and stays by my side as I make my way toward her.

"I'm sorry, she just... I just..." Leila stares at me, completely lost for words as she shakes her head.

"She fucking deserved it. Besides, it's better coming from another girl and not one of us, but I was ready for it if necessary," Eldon states, pulling me into his side as he glances over me to make sure I'm okay.

Leila nods, rubbing her lips together nervously as she

looks at me. Suddenly, her eyes widen and she digs into the backpack at her feet. "Sorry, I was hoping to catch you guys before you got near the main building so I could show you this. I just got a bit distracted with…" Her words trail off as she looks down at Genie.

She holds a dusty and tattered leather binder out and Brax takes it from her.

"What's this?" he asks as I step out from beside Eldon to take a look at it too. Creed and Zane inch closer, Genie's body left on the pathway for someone else to deal with.

"I've been researching the stone they were talking about yesterday."

"When?" Creed asks, brows furrowing.

"I've been up since four and at the library since shortly after."

"You've been awake, researching, since before the sun came up?" Brax clarifies, a mixture of uncertainty and disbelief in his eyes.

"Yes," Leila replies with a nod, rocking back on her heels as Brax flicks through the pages.

"The look on your face says you found something good…"

"Well, I found that," she states, pointing at the binder as a whole. "It's a compendium of magical artifacts, and it includes the Poten's Ruby."

"There's a whole fucking book on this shit?" I blurt,

and Zane grins at me.

"Do we need to know anything more about it other than it's coveted as fuck?" Eldon adds with a huff, trying to get a better look at the binder.

"The ruby is only part of the equation," Leila reassures. "Did you not hear the fact that there are others listed and detailed in there?"

"Is there anything of use?" Brax asks, quirking a brow at her, and she shrugs.

"I can do some more research, Brax. I can't make decisions for us." She turns to face me head on, nodding as she exhales slowly. "I trust that to be your role."

NINETEEN

Brax

After Genie's unexpected visit this morning, Raven shook off the lingering effects of her bullshit and got on with the day like it wasn't a goddamn tree that hit her. I think that's why she holds me captive despite my best efforts to keep her at arm's length. It's all gone to shit and I know it. Admitting it hurts more than I would like, but fuck, it's the truth.

I've never met anyone in all of my life who continues to get back up every time they're knocked down quite like she does—both metaphorically and physically, if the tree to the head this morning is anything to go by. She doesn't cower, she doesn't hide away, she doesn't let a single hurdle keep her down.

Even now, as we head down the hallway, her shoulders are back, her head high, and her strides purposeful. She has an inexplicable presence that I can't even put into words. I should have known I never stood a chance against her. Arm's length may not be working anymore, but letting myself hunt her down, stake my claim, and take what's mine makes up for it.

Today, my issue isn't the fact that this damn woman has me twisted up in knots.

No.

It's the fact that classes are relatively... normal.

There hasn't been a single glimpse of Erikel or any of his men. I have no fucking clue what that means or where they might be, but the reality is, if *we're* getting peace from them, someone else is paying the price of their presence. Likely on a grander scale. Which will be an issue for us in the near future, I'm sure.

Despite the impending doom, it's a relief. Not enough for my guard to drop, I'm on pins and needles, but when we step into our final class for the day to see it's an actual tutor instead of some fucker from Basilica, I heave a sigh of relief.

The moment I realize it's Figgins, my gaze drifts to Raven. Her eyes widen as she freezes in the doorway, her knuckles white as she clings to Zane at her side, and her brain short circuits for a moment before she's scurrying between the desks to speak to her.

There's no question what topic is at the forefront of

her mind.

Ari and the magical creatures in the forest.

Figgins is supposed to be the professor in charge of all of that shit, so she has some explaining to do. Intrigued to watch my girl in action, I don't bother to follow her up to the front. Instead, I take my usual seat and get comfortable.

"Professor, I need to talk to you about something," Raven blurts as she plants her hands on the desk between her and Figgins. The latter quirks a brow at my girl, likely questioning her rudeness, but Raven doesn't back down as she holds her stare.

"That will have to wait until after the class."

Raven's already shaking her head before Figgins finishes speaking. "I need to talk to you about Ari and the other creatures who—"

"Miss Hendrix," Figgins shouts with a gasp, cutting Raven off, and my spine stiffens, ready to jump to my girl's defense if necessary. "I said we can discuss this after class," she repeats, and Raven stands tall.

She straightens her blazer and purses her lips as she glares at the professor. "We can discuss this now and I will keep my expectations of you low, or we can wait until after class is done with and I'll be holding you accountable for more. Waiting until the end of the class will cement your dedication."

Hot. As. Fuck.

No one should look that good when they're being that demanding, but Raven has a way about her.

Figgins looks around the classroom, twisting her lips as she considers her options. After a few moments, she sighs, nodding. "Have it your way, Raven. Let's take this outside."

I'm out of my seat in a flash, my brothers along with me as we hightail it back into the corridor. Figgins regards us for a brief second but clearly sees that we're not going to budge on this, so she closes the classroom door behind her and turns to face Raven.

"What seems to be the issue, Raven?" she asks, lacing her fingers together as she stares expectantly at my shadow.

"Where do I begin?" Raven snaps back, already fuming and ready to cause mayhem. "Ari is trapped inside the fucking forest you force them all to be in but I can't ask you to let him out without demanding the others be released, too. Not only are you putting his life at risk, but you're also putting everyone else in danger because there are creatures in there we know nothing about."

"Raven, I know every creature in there. The academy has always operated this way. It's not going to change because your familiar doesn't like it," Figgins grumbles, which only makes Raven's eyes widen further with anger.

"You don't know, do you?" Raven rasps, her jaw

ticking as her hands clench at her sides.

"Know what?"

"That there are creatures in there that Erikel brought with him. Creatures that have the others scared."

The professor tilts her head, assessing Raven as if trying to decipher a lie. "That's not possible. It's—"

"Ari purposely went through the barrier, choosing to be in the forest to help protect his herd. They're not safe. None of us are. This is already a volatile situation, now isn't the time to be keeping magical creatures that could help us trapped to be killed off on a whim. Now is the time to be gaining their trust in the hopes of having their aid when the time comes." Raven's chest rises and falls rapidly as she throws her hands around in frustration.

"Raven, you must be mistaken," Figgins starts, shaking her head dismissively, and Raven holds her hands up high as she vibrates with agitation.

"Do I look mistaken? I'm dead fucking serious, and you're not listening to me."

"Raven, take a deep breath. Maybe we need to calm ourselves so we can repeat what you're saying in a way the professor understands," Creed offers, glaring at Figgins when he mentions her.

"I don't need it repeated, Creed. I understand what she's saying, but I'm telling you, it's not possible."

"What makes you say that?" I interject, intrigued by

the fact that Raven is throwing all of this information at her and she's refusing to let it stick.

"Because I put the wards up myself. I always know who is tethered to the forest."

I glance at Raven, knowing she doesn't have the answer, but there is something Ari didn't let us do when we last went to visit.

"When we went to the forest last week, searching for Raven's familiar, he refused to let us step through the barrier because he believed this information to be true. If there's one thing we can all be certain of, especially since it was Raven's familiar that saved us all at the outpost at Shadowmoor, that's the fact that he is highly protective of her in every way. He wouldn't choose to be in that forest if he didn't believe it to be true," Creed states, saying it far better than I could have. I'm well aware I'm a lot more caveman than him. She would have been lucky to get anything more than a shoulder barge.

Figgins at least looks to be considering his words, but I get the feeling she's going to be too stuck in her ways.

Clearing my throat, I try to tamp down my building rage to approach the situation a little more calm and collected like Creed, but nothing comes out. Thankfully, Raven takes a deep breath and takes control of the situation once again.

"Professor Figgins, all I'm asking is for you to come and take a look with us. I'm not wrong in what I'm saying.

We need these creatures. I know it in my heart and soul. Just... please, come and look with me."

The five of us stare at the professor, hope warring inside of us, until she finally clears her throat and straightens her cloak.

"Fine, but it can't happen until the weekend."

"Thank you," Raven murmurs with a sigh of relief. "We're going to need to act fast once we've been there, but I appreciate you agreeing to this."

Figgins nods, glancing over my shoulder to the classroom behind me. "That being said, you misspoke in there, Raven. You're going to have to sit out for the rest of the lesson. The rest of this stays between us," she adds, and we all mutter our agreement.

I'm up for an early finish, so it's no issue for me if we leave now.

Hiking my backpack up my shoulder, I settle my hand on the small of Raven's back and steer her away from the class without a backward glance. Creed, Eldon, and Zane are right with us and we don't slow our pace for a single moment until we're walking down the pathway to our home.

Once the front door clicks shut behind us, Raven sags in relief. She rests her chin on my chest and for just a second, I cling to her, inhaling her scent and getting my fill before it's back to business.

"That's a plan for the creatures on the agenda. We're going to have to try and shoulder it until the weekend. Is that going to be okay for you?" Eldon asks, flopping down on the sofa as he looks to Raven, who nibbles on her lip.

"I'm already feeling the strain from the distance between us. The weekend might be a struggle," she admits, and it only makes me softer on her. The fact that she so openly shows her vulnerability to us now knocks me off my feet.

"We'll make it happen," I murmur, pressing a kiss to her forehead before I drop down onto the sofa. "For now, though, I think we need to take a look through this thing." I pull the book on magical artifacts from my bag, waving it in the air for a second. It's practically been burning a hole in my backpack and I'm desperate as hell to understand everything in here, even more desperate than I am to understand *why* Leila went hunting for it to begin with.

I still can't make up my mind about her. It's exhausting.

"I'll get everyone a drink while you have a glance over it," Raven states, breezing past us all with that natural sway to her hips that holds us all captive. "But I think we should understand everything there is to know about the Poten's Ruby first."

None of us answer, our eyes glued to her sweet ass, and it's only when she turns to head back to us that we realize she's waiting for some form of acknowledgment. A knowing grin takes over her mouth and not one of us tries to cover our tracks. Instead, she takes the manuscript from my hands, sits down, and starts to read it herself.

I watch as her eyes dance over the pages, her finger lingering in certain spots for a few moments as she clearly thinks over what she's reading. When she turns the page to find the entry she was reading has ended, she flips back to where she was and releases an exasperated sigh before leaning back in her seat, offering us nothing.

"What—"

"It's the most ridiculous shit," she grunts, cutting my question off as she wipes a hand down her face and sighs. "All it says is exactly what Burton said about it yesterday, along with a listing of where in history it has been used before. This is the kind of shit we're supposed to be taught in this place. Instead, we've got the old head professor hiding the damn thing. Why hasn't someone destroyed it? What greater dangers are lurking out there?" Her frustration is clear.

Taking the document from her, I glance over the information. She's not wrong. It's ridiculous. "It states that the ruby was first documented over eight hundred years ago and is known to have been used by four men in the past; none of them currently living, until now, it seems," I say with a scoff, flicking the page back and forth. "Otherwise, it explains it has the ability to suck the magic from any being for it to be stored in the stone or transferred to another. It doesn't state where it was last seen or how to destroy it. Nothing."

"We should have known it wouldn't make that easy for us," Zane grumbles, and Creed hums in agreement.

"What else is in there?" Eldon asks, propping his chin on the palm of his hand as he leans forward.

I flick through a few more pages, scanning over the bold text at the top of the tattered pages. "There's an artifact that can be worn like a crown to stop someone from getting into your mind. There's a golden table that mutes and saves all conversations spoken at it," I continue, but Raven rushes to her feet, stopping me from reading any further.

"Like the golden table in the Nightmares Guild?"

My eyes widen at the connection and I nod. "Fuck. Maybe."

"I think that's something we need to check out," Zane adds.

"There's also the Lotus Onyx that deflects magic and an emerald gate that leads to the Realm of Shadows, to name a few. But the table is something we can investigate sooner," I state, closing the tome and placing it on the arm of the sofa beside me.

"What I'm hearing is there are a lot of magical artifacts out there that do more than is necessary. Like it's not enough to be gifted with powers already," Eldon says with a sigh.

He's right.

I thought losing my parents at a young age was dark enough. Then, being enrolled into an academy that takes your death as payment for the knowledge they provide seemed to top it off. But this... what we're facing right now; it's on an entirely different level.

The mention of the Realm of Shadows swirls something inside of me, a remnant of my parents deep in my dreams floating to the surface, and it has me itching to learn more, but I brush it off. There's enough going on around us without me clinging to the desperation that seeps through me, wanting to find my parents in a real, more controlled environment.

This crazy fucking ride has us by the balls and there's no stop to get the hell off and make a dash for it. We're here whether we like it or not. And although it's not the battle we thought we had signed up for, it's a war all the same.

One way or another, we're either royally fucked or on the road to greatness.

The sun peeks over the horizon in the distance, the clouds making it harder to see than usual, but it will rise above the fog soon enough. It always does. Without fail.

My limbs ache, waiting for the moment the warm rays touch me and soften me.

My gut clenches. I don't know how I know that feeling—the touch of the sun's warmth against my skin—I just know I do, and I'm desperate for it. I'm frozen in place, waiting for it, unable to move despite how much I want to.

The first dance of the sun on my skin is like taking my first breath, awakening me in a way I can't quite explain. But one thing is for certain, the moment it graces me, I'm no longer locked in place.

Rocking my neck from side to side, my bones crack, or so I think. When I look down, my eyes burning from the new freedom they have now that they're no longer frozen in place, I realize I'm in full gargoyle form, crouched on the top of a building, the roof sloping down to my left.

What the fuck?

Stretching out, a groan rips from my lungs, burning my throat as I shift from stone to flesh and bone.

I have no idea why or how I am where I am, but I sure as shit need to get the fuck out of here. Rushing down the slope of the roof, I prepare to launch myself at the gathered bushes at the bottom, a move I feel like I've done a thousand times, but I don't recall a single one.

As I reach the bottom, my attempt at leaping through the air is short-lived as I lose my footing and fall head first.

I brace for impact, ready for the pain to ripple through my body, but it doesn't come as I continue to fall for what feels like a lifetime.

Just when the nausea eases in my gut, I slam into the ground without warning. I take a second to feel the blades of grass beneath my palms, hoping to calm myself, but it's impossible.

I don't know where I am. I don't know what the fuck I'm doing. Yet I'm stuck here whether I like it or not.

Pushing up, I glance around my new surroundings and my heart freezes in my chest.

What the fuck?

I'm… home… again.

How?

I stare up at the house, waiting for it to grow legs and run the fuck away, but after a couple of minutes, it doesn't do anything, so I slowly clamber to my feet. A hint of musky vanilla floats in the air, a smell I haven't had the pleasure of in a very long time, and it makes my gut ache at the memory.

Walking the path, I take the porch steps slowly. Filled with fear that I'm going to get ripped away, just like I did last time, I take measured steps in an attempt to prepare myself, but as I near, I hear my parents laughing on the other side of the door.

It has to be a dream. It has to be. I should wake up. I

know I should, but I can't deny myself the guilty pleasure of being in their presence again.

Lifting my fist to knock on the door, I startle when it opens before my knuckles hit the wood, and my father stands on the other side.

"Son."

One word.

One word and my heart cracks in two.

The word is accompanied by the sound of scurrying feet in the distance, and a moment later, my mother appears behind him.

"Brax."

Fuck.

I shouldn't put myself through this. It hurts too much, but I crave it like I crave oxygen.

"This is a dream," I rasp, my chest aching, and my mother shakes her head.

"No, son. This is where we exist."

"Exist?" I repeat, confused, and they both nod nervously.

"Then why am I here?"

A look passes between them, a look I can't quite decipher, before my mother takes a step closer. She was always the one better with words.

"We've been trying to understand it since the last time you were here, but it doesn't quite make sense. You

should have stayed the first time you were here, but you disappeared just as quickly as you appeared. Then the second time, my heart broke all over again, because you didn't stay for long. Now, I have no clue about this."

I frown.

I'm assuming this is where I came the last time I saw them, but the first time... I don't understand.

"Where is here?" I ask, my fingers flexing at my side as nerves get the better of me.

They look so real, so present, I could just reach out and touch them. But the fear of my hand going right through them like projections makes me refrain.

"Honey, we're in the Realm of Shadows."

TWENTY

Raven

A sudden jolt beside me stirs me awake in a panic. My heart races as I pry my eyes open to find Brax sitting up in the bed. Even in the darkness of the room, I can still make out the crinkle of his eyes, the tightness of his shoulders, and the smallest tremble to his hand as he runs his fingers over his cropped hair.

"Brax?" He startles at my voice, his head whipping around to face me in an instant as he frantically searches my gaze. "Is everything okay?" I whisper, knowing it's a dumb question.

He slumps back against the headboard as the other guys sleep around us, dragging his hand down his face as he exhales. It takes a moment, but when his eyes find mine again, I see the truth before he even speaks it.

"No."

My heart aches the moment the word leaves his lips and I shuffle to sit up beside him, trying my best not to wake Eldon as his arm drops from my waist. Brax stares up at the ceiling while I watch his chest rise and fall with each breath, slowly calming with each repetition.

"Do you want to talk about it?" I finally ask when his head tilts my way once again, and he sighs before nodding ever so slightly, but no words follow. I give him a few minutes to try and piece it together, but when he exhales in frustration I know it's not going to be as simple as that. "Do you want to talk about it *now* or in the morning?" I prod, trying to get a read on what he actually needs from me. I want to reach out and lace my fingers with his but I can't tell if that's going to make the situation better or worse.

He purses his lips, taking another deep breath. "I've been having dreams." His voice is groggier than I expect, a hoarseness I've never heard before, and it twists something inside of me. His emotions are thick with whatever this is. A few minutes pass, but I don't push. He needs me to be patient with him right now, and if it's time he needs, it's time he'll get. "Dreams where I see my parents."

Fuck.

I can't help it, I reach for his hand, and despite the worry blossoming inside of me, when my fingers touch his, he turns his hand for my palm to touch his. I squeeze, trying to silently communicate how much I'm here for him, and to my surprise, he returns the gesture, warming my aching soul.

"What kind of dreams?"

"I don't even know if they're actually dreams, I just don't know what else to call them," he admits, making me frown.

"What do you mean?"

His tongue sweeps over his lips as he tries to find the right words to explain. "I think that I'm traveling to wherever they are." My eyebrows furrow deeper as he looks at me, the question clear in my eyes so I thankfully don't have to ask. "The Realm of Shadows."

"The Realm of Shadows?" I repeat slowly, barely more than a whisper, as he shakes his head in disbelief.

"Apparently."

"Where is that?"

"I don't know." He shrugs. "They said it, and then I woke up. Again."

I hate to be the one to question it, but I need him to be sure. For his sake more than mine. "Do you trust in—"

"I've dreamed about them three times since you brought me back from the dead, Raven."

I gape at him.

Well, fuck.

"You think it's linked?" I ask, silently scared of the

answer, and he shrugs.

"I can't be sure," he murmurs, but I know he feels it in his gut because Brax isn't the kind of guy to voice his thoughts if he doesn't believe them to be true.

"But it makes sense," I breathe, worry clawing at my insides.

"None of it makes sense, Shadow."

Damn. That's fucking true.

"What are you thinking?" I ask when a couple of minutes pass. I can practically hear the cogs turning in his mind.

"I'm trying to find where I remember the mention of an emerald gate. If it can lead to the Realm of Shadows, then fuck, I could visit without being asleep. I have no control over any of it. I'm completely helpless and I'm always ripped away too soon."

"Do you want me to look with you?" I offer. Sleep is lost on me now, just as it is on him. There's no point pretending otherwise.

His hand tightens on mine. "You don't have to."

"I want to," I reply quickly. "Whatever you need, I'm here." He turns to me, the corner of his mouth turning up slightly as he nods. "Are you okay?"

"Yeah."

He's not. I know he's not.

"Are you sure?" I hate that I'm pushing, but mentally

berating myself isn't working. It seems my filter doesn't work in the midst of the twilight hour. "If there's anything—"

"I'm good," he interjects, and I know I deserve the blunt nudge to shut the fuck up.

Silence descends over us, but his hold on my hand doesn't change, so I shuffle closer, resting my head on his shoulder.

"Do you still see the shadows?" he asks, catching me off guard.

"Yeah."

"Now?"

"No. It seems I'm as helpless to them being here as you are to the timing of your visits to the Realm of Shadows," I state, and he huffs in agreement. We sit side by side, basking in the silence for a little while longer until he speaks again.

"Do you think you're going to go back to sleep?"

"No," I admit. My mind is too wired for me to even consider going back to sleep.

"Do you want to sneak out and continue training with your mirror magic?"

This man knows me far too well.

"Yes, please."

My body aches. We've repeated the process again and again to the point that the sky is starting to lighten. I hate that the sun isn't visible. Ever since Erikel arrived, it's been clouded by whatever shit he's doing. After growing up in Shadowmoor, I clung to the sun here. It was a sign that my life was changing, that I was growing, and now it's gone again. At least it's not complete darkness, but it's still tainted.

"That's it, Shadow. Let the feeling run through you this time. You're so close to controlling it completely," Brax encourages, and I take strength from his words as I calm the panic growing in my chest.

My eyes are closed tight, every inch of my body acutely aware of the fact that it's turning to stone. It's one thing to let your arms shift and the weight knock you off balance. It's something else entirely to let it consume your whole body.

I feel like I'm going to fall backward at any moment, the weight of my body completely knocking me off balance, but it makes me feel strong too, so I push on. Brax's encouragement and praise are helping. I like him snappy and all alpha when he's between my thighs, but right now, in this moment, when his tone is softer and his words more gentle, I like him even more.

"That's it. Now open your eyes and try to focus on your balance." I exhale slowly before I try, and it takes a few attempts for me to finally settle my gaze on his without falling to the side. The smile on his face is a rare one; one I'm committing to memory for all of eternity. "Perfect. Now, do you think you can take a step forward?"

I balk. "No way." The sound of my own voice startles me. It's raspier than usual, deeper, and it's strange to even associate it with myself.

"You've got this, Raven. You know you do. I'm right here with you."

My gaze narrows on him. I think I take back every positive thing I said about his encouragement and praise. It's starting to drive me insane. It stops me from backing out and quitting, and as much as I need it, I don't want it. I want to give up like a baby, maybe even throw a tantrum, but I know he won't let me get away with that.

"Come on, Shadow. If you can walk to me, I'll let you punch me in the gut. Gargoyle fists and all," he offers, and his persuasion instantly has my interest piqued.

That definitely does sound enticing.

The grin on his face makes it clear he knows he's got me right where he wants me, and I'm a damn sucker for him once again.

Exhaling, I turn my attention to my feet, toying with the weight as I attempt to lift my foot off the ground. It's worse than the whole moving my arms situation the last time we were doing this, but he definitely lured me in with the desire to get him.

"You need to stop thinking about how heavy it is; you're letting it become a whole mind-over-matter scenario, which is only going to make it all feel heavier," Brax points out, and I give him my best death glare, which does nothing to affect him.

Fucker.

I let go of his magic and the power I was drawing from him quickly disappears, leaving me to sway on my feet for a second before I regain my balance.

"I need to start fresh then," I state before he can moan at me for dropping the magic. "I need to grab the thread and move straight away so I don't get in my head," I add, and he nods in agreement.

"Realistically, that's how you're going to attack in a real-life situation."

"Who knew you had such words of wisdom?" I snark, and he folds his arms over his chest, cocking his brow at me while I smile at him from ear to ear.

"Do I even want to know how long you two have been out here?"

I spin to see Creed in the open doorway leading into the house. His hair is messy, his eyes tired, and his smile soft as he glances between us.

"Longer than I want to admit," Brax grunts, relaxing his magic.

"Have you been practicing mirror magic again?" Creed asks, and I nod. "Am I the only one you haven't done this with now?"

"Yeah."

"Want to give it a try before we have to leave for classes?"

I'm not looking for permission, but my gaze travels to Brax. We were about to go again, channeling his gargoyle, and I don't want to cause an issue by switching it up.

"You're good, Shadow. It'll be good for you mentally. Next time, you can come at it quicker, and hopefully, you'll smash it." He squeezes my shoulder, pressing a kiss to the top of my head, and I bask in the feeling.

"I'll smash *you*," I say with a smirk, and he chuckles.

"You wish," he retorts before heading for the house, leaving me to gape after him.

"That's not what I meant," I holler, my cheeks heating with embarrassment, but both Creed and Brax just laugh at me.

"If that's what you have to tell yourself to sleep at night, then okay," he says with a grin and a wink before disappearing inside.

Such a fucker.

"Are you ready? Or do you need a minute?" Creed asks with a cock of his brow, and I flip him off. He chuckles, and even though it's at my expense, the sound makes it all worthwhile.

"Get your ass over here so I can use your magic," I say with a pout, which makes his smile grow wider as he approaches.

"I love it when you use me," he murmurs, coming to a stop in front of me as we're toe to toe. Fuck. I gulp, my mouth drying as I lose words once again. "Come on, let's focus before we get completely distracted," he adds, like he's not the reason for my distraction, as he pulls me from the thoughts in my head, and I nod.

"I'm nervous," I admit. "With Brax, sharing a piece of my mind with him was a complete accident. I've seen what you can do. I don't want to fuck it up and hurt you." I think that's secretly why I've been holding back from him. Circumstances made it easier, but now I can't hide from it.

"You won't hurt me, Raven. Not even by accident." I part my lips, ready to push back, but his fingertips cover my mouth as he stops me before I can even begin. "I'm going to talk you through it, okay?" I shake my head, but he gives me a pointed stare until I sigh. Relenting, I nod instead. "That's my girl," he breathes, dropping his hand back to his side as he takes a step back. "The best way to focus is to stare into my eyes, think of what you would like to see, and if my barriers are down, you'll see it in your mind. For you to hurt me, that's got to be what you envision."

I exhale, shaking out my arms as I nod once again, trusting his word. "What are you happy for me to see?" I murmur, my pulse ringing in my ears with nerves.

"Anything at all."

"Will you know what I look at?"

"I will, but those without psychic abilities wouldn't."

Nibbling on my bottom lip, I tilt my head. "Do you want me to see if I can delve into what happened in Pinebrook?"

He stares deep into my eyes, caressing my soul with his dark, onyx eyes as he considers my offer. After the other day, he has to know that it doesn't matter to me, but I can see the way it's haunting him and I hate it. I hate it so much it hurts. If I can offer him even a glimpse, I will, even if it's painful to see.

For him, for any of the Bishops, I would give my all, no matter the consequences. It should be embarrassing because I really haven't known them all that long, but there's no turning back now.

"Please," he rasps, his eyelids shuttering a little at his admission.

"I'll try."

Nerves rack my chest as I watch the flickers of magic dance around his head. It's so elegant it's almost distracting watching the charcoal-gray swirls beckon me closer. My fingers tingle, curiosity getting the better of me as I reach up to grasp it.

The second I latch on, my eyes slam shut and the world goes black. All I can hear is the sound of my breath as even the breeze around me comes to a stop. I choke up, stuttering over what I want to envision. I feel like I'm intruding, which I technically am, but at his request. It just takes a moment for my mind to understand that fact.

Inhaling, I fill my lungs with so much air that my chest burns before I exhale softly.

I want to see what happened in Pinebrook.

I'm unsure if I'm being too vague or not, but the second I think about it, smoke seems to fill my vision. My heart gallops in my chest, my nerves getting the better of me.

Clouds form in my mind, the sound of screams consuming me as nausea swirls in my gut.

Fuck. Fuck. Fuck.

Dread fills my veins, and horror rocks my bones, but a blanket of safety consumes me.

A flicker of gold among the carnage catches my attention and I settle my focus on the shine of it under the warm sun. "Stay here, son. Stay safe until I tell you it's okay to move." Wide onyx eyes flash before me, the owner of them settling before me, and I gasp. "I'm sorry about this," he adds, lifting his hand to my face, then he's gone.

Gone.

The screams continue, the chants and roars of anger mingling with the fear as I remain rooted to the spot. A minute passes into what feels like an eternity until a whisper breezes against my ear.

"Now, son. Come now."

All at once, my feet are moving before I can understand, the scenes before me overwhelming my senses as death stains every inch of the cobbled street I stand on. I search for him, for the onyx eyes I'm so familiar with, but a knock from my right side makes me stumble. Another glimmer of gold and everything goes black once more until I'm hovering above a pile of dead bodies.

I stumble back with a gasp, my heart racing in my chest as I stare at Creed, who is looking back at me with the same level of surprise on his face that must be showing on mine.

"Creed," I breathe, my hand pressing to my chest as I try to calm myself down. "Is that... was that..."

"My father. He protected me from it all." He runs a hand through his hair as his face tilts toward the ground. "But that doesn't make sense."

"It does, Creed. It makes complete sense. The reality of the situation is just a little more complicated than we even considered," I reply, but he still keeps his gaze downcast. I can't even imagine what he's feeling right now, but if he knows what I saw, then he knows exactly what I know.

His father protected him in Pinebrook. Kept him away from the destruction and made sure there was no blood on his hands. When all was said and done, he wiped the surface of Creed's memory.

Those aren't the actions of the golden warrior everyone fears. Those are the actions of a father who loves his son.

TWENTY ONE

Raven

The morning passes just as easily as it did yesterday. No Erikel, none of his men, not even a glimpse of Sebastian. My gut clenches with the worry this brings, but I focus on the relief we get to bask in for a moment instead.

Pulling out the seat beside Leila, the Bishops choose their spots around the table in the dining hall, giving me the pleasure of Zane on my other side, with Eldon sitting straight across from me, leaving Brax and Creed to flank him.

"Have you had any luck with the book I brought you?" Leila asks as I choose what I want for my lunch.

I look up through my lashes toward Brax to find him glancing at me already.

"No, not yet. We had a look through it, but it all kind of blurred together. So I'm going to take another look tonight," I explain, and she hums in agreement.

"I'll keep searching, and if I come across anything else, I'll let you know."

"Thank you," I breathe, turning my attention to my friend. That's what she is. I was dumb to put a lot of shit between us because she kept the guild a secret. Especially since she has proven herself again and again since then, even when it hasn't been necessary. I need to get over the usual niggle in my gut I get when it comes to trust.

"No worries."

I opt for the buttermilk fried chicken and the table settles into a comfortable silence as we all eat. I feel relaxed and at ease, except for the tiniest bit of tension in my shoulders when I think about whatever is to come next. I can't shake it, but it keeps me alert, so it's probably a good thing.

I almost wish we were back to dealing with Genie and her bullshit. At the time, it was irritating as fuck, but now, I would take it over the mess with Erikel and his men any day. It was playground shit in comparison to this. Now we're dealing with real realm problems.

Shaking my head, I pull myself from thoughts of what was and what could have been. There's no use having my head buried in the past. Instead, I consider what tomorrow will look like now that we've convinced Figgins to meet us at the compound. Something good has to come from it. It *has* to. My soul is feeling a little frazzled with the separation from Ari now and the need to be closer to him is getting more difficult to suppress. Those are just my selfish reasons, nevermind the fact that they're in danger in the forest with the unknown creatures.

Fuck.

Maybe I shouldn't think about that either.

The only thoughts that will lighten my mood revolve around the Bishops and I'm sure, on some level, that's not healthy, but fuck if I care. The only issue is, if I start to delve into my thoughts of them, I'll either get stuck on the almighty *L* word that plagues me or twisted up in knots over thoughts of them touching my body.

Laughter pulls me from my head completely and I look up to see a group of people walking through the doors leading into the dining hall. It doesn't take even a second to recognize them.

Erikel's men.

The students from Shadowgrim Institute.

They're back. Which I can only assume means one thing: Erikel's back, too.

Great.

My fork clatters to my almost-empty plate, my appetite gone. Everyone watches their every move, and it's clear when the group continues to grow that there are more here than before. I can count at least fifteen of them and my gut clenches.

The swagger oozes from them as they saunter between the tables, fully aware they hold everyone's attention. Their egos could definitely do with a good ass kicking and I would *love* to be the one to do it.

"Where do you guys usually throw a party?" the guy at the front asks, flanked by his friends on either side. The question is aimed at a girl at a table two rows from us and I can see her gulp nervously from here.

"Uhh, down by the mausoleums," she mumbles before slamming her lips closed.

"Nice," he replies with a smirk. "I'm Ruben. My friends and I have just been enrolled at the academy, and what better way to celebrate than with a party tonight, yeah?" His smile widens as he glances around the room. His eyes hover on our table for a brief second before he continues to scan the other students. "Everyone is invited, of course," he adds, patting the girl on the shoulder a few times before continuing to prowl across the room.

They make a scene of rearranging two of the tables in the far corner, pushing them together so they can sit as one. The crowd is quickly forgotten as they get comfortable and eat, laughing and boasting louder than necessary.

Turning my attention back to our table, the first thing I notice is the frown on Brax's face, the corner of Creed's mouth tipped up in a sneer, the ticking of Zane's jaw, and the white of Eldon's knuckles.

"The party is definitely to get intel on us," Leila murmurs, her nose wrinkling with a mixture of worry and certainty, and I nod.

"Possibly. I guess creating a buzz is a far easier way to get us to let our guard down, and what better way to get the hive buzzing than by placing students here? Probably way more effective than relying on those they put in charge of us. I imagine they think we'll see them as our equals," I reply, twisting my lips in thought.

"If that's the case, then maybe we play them at their own game." Leila seems concerned with her own idea, but as I stare at her, it makes more and more sense.

"Maybe we do," I state, turning to the Bishops. "I hate to say it, but we're going to that party."

Black silk clings to my body, dainty straps holding it in place as I twist from side to side in front of the mirror. What I want to do is curl up into a ball under a thick duvet and snuggle the night away, but me and my bright ideas have us getting ready for the damn party.

My hair is twisted into a bun on top of my head, revealing the swirls of black that now intertwine with the pink. We're embracing them tonight. Besides, it fits with my dress and smokey eye make up.

Grabbing my clutch, I step out of the bathroom and falter in the doorway when I find all four of my men dressed and ready, lying side by side on the giant bed while they wait for me.

Brax is the closest, in jet-black jeans with a matching fitted tee, making his muscles look even bigger somehow. Eldon is beside him, in dark blue jeans and a white shirt, while Zane lies in a pair of cream chino shorts and a navy button-up on his other side. Creed is the farthest away from me, wearing an emerald-green t-shirt and black shorts. The green makes his dark eyes glisten as he looks my way.

"I don't think we should go," he rasps, eyes raking over me from head to toe, and the others quickly glance my way too.

"I agree," Zane says with a nod, and I roll my eyes at them.

"Please, we're not going to be having any fun. No drinking, no dancing, just listening. I may as well look cute while we do it," I state, and Eldon shakes his head at me.

"You're sinfully delicious, Little Bird. I want to unwrap you now," he says, his blue eyes darkening as he moves to stand at the bottom of the bed.

"Everyone else is going to see how hot she is," Zane grumbles, following suit and folding his arms over his chest as he stands beside Eldon.

"For sure, but that's why we have Brax. If anyone

tries to do anything more than look, he can smash them in the face with that right hook of his," Eldon retorts with a chuckle, making me grin.

Nodding, I take a step toward the door. "Good. If that's settled, are we ready to go?" I ask, and I almost make it to the open doorway before I'm swept off my feet.

The thickness of the arms banding around my waist tells me it's Brax, which is confirmed when he growls in my ear. "You're going to have me punching every fucker tonight. Behave, Shadow."

Damn.

My thighs clench and I really consider my options. Staying home with the four of them seems way more fun right now, but the thought of a future where we get to just be ourselves, free to be like this all of the time, makes me stick to my plan.

Brax carries me outside before placing me back on my feet. I'm half expecting to see Leila, but I quickly remember the last lesson of the day. Fitch was waiting outside of the classroom doors when she stepped out, and when she mentioned the plan for the party to him, he completely forbade it.

That's not an argument we need to get ourselves involved in, so I promised to keep her informed about anything we learn. I can't imagine what it's like to have a parent care so deeply and react so protectively. I'm sure for her it's constricting and annoying as fuck, but from the outside looking in, it almost seems… nice.

My fingers lace with Brax's as Eldon appears at my other side, placing his palm against the small of my back. Creed takes the lead position in front of us this time, and Zane silently holds back a step.

Imagine what it would be like for us to just walk normally. Even if there wasn't a war building around us, I get the distinct feeling that the four of them would still behave this way. Is this their version of being protective? The answer is obvious and I relax, my heart swelling with appreciation as we head toward the music in the distance.

The marble mausoleums appear by the outline of the forest, and the gathering of students grows. Laughter echoes around us in the night air, lanterns and orbs glowing just bright enough for us to see where we're going once we step off the lit path.

It doesn't take long for me to spot Genie dancing with some of her friends as the party comes into full view and my nostrils flare with anger at her mere presence. I should make a scene and slam a damn tree into her, but I have to remember that tonight is about something else. Something far more important than the playground bullshit she brings.

Brax pulls me along to a table in the middle of everyone else, offering us a good vantage point of conversations going on around us as well as a spectacular view of who is mingling with whom. One thing we need to be making a note of is who is effortlessly befriending the guys from Basilica.

That will be a giant red flag for me, but it will also allow us to see who can and can't be trusted, and if they're a member of the guild with no given agenda, then I'll be bringing that shit to the next meeting.

My hips sway to the beat as my men all stand around the small circular table with me. I instantly regret declaring a ban on drinking and dancing because now that I'm here, I'm itching to do both.

As if sensing my thoughts, Zane taps my shoulder. "Maybe we should get drinks so we look like we're here to do more than just spy on people," he offers, and I nod in agreement. He smirks, seemingly pleased with himself, before he saunters off with Eldon to do just that.

Creed's dark eyes turn my way at the same time Brax shifts to stand behind me. With my back pressed to his front and his arms barricading me in, I'm breathless. Creed smirks knowingly as Brax leans in, pressing a kiss to the sensitive spot at the base of my neck.

Fuck.

The control I was commanding earlier is quickly slipping. I should tell him to stop, make him focus, but fuck, my words are lost right now. I continue to sway my hips as I watch the students around us. I'm focused and paying attention…barely, but it counts.

"Silk feels phenomenal against your skin, Shadow," Brax whispers against my ear, making me shiver as I try to remain as relaxed as possible, but it's far easier said than done.

"Dammit, Brax," I bite, practically panting, and despite my internal warring, I pout when he moves, returning to my side as Zane and Eldon return with drinks.

I offer a stern glare to my gargoyle, who simply winks in response before turning to Zane for the sweet yellow drink in his hand. I need it. I need it right now. The glass is barely in my hands before the liquor is burning its way down my throat, leaving me wanting before I've had a chance to swallow the first.

Fuck, if I don't calm down, I'll be the one running my loose lips to the enemy just to get a rise out of my men for leaving me so needy. I'm my own worst enemy. I know it, but I can't help it.

"Woah, Dove. What did I miss? What has you so riled up?"

I look up at Zane, my jaw slack for a second on being called out, but it's Creed who answers him anyway. "It seems she's struggling with us 'blending in,'" he says mockingly with exaggerated hand gestures.

He knows exactly what Brax was doing, and blending in definitely wasn't on his agenda. I don't think.

"No, I—"

"She needs a distraction. Otherwise, none of us will get any intel from this fucking party, and that's the only reason we're here," Brax grunts, but I don't miss the fact that he's rearranging his jeans at the same time as putting all the blame on me.

Fucker.

"Maybe I should be distracted by your cock in my mouth. Put us both out of our misery. Do you want me to take care of that now?" I ask, cocking a brow at him as I stroke my hand over his tight jeans, the bulge of his thick dick obvious.

His teeth clatter as he bites back a hiss, and one of his hands lands over mine, pushing my palm harder against the material.

"Don't play games with me, Shadow. I'll have you on your knees in front of everyone here and you know it." My breath hitches, excitement swirling in my core. Right now, that sounds like an excellent idea.

"Our girl is clearly needy, but like fuck is she being taken care of in front of all these people," Eldon grunts, tugging Brax's hand from mine. "Since you got her all worked up with no prize, you can stay here and observe," he continues, intertwining my fingers with his. "I, on the other hand, am going to give her exactly what she wants."

I gulp as I look up into Eldon's mischievous eyes. I

should say no. I should stay and fucking focus. I should do anything but be distracted tonight, but when he tugs at my hand, I'm powerless.

My teeth sink into my bottom lip as he guides me through the crowd, bypassing the growing number of tables filling with newcomers, before slipping inside the closest mausoleum. The cool air wraps around me as he closes the metal gate behind us, secluding us from the rest of the party.

I can still hear the music and the murmurs of the party-goers, but it's all muted in the background.

"In here? Really?" I breathe, looking around. There's a stone tomb in the middle of the space, which is a lot bigger than it looks from the outside, with a cushioned bench against the far wall. A few trinkets are lined up along the little carved-out alcoves, but otherwise, it's cobwebs and dust that decorate the place.

"Little Bird, if I bent you over that tomb right now and slammed two fingers into that sweet pussy of yours, they would come out wet. Try and tell me I'm wrong."

Fuck.

Pouting at his accurate assessment, I'm not ready for the move when he grabs the back of my thighs and effortlessly lifts me into the air. My arms tighten around his neck, and my legs around his waist, as he runs his nose along mine. His hands find their way to the globes of my ass and the way he palms them has me clenching even tighter around him.

"You're not wrong," I breathe, and he smirks.

"How do you want this, Little Bird? Fast and to the point to give you exactly what you want, or do you want to walk out of here looking well and truly fucked?" I nibble at my lip. The latter sounds the most appealing, but we're supposed to be here for a reason and I'm disrupting it all with my needy pussy. "Nevermind, I'll make the decision for myself," he rasps, ghosting his lips over mine before he strides across the room.

My back stiffens, bracing to feel the cool stone of the tomb beneath me, but to my surprise, the chill doesn't come. Instead, I'm hoisted higher in the air, my grip on him completely gone as my thighs hit his shoulders and my back connects with the wall.

"Fuck." I gasp at the exact moment he nips at my pussy through my panties, and it turns into a drawn-out moan.

I scramble to brace myself against the wall, but there's nothing to hold on to, leaving me completely at his mercy. Until I remember that he told me to use my magic to hold me against the wall the other day. Settling my magic in my chest, I feel much steadier just in time for him to make my panties disappear.

The next lap of his tongue melds between my folds and I groan. The stone wall is rough beneath my palm, so I reach for his hair instead, which makes him hum hungrily against my clit.

"You're going to come on my tongue, Raven. Then I'll fuck you," he murmurs against my sensitive skin.

I nod, even though he's not looking at me, and his lips find my pussy once again as I cry out from the flicker of heat dancing over him.

He's using his magic.

Fuck.

Heat ripples from him to me, mixing with the desire already warming my body, and I feel like I'm going to combust.

Swipe after swipe of his tongue, pleasure claims me, and when his fingers plunge into my core for the first time, warmth dancing over the tips, I come apart. Wave after wave of my climax crashes into me. I cling to it, my moans getting higher and higher as I grow breathless, and Eldon doesn't stop until my hold on his hair softens and I release my magic to slump back against the wall.

All too quickly, he's lowering me to my feet. I clutch his shoulders for stability and he smirks down at me, his chin glistening with the evidence of my release. Reaching up on my tiptoes, I swipe my tongue along his bottom lip, tasting myself.

"Fuck, that's hot," he grunts, pulling me close so we're chest to chest before claiming my mouth. He takes charge, delving his tongue between my parted lips, and no matter how much I try to fight for dominance, he wins.

Succumbing to his touch, he inches backward and I willingly follow while we remain attached at the lips. I know we're near the tomb now, and his desire to bend me over it is close to being fulfilled, but there's something I want to do first. Something I was denied the other day.

I push off his chest, tearing our lips apart, and his dark gaze narrows. But it doesn't last long as I drop to the floor, the harshness of the ground biting into my knees. I relish in it.

"I want you on my tongue."

His tongue sweeps out over his bottom lip as he stares down at me. "You want to taste me, Little Bird?" he murmurs, and I nod, reaching for the zipper of his jeans. I know they can be magically and effortlessly removed, but there's something about the urgency of needing each other that there's no time to remove clothes that has me wound tight.

Unbuttoning his jeans, the sound of his zipper echoes around us, and I smile excitedly as his cock springs free. There's no building up to this, no slow start. I want him, and I want him now.

I wrap my lips around his length, sucking him to the back of my throat in one swift move.

"Holy fuck, Raven. Just like that," he gasps, his fingers

lacing in my hair. His hold tightens when I repeat the move, and with every swipe of my mouth, his panting grows louder.

Trying my best to relax my throat, I take him deeper and deeper until gagging is unavoidable, but he likes that just as much. I look at him through my lashes and find his jaw hanging loose as he gapes at me. His hold on my hair tightens as he steadies me, flexing his hips instead, and I gag around his length again.

"Fuck, Little Bird. I shouldn't like that," he rasps, retreating slowly before slamming to the back of my throat and making it close around his cock. "I really shouldn't," he repeats, slipping from my lips.

"Don't stop until my mascara is running down my face," I murmur hoarsely, clinging to his denim-clad thighs eagerly, and his eyes widen as he stares at me in wonder for a moment.

He doesn't ask me if I'm sure, he doesn't doubt my choice, he does nothing but exactly what I ask. With his cock resting between my lips again, he fucks my mouth vigorously, making my thighs slick with my own pleasure as he takes and takes. Again and again, I gag around his length, and I watch as his eyes roll to the back of his head at the same time as tears track down my face.

All at once he's gone. He goes as far as to take a step back from me as he braces his hands on his knees, heaving every breath as he looks at me through half-mast lids.

"Raven. Fuck, I swear to the heavens, I want that pussy out for me right now. Tempting me with that fucking mouth of yours. I almost sprayed down your throat so many times, but I want to paint your insides with my cum. Make it happen, Little Bird."

I gape at him in surprise for the briefest moment before I kick into action. Pushing to my feet, I gather my dress around my waist as I climb up onto the tomb, lying with the full length of the stone beneath me.

His eyes darken as he circles me, stopping where my feet are pressed against the tomb, offering the perfect view of my pussy with my knees bent and parted.

"Good girl." Climbing onto the tomb, he inches closer, his clothes still in place as he settles between my open thighs. "I want to fuck you bare," he murmurs, and I nod.

"Do it. I'm on protection."

He stills, looking down at me with furrowed brows. "You've been on protection this entire time?" he asks, and I nod lightly, confused about where he's going with this instead of doing it. "So, to clarify, I could have been fucking you bare all along?"

"Uhh, yeah?"

"You're in trouble, Little Bird. Withholding that piece of information from me. You better believe we're going to make up for that," he growls, grabbing my thighs and pushing them against my stomach as he aligns his cock with my entrance.

He slams inside of me hard and fast and I scream. Blindly grabbing onto his arms, my nails dig into his flesh as he doesn't give me a second to adjust. He slams into me, unrelenting as I hold on for dear life.

My vision blurs, my pulse ringing in my ears as he leans down and bites at my pebbled nipple through the material of my dress, making me unravel beneath him. My lungs burn with the scream that explodes from my body, consuming me as I milk his cock with everything that I am.

"Shit, Raven," he moans, and I feel it—the moment he finds his release—the pulse in my core, the ropes of his climax clinging to me as we shatter together. Sweat coats our tangled limbs as we slowly come down from the highest of highs. I gasp when he pulls his dick from my pussy, but it's quickly soothed by his lips peppering kisses over my face. "You do look stunning with your mascara down your face, Raven," he breathes against my lips, and I sigh, basking in the afterglow when a loud cackle freezes us in place.

"Sebastian, where have you been?"

We both glance toward the opening of the mausoleum, but no one is standing there. They must be on the other side, unaware we're in here.

"Ruben. Erikel said you would be joining us soon. I had some things to take care of, but I'm here to join in the celebrations now."

Yup. That's definitely my brother.

Glancing at Eldon, he nods and we both climb down from the tomb as quietly as possible, fixing our clothes as we edge closer to the wrought-iron gate between us and *them*.

"I didn't think I'd be here celebrating joining a damn academy when I graduated two years ago, but apparently, it's about the bigger plan and I'm here for the ride. As long as I'm out of Basilica, I'm at Erikel's beck and call, and you know it."

"It will all be for the greater good. We've got some smaller hurdles to overcome here first, but once we have everything we need, we're heading to the capitol. Once we've brought down The Monarchy, we'll be doing whatever the fuck we please when we call this place our own," Sebastian replies, a fierceness in his tone that's not the same as he uses with me.

"Small hurdles are nothing. You tell me what you want done and I'll fucking do it. Anything to get us to the end goal as quickly as possible," Ruben states eagerly, and I glance at Eldon, who is frowning just as hard as me.

"I was hoping you would say that because I need somebody dead," Sebastian explains, his voice getting quieter as they seem to step away. I have to strain to hear Ruben's response, and it sends chills running down my spine.

"Tell me the name and consider it done."

TWENTY TWO

Raven

I wake the moment I feel them. My senses are on high alert as I take a moment for my brain to come to life before I even consider opening my eyes. It's like there's a disturbance but no hint of a creak, a rustling breeze, or anything else to signify their presence, yet I know with all that I am that they're here.

Taking a measured breath, I slowly flicker my eyelids open and there they are.

Silhouettes touch every surface. Some move fast, others slow. A large portion seem to travel together, while some move in the opposite direction alone. The walls, the floor, the ceiling, the bed sheets, my men. They're everywhere.

I wish I could communicate with them, understand what's drawing them here and question what it is they seem to need. Not to get rid of them, but to help. I don't know why it feels like they need my help, but it does, and I can't back away from it.

As if sensing my thoughts, they all still at once, making my heart freeze in my chest.

All but one.

One outline appears among the others, with arms hung loosely at their sides as they slowly grow in size along the far wall. Rising above the rest, it stands tall, as if looking directly at me, and it's the first time it feels like they're acknowledging my presence in some way.

Why now?

What can't I see?

"Are you seeing shadows?" A squeal burns my throat as I try to suppress it, but it's impossible. Whipping my attention to my left, I find Brax propped up in bed with the book on artifacts in his lap. *How long has he been awake?* "Raven?"

I clear my throat, pulling the sheets higher up my body and fixing them tightly around me. I don't know how I haven't startled any of the others awake, but they're all resting peacefully.

"I was," I finally admit, turning back to him.

"They're gone now?" he asks, cocking his brow, and I nod. "Are you okay? Something seemed to have your undivided attention."

I gulp, shaking my head as I try to find the words.

"There was one. Bigger than the rest, or maybe not actually bigger, but more prominent, and it was like it was seeking my attention."

His hands pause on the tome in his lap as he gives me his full attention. "In a good way or a bad way?"

"I'm not quite sure, but my gut says a good way," I reply, and his shoulders relax.

"Good, because I will fight like fuck for you, but I'm not sure how well that would go against a shadow I can't actually see."

I smile, burrowing down under the covers a little more as a yawn parts my lips wide. Relaxing against the pillows, I take him in, watching as he flicks through the pages, back and forth, comparing artifacts.

"Find anything in there?" I ask, my eyes lulling a little as exhaustion starts to cling to me once again. It's like the shadows have left and taken my energy with them.

"I think so. Especially this emerald gate. It really is believed to lead to the Realm of Shadows. I had glossed over it the other night, but I couldn't sleep trying to remember where I had heard of the realm before that wasn't from my parents. Which has led me here."

"So going there physically and not in a dream could actually be possible?" I ask, wanting to clarify with my tired brain taking hold again, and he nods.

"I think so, but I'm sure it's not a surprise for you to

learn that the text doesn't reveal *where* the gate is."

I sigh. Of course not. Nothing is set to make our lives easier right now. This isn't going to be any different.

"Anything else worth noting?" I ask, yawning again.

"There could be, but don't worry about it, Shadow. Sleep. We're going to the compound when you wake up in the morning and you need to be fully rested."

I hum in agreement, but I have no idea if he hears it because a moment later, I'm fast asleep again.

The feeling that washes over me as I step through Brax's portal is almost soothing, something I cling to as the compound comes into view.

It will never cease to amaze me just how much it looks like any other forest, but the wards protecting it and what potentially lurks inside are far from normal.

The five of us hurry across the open grass field to get closer, repeatedly scanning from left to right in search of Professor Figgins. If she doesn't show, I'm going to have to be much more forceful in my approach, but the way her eyes shone the last time I saw her makes me believe she'll be here.

She has to be.

"Ari, can you hear me?" I wet my lips nervously as we

approach the tree line.

"What are you doing here, Raven?" I can hear him, but I can't see him anywhere.

"I'm here to help, to put things right for you," I insist, my soul tugging me toward him, but the anger I can feel drifting off him in waves tells me that's not a good idea.

"It's not safe. You shouldn't have come."

Zane tugs my hand and points at my face. I realize my eyebrows are pinched, and my jaw is tense.

Ari, I mouth, but that doesn't seem to ease the concern etched across his face.

"Good, you're already here. I don't have much time," Professor Figgins states, appearing out of thin air in a long black cloak with the hood pulled up.

"What's the hurry?" Brax asks, folding his arms over his chest as he stares her down, waiting for a response.

"I don't believe that's any of your business," she retorts, cocking a brow back at him, but he doesn't falter under her gaze. The two of them stare each other down, refusing to give in, and I sigh.

"We really don't have time for this," I grumble, breezing past the pair of them to get closer to the compound. I still can't see Ari anywhere, but I can feel him, and I can't decide if that's a good thing or a bad thing.

As if sensing my uncertainty, a flicker of golden feathers flashes through the tree line and hope blossoms inside of me. My soul calls out to him, desperate to have him near, but no matter how much I rock back and forth on my heels, he doesn't come any closer.

"Ari."

"Why are you here, Raven?"

"I already told you."

"Why?"

I can see his wings flutter at his sides, but he still doesn't make any effort to turn and face me and my gut twists with worry.

"Raven?" Creed looks at me in wonder and I realize they're not even getting to listen to half of the conversation like they usually would, so they have no idea what's going on.

Clearing my throat, I turn back to Ari as I feel the others inch closer to me. "Ari, we're here to prove to Figgins what is going on so we can safely get you out of here."

He scoffs. *"You're wasting your time. She's as useless as a glass hammer,"* he retorts, and I pray like hell he's not right. *"Besides, I've told you over and over again that it's not safe, yet you continue to defy me by coming here."*

"Excuse me, asshole, I don't defy you, and even if I did, you're not my boss," I grumble, clenching my hands at my sides, trying to rein in my temper. "Besides, we know it's not safe for me, but we know it's also not safe for you and Gia, and I'm trying to protect you."

"What is he saying?" Figgins asks, pulling her hood down to look at me properly. This close, she looks tired, her eyes seem a little sunken, and the bags beneath them are darker than they were a few days ago.

I wonder what's causing her trouble? Does it link to Erikel too?

Shaking my head, I focus. "He thinks you're going to be useless and he's adamant we shouldn't have come because of how unsafe it is."

"As useless as a glass hammer. If you're going to throw me under the rock, you may as well do it accurately."

Biting back my smirk, I clarify. "Sorry, his exact words were 'as useless as a glass hammer'."

Figgins raises her eyebrows at me as Zane and Eldon snicker behind me, but if anything, she doesn't seem offended, more that she wants to prove Ari wrong.

By all means, please do.

She steps past me without another word, lifting her hand before her when she gets close enough, and I watch as the ward around the compound ripples beneath her touch.

"She shouldn't do that."

"Ari said you shouldn't do that," I repeat, feeling like a damn parrot.

"I created it, I think I'm good."

"Did you warn her that it may have been tampered with?"

"Yes."

If Ari was standing in front of me right now, I'm certain he would be giving me the stare. The stare that questions whether I'm telling the truth or not.

Fucker.

"Hmm, I understand what he means, though. It feels… different somehow."

I stick my tongue out like a childish brat, knowing he's likely not paying me any attention, but it feels good anyway.

Ari sighs. *"I thought you told her stuff."*

"I did," I grumble, waving my arms at her. "It doesn't mean she wanted to listen, though," I add, earning the stare from Figgins this time, but I brush it off. I'm not wrong.

A screech rings out around us, making me pause as panic consumes me. It's high-pitched but deep all at once, a sound of dominance, not fear, and I know it's what's got Ari all worked up.

"It can sense your presence because she touched the barrier. You need to go."

"No, I'm not leaving you."

"What is he saying?" Figgins asks, and I start to feel irritation creep up my spine. I don't have time to keep repeating every last thing.

Fuck.

"He thinks the creature knows we're here because you

touched the barrier."

Her hand quickly drops away like it's been burned, but if what Ari says is true, it's too late for that now.

Another screech burns through the air, and I'm quickly surrounded by my men.

"Raven, if it's not safe, we can't stay," Creed states from my right, scanning the forest for the creature.

"I'm not leaving him, Creed. Not until we have some way of saving them, at least," I insist, worry sinking its claws into my flesh as I scan the forest once again.

Purple, blue, and green iridescent colors shimmer to the far right, I spot it around Brax's wide frame. "Over there," I say with a gasp, watching as the colors pounce through the trees.

I can't make out what it is, which only stokes more fear into my veins.

"Raven. Go," Ari orders, but I continue to ignore him. He's moving in the next moment, his feathers and fur rustling with the wind from his speed.

At first, I think he's running from the danger, but when he doesn't change course or dart away from the shimmering iridescent colors, I realize it's the complete opposite.

"Ari, no!" I yelp, and the creature turns my way, freezing as its dark gaze connects with mine.

Blacker than black eyes pierce mine, scales shimmering in the light that breaks through the trees. Paws with claws like steel curl into the moss beneath it as its body ripples with every breath it takes.

"What is that?" I whisper, my heart racing in my chest.

"I-I... I think it's a... it's a Drake."

I tilt my head to find Figgins, who is rooted to the spot and gaping at the creature as intently as I am. "A Drake?"

She nods. "A wingless dragon. I've never seen one in my life. They're mythical, not of this land. Or at least, I thought they weren't," she rambles as her trembling fingers lift to her mouth.

It screeches again, gaining my attention as it leaps through the air toward us. We should run, we should hide, we should definitely get the fuck out of here, but we're all frozen in place, taunting destiny as it barrels toward us through the trees.

I grab hold of the back of Brax's t-shirt, choking on my own breath as it pushes off the ground and leaps toward the barrier separating us. I'm certain it's going to break through the ward with ease, but before I can find out, it's catapulted sideways as Ari launches himself at it.

"Ari," I breathe, hearing him grunt as the Drake continues to screech, but this time, it's not a dominant call; it's one of pain.

Ari doesn't stop there. He refuses to give the Drake even a sliver of a chance as he attacks. It's too much, but my eyes are glued to watching them.

"Don't look, Raven."

"Ari," I manage, unable to find the words.

"Don't look, please."

Fuck.

Fighting my internal need to keep my gaze fixed on him, I focus on the emotion pouring into me from my familiar, letting it guide me forward so my forehead rests on Brax's back as I cling to his t-shirt.

I may not be able to see, but the sounds tell a pretty good story, and when pain aches through my limbs, I know Ari has been hurt, too. But any chance I have to panic over it is short-lived when a piercing cry rings out from the Drake before silence follows.

A few moments pass, but the feelings I can sense from Ari have me still hiding away until Zane runs his hand down my spine. "You're good now, Dove," he breathes, and I slowly lift my head.

I can't see the Drake, but my Griffin is a few meters away on the other side of the barrier. I gasp when I get a good look at his face. Three thick, deep and jagged marks run down his face, and my heart lurches.

They're not from today, though. They're slowly starting to heal, which means they were already there before we got here. Is that why he was hiding?

Stepping around Brax, I half expect him to force me back behind him, but he doesn't. I move closer to the barrier, careful not to touch it as I stare up at Ari's defeated face. I want to stroke his fur and feel the comfort the nudge of his beak gives me, but I can't.

"What the fuck was that?" I ask, wrapping my arms around myself as a chill seems to spike the air.

"Drakes. They're what Erikel brought in. It's what he's hiding here."

I quickly repeat his answer to the others, settling my gaze on Figgins, who looks as white as a ghost.

"That shouldn't be in there," she mutters, shaking her head in disbelief.

"Does this mean you're *finally* listening?" My chest tightens as I wait with bated breath for her answer.

She turns to face me head-on. There's a sadness in her eyes and the smallest of smiles on her lips, which doesn't fill me with hope.

"It does, but that doesn't mean anything anymore because I'm no longer the one in control of the ward. I can't set them free."

TWENTY THREE

Zane

Raven sits with her head in her hands, Eldon and Creed on either side of her, while Brax and I pace. He's behind the sofa, and I'm in front, walking in tandem as we struggle to contain our building frustration. I had hoped everything Ari had said last time wasn't true, but unfortunately, we're not that lucky.

It's truer than true.

That creature...fuck. That was something else. By the looks of Ari, there are plenty more of them, and he's been left alone to fight them off. I don't know what fate we've been destined for, but the fact that the shit we're dealing with continues to multiply doesn't bode well with me.

"If they're trapped in there by someone else's magic, how can we gain access to free them? How can we do anything at all to help?" Raven sits back in her seat with a huff, dragging her hands down her face as she struggles to handle the helplessness consuming us all.

"I don't know, Shadow, but we'll figure out a way to do it," Brax promises, rubbing at the back of his neck. Shit. I know things aren't looking good if it's Brax who's the one doing the consoling.

"On top of everything else?" Raven adds, throwing her hands out in frustration. "This is too much for one fucking realm, nevermind one group of people."

"One person." Creed leans forward, bracing his elbows on his knees as he looks at our girl.

"Huh?" Raven looks at him, clearly confused, but I understand exactly what he's saying.

"The person who has the power to face all of this is you, Dove," I murmur, pausing my strides to turn and face her head-on.

"Me?"

It's almost cute how she still doesn't see how powerful she is, how much she can change the course of the world. The self-doubt and disbelief are etched into her very soul, making it clear as fuck that we need to help her realize her strength. Now more than ever.

I nod, crouching before her. "And we'll be here at your side every step of the way."

She nods at my words, but I know they're not truly sinking in.

Rising, I exhale heavily as the weight of the world continues to try and crush us.

I feel helpless.

Eldon starts explaining something to Raven, distracting her, and I take the opportunity to slip from the room. I close my bedroom door behind me, falling back against the wood for a moment as defeat takes hold of me.

I give myself ten seconds to get over it, and even though it still clings to me when I stand properly, I push through the irritation and pull out my shell from my nightstand. My fingers dance over the device with muscle memory. The tone fills the air a moment later, and it hangs there for almost a minute before it cuts off.

This is exactly what it's been doing since everything went to shit.

Repeating the same motions, I try again, but once more, my father's voice doesn't magically fill the room.

Fuck.

Trying one more time, I'm left just as disappointed as I was the first time around when it cuts out, leaving me all alone with my bubbling agitation. I'm not going to get anywhere with it again today, and I need him now more than ever.

I launch the shell across the room, letting it clatter against the wall before bouncing on my bed while I stand, panting with every breath as my frustration turns into fury.

I've never felt more helpless and useless than I do right now. Raven deserves more from me, and I'm offering her nothing. Nothing of value, at least.

A knock comes from my bedroom door, halting my internal raving, and a second later, Raven's head peeks around the frame.

"Hey, is everything okay?" she asks, her eyebrows pinching with concern, and I'm left even more irritated. She doesn't need this from me on top of everything else. Her mental load is already at full capacity, and I'm just making it worse. But it's too late now. It's clear I'm struggling. To deny it would only drag out the situation, and I want that even less.

"No. No, it's not, Raven." Admitting it lifts a weight from my shoulders. "I've been trying to get a hold of my pops. I'm trying and trying but he's not picking up. I'm getting nothing at all. It's been like this since the night he left. We need his help. *I* need his help."

Her shoulders sag, and a soft smile turns the corner of her mouth as she steps farther into the room. "Then it's simple, Zane. We go to Lyra."

I immediately shake my head. "I've thought of that so many times, but it's too risky. She's probably under the power of Erikel."

Raven waves me off as my brothers step into the room behind her.

"We won't know unless we go to find out."

Since when did she talk with such reason in a time of pressure?

Nodding, I take a deep breath, letting my shoulders relax back as her smile grows. She spins for the door, side-stepping Brax, Eldon, and Creed before turning to glance at me.

"You coming?"

"I would follow you anywhere."

Our footsteps echo off the marble floor as we make our way through the double doors of the main academy building, Lyra's office now in sight. We saw a few other classmates on our walk over here, but the second we stepped inside, you could tell it's the weekend because it's empty as hell.

Shit, even Lyra might not be here, but when Raven is on a mission, she's *on* a mission, and we're happy for her to guide us to Hell if necessary.

Raven takes the lead as we get closer, knocking on Lyra's door without a moment's pause. I'm certain we're going to get no response, and the walk back will hopefully calm us all down, but to my surprise, her voice replies from the other side.

"Come in."

Raven looks over her shoulder at me with her eyebrows raised and her fingers crossed, and the rest of us take her lead as she steps into the room. I kick the door closed behind me, doing a quick sweep of the room with my eyes, but nothing out of the ordinary stands out.

"Lyra."

"Raven," the administrator retorts, cocking a brow at my Dove. "To what do I owe the pleasure?"

Before I even realize what I'm doing, I step forward, accidentally shouldering past Eldon to get there quicker. "I've been having trouble with my shell. It's not working."

Fuck.

I'm quite certain we were going to downplay this until we were sure she could be trusted, but apparently, my loose lips have other ideas.

Raven glances back at me with worry in her eyes as she clears her throat. "Yeah, we seem to be having some trouble with Zane's shell. Are replacements an option?" she asks, turning back to Lyra, who is already shaking her head.

"No. They've been disconnected," Lyra explains without lifting her gaze from the parchment in front of her.

"Disconnected?" I blurt again, feeling my brothers glance at me sideways while Raven's gaze seems fixated elsewhere in the room as if she's watching something. "How is that even possible?" I add. My worry has been around my father's safety, along with my mother's and sister's, but if it's the shell that's having problems, then hopefully, my family is okay.

Lyra frowns, the quill scrawling with magic in front of her pausing briefly as she glances up. "I don't know."

"Are we still able to speak to our families in the booth?" Raven pushes, and I nod.

"No." Lyra's gaze drops back down to the parchment again.

"How come?" Raven asks, leaning forward to brace her palms on the desk.

Once again, Lyra frowns, deeper this time as she shakes her head. "I don't know."

"Are we able to generate a gateway to go and see them?" Eldon interjects, folding his arms over his chest, and Lyra shakes her head again, not even bothering to answer him verbally this time. "It was worth a try, at least," Eldon mutters under his breath.

"Was it?" Lyra retorts, lips pursing as she stares at the parchment.

I part my lips to tell Raven this was obviously pointless, but not a single word comes out as I gape at Raven, thrusting her hand into the air. She tugs on what seems like nothing, her hand coiling around an invisible rope or something, and it takes a moment for me to connect the dots.

She has hold of Lyra's magic.

Raven takes a few steps toward the administrator, going around the table to get closer to her, gasping as she continues to look down at her hand. I don't know what I'm expecting my unpredictable Dove to do next, but the soft words that leave her mouth aren't it.

"Lyra, are you okay?"

"No," she blurts, clapping a hand over her mouth before she bursts into tears, sobbing uncontrollably into her hands.

What the fuck?

Raven gives her a moment, waving Creed closer as the rest of us keep a fair distance from the crying female. That's not my area of expertise. Definitely not. When her cries calm a little and she swipes the tears from her face, Raven places her free hand on Lyra's shoulder.

"Why, Lyra? What's going on?"

"I don't know," she repeats, her face scrunching up in anger as the words seem to make her cry even harder again.

Raven tilts her head to look at Creed, and a conversation happens between the pair of them that doesn't involve words because a second later, Raven is clutching something beside him too.

His magic.

"I'll be gentle, Lyra. I promise."

Eldon and I glance at each other out of the corner of our eyes, confused as fuck as we watch Lyra's eyes fall closed and Raven's follow suit. All I can hear is the ringing of my pulse in my ears as silence descends over the room until Raven steps back with a gasp.

"Raven." I can't help but call her name, and she turns to look at me without hesitation.

"I saw into her mind, mirroring Creed's magic. She was forced to do a lot of things but doesn't know what because one of Erikel's men seems to have put a blocker on her," she explains, making my eyes widen in surprise. That definitely explains why she doesn't know shit.

"How are we going to help her? Blockers can only be undone by those who set it, and that person isn't here. Even if they were, I don't imagine them aiding us," Eldon states, and I nod in agreement.

Despite Eldon's facts, Raven smiles. "That would be the case, but it seems Erikel's men aren't as clever as they think." I'm about to ask why that is, but the second Raven drops both of her hands to her sides, releasing the magical strands, she turns to explain. "He was bragging to his friend that exact information before he put the blocker on her. So I know exactly what to do."

She turns away with that while the rest of us stare at her with wide eyes, Lyra included. Raven crouches down before her, sandwiching one of her hands between both of hers. "Melody. My. Broken. Take. Dirty. Word. Final."

A whoosh of orange floats from Lyra as she groans, her

head tilting back to the ceiling, and I gape in horror.

What the fuck?

A moment later, she slumps in her seat, sagging against the cushion as she squeezes Raven's hand. Her chest rises and falls as she pants and slowly blinks.

"Oh, my goodness. Thank you. Thank you. Thank you," she chants, sitting up straight in her seat as she lets go of Raven to brush a loose tendril of hair back off her face. "For real, thank you," she adds again, and Raven stands.

"It's okay."

"Honestly, I can't explain how it feels to be trapped inside of yourself like that. I was here, but I wasn't truly here. It was horrible. I don't know how I'll ever repay you," she rambles, and Raven simply smiles at her.

"If you can help get us in contact with Monarch Denver, I'll consider us even."

Lyra rubs her lips nervously as she brushes her hands over her skirt and stands. "Come."

She rushes to the corner of the room and I frown. There are just walls, but with one sweep of her hand, a door appears.

"You're expecting us to go into some random room?" Brax states, not moving an inch as he cocks a brow at her.

"Sorry, this is my… space. It's concealed in case I need to hide. It also allows me to use my magic when people think I'm not here," she adds, looking at Raven, who smiles in understanding.

"Thank you, Lyra." Raven steps into the small space, not bothering to see if we're going to follow or not, but that's probably because she knows for a fact we will.

"Use this system here. It's set up separately from the rest of the academy," Lyra explains as we all filter into the room. It's a lot bigger than I expected, with a desk, sofa, and access to a bathroom.

I murmur my thanks as I take a seat beside Raven on the sofa, pressing the necessary keys for my father. The tone fills the room as the others get comfortable too, but it doesn't last very long before my father appears in front of me.

Fuck.

Relief bursts from me as he comes into view. It might be a projection, but it's still him.

"Zane. Damn, Zane, is that you?" His voice booms around us, embracing me in an invisible hug, and I smile. "Are you all okay? Raven, Brax, Eldon, and Creed? All of you?"

I nod, as do my girl and friends, and the smallest light of hope forms in my stomach. "Hey, Pops." My father smiles from ear to ear, but it's not lost on me how tired he looks. He looks as if he's aged ten years since I saw him just a few weeks ago. "Are you okay?"

"Fuck that shit. Am I okay? Are *you* guys okay? You're the ones trapped in there, nevermind me."

"Have I mentioned before that you're the coolest?" Eldon interjects, wagging a finger at my father, who chuckles.

"Maybe a time or two. At least it doesn't seem to have knocked your spirits," he replies, but his brows bunch together when he takes a closer look at us. "Or maybe it has."

"We're surviving, Rhys, but it's all fucked to Hell," Raven admits with a scoff as she tries to contain her own emotions, and my father swipes a hand down his face.

"Tell me. Tell me everything."

So I do. I recap every last detail, even though recapping it again is hurting my brain. He curses at the villagers from Pinebrook, he sighs at the lack of leadership from Burton and the others, and he gapes in horror at the mention of the Drake this morning. I even explain what happened to Lyra and how she's helping us now.

"You were right, Raven. It is all fucked to Hell," he replies when we're finished.

Raven hums in agreement. "Can I ask if you've heard anything about my parents?"

Her head dips down, like she's embarrassed to ask, but the second my father glances away for a moment I know there's something there.

"Pops?"

He turns back to us with a sad smile. "I have, but unfortunately, Raven, things are a little difficult with your father right now."

Raven huffs. "I'm not shocked."

"No, no. He's… his mind has been tampered with," my father blurts, swiping a hand down his face. "Your mother is at our home, and so is your father, but he's… we have him sedated and confined until we can remove whatever is controlling him."

"Controlling him?" Raven sits straight in her seat, gaping at the projection.

"Yeah. We can't tell how long it's been going on, but what's important right now is getting you guys out of there. I'll handle him, I need you to remain focused."

Clearly, a lot is happening that we don't know about, but he's right. We've got enough to handle already.

"Okay. Thanks, Rhys," she murmurs, and my father nods.

"On the outside, The Monarchy is putting together an army," he starts to explain, and the five of us glance at each other in surprise. "The Monarch you brought back hasn't been returned, and even if he had been, they wouldn't have upheld the agreement. We're days out still, that's the only issue, but I'm riding the other Monarchs hard to make sure this is everyone's priority," he insists, and my heart swells.

I know I'm lucky to have him as my father, and I know we're lucky to have him fighting in our corner, but more than that, I'm lucky he blindly supports us no matter what.

"You're coming for us?" I ask, wanting to hear the words, and my father nods.

"I'll always come for you, Son."

CURSED SHADOWS

TWENTY FOUR

Raven

I run my hands down the lapels of my blazer as I take a deep breath and smile at myself in the mirror. I might be wearing this stuffy uniform, trapped in this damn academy with the enemy as our leader as I await his next move, but determined positivity keeps the weight of the world from my shoulders for the first time in a long time.

It's Monday morning, which is a fresh day and a fresh start.

After speaking with Rhys over the weekend, there's been a lightness among us that I've never actually felt before. Hope is real and it's present in all of us. The Monarchy is coming, we just have to bide our time, remain alert and vigilant, and everything is going to be okay.

We've seen it all by now. It's surely impossible for anything to shock us.

Hitching my backpack up my arm, I head out into the lounge with a noticeable bounce in my step to see my guys laughing among themselves. Seeing them smile makes me grin wider. Creed notices me first and jumps from his seat. His arm is around my shoulders in the next breath and he's hurrying me toward the door.

I giggle. I don't know why, I just do.

Fuck.

The floor vibrates with the footsteps of the others chasing after us and we're laughing freely as we step out of the front door to where Leila waits. We manage to calm down as she raises her eyebrows at us.

"Good morning, you guys," she says with a smirk, falling into step with me as we head up the path.

I lean my head on Creed's shoulder. "Morning, how's everything with your father?" I haven't seen her since he refused to let her come to the party, and the way her face scrunches up says it all. "That fun, huh?"

"The funnest," she retorts with an eye roll, and I grin. "Did you learn anything good at the party?"

I don't doubt myself for a single second as I catch her up with exactly what we heard Sebastian and Ruben talking about. It's not much, but it's something. My gut tells me the target is on *my* back, but I'm not going to let that drag me down. I'm quite sure my brother has had his sights set on taking my life since I got here, I don't see that changing any time soon.

"So I didn't miss out on anything fun then," she says with a sigh as we approach the academy building, and I shake my head.

"Well, that depends," Eldon starts, a sparkle in his eyes as he waggles his eyebrows. "Raven and I—"

"Shut up," I grumble, and Creed shoves him on my behalf, but that only makes him laugh louder.

Leila shakes her head at him and steps in closer, nudging her arm against mine. "There's a meeting tonight," she breathes, keeping her voice low, and I nod, glancing at the others.

"Perfect, what time?" I ask, my mind already going a mile a minute.

"Seven sharp."

I nod. "Are you free beforehand?"

Her eyebrows rise. "I can be. Is everything okay?"

"I hope so," I reply, taking a deep breath. After much consideration and a lot of back and forth, I've decided I'm going to trust this girl wholeheartedly or not at all. So here we are. "I want to be in that meeting room before anyone shows up. Can we make that happen?"

"Definitely. Is there a reason why?" She seems more intrigued than suspicious, and I don't know why, but it gives me the confidence I need.

"There's mention of a table in the book you gave us. I

want to know if it's the one down there."

Adrenaline courses through me as we cut across the grounds of campus, discreetly heading toward the Nightmares Guild chamber an hour earlier than the meeting. Fuck stealth mode when you have a hot guy who turns invisible on demand.

My fingers are laced with his, Leila on my other side, while Eldon has his hand on Zane's shoulder, creating a chain with Brax and Creed connecting too.

Leila has her free hand clapped over her mouth as she tries to hold back a giggle of excitement. Her being here is another show of trust, but also her presence means I can't get distracted by the Bishops either.

My kryptonite is my men, in every way. Both a positive and a negative. I'll protect them until death, but they distract the fuck out of me.

Slipping through the bushes, the entry point to the guild comes into view. We take our time, making sure the coast is clear before heading down the steps. I hold my breath, but no one appears as we reach the bottom and head into the main room. All that greets us is the golden table standing as prominent as ever in the center of the room.

"What do we do now?" Leila asks as we move closer.

"Honestly, I don't know."

Zane drops the magic and I release both his and Leila's hands. I run my fingers over the table, unsure where to even begin, and the others do the same. Nothing seems out of the ordinary, it looks like any other table.

Doubt swirls in my gut as I drop to my knees and crawl underneath. Scanning the length of the gold from left to right and back again, I come up empty handed. It doesn't help that I don't know what we're supposed to be looking for.

I sigh, ready to give up when the smallest glint in the far corner catches my eye. Inching closer, my nerves frazzle. The closer I get, the brighter it shines. Reaching out, everything slows around me. I should call out to the others, but my tongue is like lead in my mouth.

Grasping it, I gasp as my eyes slam closed and images infiltrate my mind. Murmurs mingle, consuming me as person after person appears on the back of my eyelids, revealing conversation after conversation that the table has stored.

Holy fuck.

It really is the artifact from the tome. But if I don't gain control of what it's showing me, I won't walk away any wiser. Taking a deep breath, I think about what I want to focus on, hoping that will narrow down what plays for me.

I'm intrigued as hell by the other artifacts now, and I think that's what makes everything else disappear but Burton.

He's sitting at the table with his elbows braced on top and a grin on his face.

"The artifact is hidden," someone explains, making Burton's smile widen.

"Good."

"Do you think anyone is on to us?"

I don't know who is talking. I recognize the voice, but I can't place it.

"On to us? Why would they be on to us? We're aiding everyone, keeping them safe from the Basilica realm. If anything, they'll be praising us," Burton retorts. "Besides, it will be safe in the mountains of Ashdale. Especially with the desert surrounding it. No one is going to find it."

The pair of them chuckle and my gut clenches.

"With the table and Poten's Ruby, we're going to have quite a collection," the other person states, and Burton nods eagerly.

"You're forgetting that I also have the location of the gateway to the Realm of Shadows," Burton adds, causing my eyebrows to lift in surprise. I can't decide if this man is helping the realm or helping himself, and I don't like it.

"Three. You have access to three artifacts. You know what that means, don't you? The more you gather, the more intense the artifacts become, they're stronger, more indestructible."

"I know. That's the point," Burton states, leaning back in his seat with a sigh which echoes with relief. "It's perfect."

"What else is on your list?"

My eyebrows bunch together as I try to place the other person's voice, but I keep falling short even though it sits on the tip of my tongue.

"I want eyes on the golden warrior. My gut tells me he's got something, possibly the onyx with the way nothing affects him," Burton says, choking me with more facts. "And I want the crown, but the whereabouts of that have been hidden for the past ten years and no one has a clue where to begin. The last known sighting was in Amberglen, but some believe it to be with The Monarchy."

I need to be making a note of all of this.

Holy shit.

The vision fades and I drop my hand, letting the real world come back into view.

"Raven?"

"Yes?" I croak, shaken with shock.

Creed crouches down to meet my gaze, surprise flitting through his gaze. "Did you see all of that?"

My eyes widen as I nod. "You guys saw it too?"

"Yeah, it played out like a projection on the table."

Crawling out from under the table, I stand, dusting myself off as I glance around at everyone. "Did any of you guys manage to see the other person? I could only see Burton."

Eldon shakes his head, but as he opens his mouth to speak, the thud of footsteps garners our attention.

"Fuck. Quick, this way," Leila whisper-shouts, waving for us to follow her farther into the room where a small alcove sits in the shadows. She tucks herself away in the corner and the rest of us follow suit. Zane accesses his magic, and without a word, we all connect once again to become invisible.

My heart races in my chest, but the curiosity over who it could be is short-lived as Burton steps into the room. Fitch is a step behind him, dragging someone along with him, and my frown only deepens when I see it's Sebastian.

Burton tugs at the lapels of his blazer as he circles the table. "I'm assuming no one saw you," he says, turning to watch Fitch release Sebastian in the middle of the room, who sits defeated where he's left.

"Of course not. But we don't have long. The meeting was called for seven, which is in thirty minutes," Fitch explains. "Why is he here anyway?"

Burton's jaw tightens as he shakes his head at Sebastian. "His control is wavering. His decisions are faltering. Guilt seems to have taken over him since he secured the target from Ruben."

His what is what now? Why does Burton know about that? I thought that order had come from Erikel, especially since it was passed on to one of his men. Nausea burns the back of my throat as they talk about Sebastian like he's not there, and he remains silent and still.

"How do you want me to handle it?"

"I'm sure punishment with a fresh load of magic will do the trick," Burton bites, and Sebastian whips his head up, fear in his eyes.

"Please," he rasps, trying to move back, but Fitch already has him by the collar.

I blindly clutch Brax's hand as magic lifts Sebastian just off his feet. His school blazer, shirt, and tie are removed, revealing his back. My free hand cups my mouth as horror burns in my eyes.

His flesh is red and raw. Line after line of pain and brutality cover his skin, and the source of it now rests in Fitch's hands.

A whip.

I glance at Leila out of the corner of my eye to see the same horror written all over her face. Any inkling that she had any knowledge of this is dismissed with the pain and disbelief that makes her tremble.

"Three lashings. Let's make sure he has a reminder for the next few days," Burton orders, and Fitch doesn't need any further encouragement as he pulls his hand down and lets the sound of the whip cut through the air before it connects with Sebastian's back.

Fuck.

Emotion clogs my throat. My brother is an asshole. There's no lie in that, but has that been his own doing…or theirs? Either way, I can't watch. It's too painful.

The second and third lashes of the whip have Sebastian crying out, the sound is raw and jagged, but I force myself to remain where I am. I don't have the whole picture, and until I do, I can't reveal us.

"Now, remember your place, Hendrix," Burton hisses, and I open my eyes in time to see him place his hand on Sebastian's face, fingers splayed as he chants something under his breath. My brother falls to the floor a moment later.

I sense Leila's panic and movement, and when I turn to face her, I see the tears tracking down her face.

"I can't go home to him. I can't," she whispers, her bottom lip jittering with every word.

"You have to, Leila. This is bigger than us. Bigger than everything, and they can't know that we know," I breathe in response when I'm sure they haven't heard her. She shakes her head vigorously, but Burton moves around the table, regaining our attention.

"Prepare for the gathering and get rid of him," Burton

hisses, waving a hand at Sebastian's limp body on the floor. I expect Fitch to dismiss him, but before he can grab Sebastian, Burton has him by the scruff of his collar. "Do your job, or the next time, it won't be a lashing; it will be your life. You thought you could hide this little guild from me? You fool."

I frown, my heart racing so fast I'm certain it's going to burst from my chest. Hide the guild from him? He's the leader, what the fuck does that mean? I glance to Creed beside me, who shakes his head, obviously just as confused as I am.

"We even had to kick your daughter out of the guild to keep up with the ruse," Fitch adds, taking Sebastian from Burton's hold and tossing him over his shoulder. He's unresponsive, but they continue to vocalize their disappointment in him.

Fuckers.

Who is Burton's daughter, though? The only girl I know that's been kicked out is… Genie.

She isn't, is she? Surely, we would know about that connection, right? A quick glance at Eldon confirms he didn't know that either.

We're all fucked with the information overload.

"This is already making me dizzy," Burton groans, swiping a hand down his face, and I watch in shock as his features change. His eyes darken, a scar appears, his hair lengthens, and his pristine suit morphs into layers draped with a fur coat.

Erikel.

Erikel is…Burton?

What the actual fuck?

I'm certain I'm going to pass out. There's no denying it.

"Fitch, are you certain Burton has been disposed of properly? I can't add to my troubles," Erikel rasps, cracking his neck from side to side, and Fitch nods.

"I'm sure. Ruben did exactly as we asked and I made sure to dispose of him myself. Burton is gone."

TWENTY FIVE

Creed

My head is spinning and I don't know which way is up. If we thought things were fucked before, they're even worse now. I don't have a clue what's going on, and I'm pretty certain the others don't either.

Erikel is a... fuck, I don't know what he is, but that was some extreme magic right there.

"We need to get the fuck out of here so we can come back in with the others," Brax mutters, and Eldon frowns.

"Do we want Erikel to know we're a part of the guild?" he asks, raising a valid point, and Raven sighs.

"I'm sure if Genie is his daughter, then he already knows," she bites, her shoulders bunching with a mixture of annoyance and anger.

Fuck.

Genie is his daughter. Genie. Is. His. Daughter. Or

that's how it sounds from what Fitch said moments ago.

"How does someone from the Basilica Realm get into Silvercrest Academy?" I ask, completely bewildered, and Zane shrugs.

"I don't fucking know. How does any of this happen?" he grumbles, shaking his head in disbelief.

Fitch leaves the room with Sebastian over his shoulder while Erikel drops down into a chair by the table. He leans back, stretching his arms out from side to side before he slowly transforms back into Burton.

My mind is blown. If I hadn't seen the shift, I would swear it was Burton himself in front of us, but based on Fitch's words, he's dead, so that can't be possible. Why bother making Raven bring him back from the dead that night? Was it all just a ruse to be able to take his place because everyone believes he's still alive? That's fucked up.

"Let's get out of here," Raven whispers, keeping the connection between everyone as we all fall into step, silently tiptoeing around the room. My breath is lodged in my throat, and I'm certain I'm going to pass out from trying to be so quiet, but to my surprise, we make it to the staircase without interruption.

Zane gets one foot on the first step but quickly has to move as Fitch storms back down the steps in a hurry. He rushes past us as we press as tightly as possible against the wall, and when he saunters back into the main room, completely oblivious to us, I heave a sigh of relief.

We make it up the steps and outside without any further interruptions, coming to a stop when we're firmly hidden away from view.

"Are we good here?" Zane asks, and I notice the tiredness clinging to him.

I double-check around us before I nod. "We're good, drop the magic."

He does instantly, sagging in relief. "Are you okay?" Raven asks, panic in her voice as she grabs his arm, and he nods with a grin.

"Yeah. I'm good. Sorry, Dove. It's just the magic. It's exhausted me," he explains, and she quickly wraps herself around him comfortingly.

"Thank you," she breathes, and the rest of us all murmur our appreciation too, Leila included, although hers is a little more muffled around the silent sobs burning through her as she tries to keep it bottled up.

Raven releases Zane and drops to the ground, sitting cross-legged on the grass, and the rest of us follow suit except Brax, who continues to keep an eye on our surroundings. She rests her head on Zane's shoulder and holds Leila's hand in a show of support as her crying calms.

"What is Erikel?" Raven asks, and I shrug, unable to recall the name for it, but Eldon does.

"He's a skinwalker, someone who can change their appearance to resemble someone else."

Raven shivers, her face scrunching in distaste, and I can't blame her. "I didn't know that was a thing."

"It's rare. He's technically classed as a shifter," Brax adds without looking at us.

"Well, either way, we're going to be okay. The Monarchy is coming soon. We just have to try and keep our heads down and get through all of this alive," Raven declares, and Leila gapes at her.

"They are?" Hope is thick in her voice and Raven nods.

"We don't know the exact details, but we know they're coming. You're going to need to get your head on straight and consider how you're going to approach your father until then. I know it's scary, and I wouldn't want to do it either, but if he learns that we know he's working with Erikel, fuck knows what he'll do. You saw the state of Sebastian." Raven gulps. She's shaken by that, by what she saw mottled into Sebastian's back. If I'm honest, it threw me off too.

Silence descends over us as we all recall the lashing Sebastian got. If you had asked me yesterday if he deserved it, I would have answered with a resounding yes, as I'm sure my brothers would have done, too. Shit, I would have asked for the whip to do it myself, but now…nothing seems real. There's no guessing what is and isn't true anymore.

Fuck.

Wiping a hand down my face, I sigh.

"Do you think Sebastian is going to be okay?" Leila asks, and Raven's lips twist with uncertainty.

"They seem to want him alive. But if what they were saying is true, and we piece the rest together for ourselves, then it seems as though he's under some kind of magical control. But for how long, I don't know. Have any of us ever met Sebastian without the influence of it? I don't know, but that was horrific," Eldon states, referring to the lashing, and I nod in agreement.

"Damn, thank goodness you all agree," Raven murmurs, tucking a loose tendril of hair behind her ear. "I thought I was going soft on him for all the wrong reasons. I'm certainly not saying he's suddenly a high priority for me, but that wasn't fun to witness."

Everybody hums their recognition of the truth. Everyone but Brax. I'm sure he's twisted up about it more than the rest of us. He's the one who promised to kill him. Promises are life vows to my brother. He doesn't falter from them. That's a concern for another day though. We have enough in front of us to deal with as it is. Especially since we need to head back in there and pretend like we didn't just bear witness to any of that.

"So you think the Burton in the vision was the real Burton, and not the new Burton?" Leila asks, sending my head into a spin with the number of times she said Burton.

"Who fucking knows?" Zane grunts, rubbing at the back of his neck. "When I replay it, I think the projection was the real Burton, which still doesn't fill me with joy because he was also conniving beneath the surface, and now we can't question him on any of it because he's dead."

Dead.

"At the hands of Ruben too. That must have been the conversation we heard at the party," Raven clarifies, and Leila scoffs.

"Why would my father not allow me to go to the party because it was full of Erikel's men when he's..." A sob bursts from her lips and she covers her mouth for a second before finding the strength to say it. "He's one of them." Tears pour from her eyes, betrayal claiming her, and it's impossible not to feel sorry for her.

I don't trust her as much as Raven does, but I also know it takes a lot for Raven to believe in the goodness of people, which is the only reason she's here. As much as I'm glad she's now aware of what her father is capable of, I half wish she wasn't here having to deal with the consequences of that.

I don't even know where to begin with all of that information, nevermind her. It doesn't help that every time we uncover a new level of the information we're receiving, it opens something else up. I don't think we're ever going to get to the bottom of this. Knowing where it all began is impossible.

"I think we need to join the others," Brax states, nodding in the direction of the guild, and we all stand, brushing the loose grass off us as we watch the other members heading down the stairway.

"Are you going to be okay?" Raven asks, looking to Leila, who nods meekly.

"I have to be. It's bigger than me and my feelings," she admits, wiping the remaining tears from her face before pressing her hands to her eyes. I notice the icy white on her fingertips, but it's only there for a moment before it disappears and she drops her hands back down.

"Did you just cover the fact that you've been crying?" I ask, noticing that her red puffy eyes are all gone.

Leila smiles from ear to ear, pleased with herself as she nods, and Raven giggles. At least we're heading down there with a calmer vibe than what we left with.

The six of us head toward the stairs, as relaxed as we're going to be, but my shoulders stiffen when I notice the telltale armor of the golden warrior, my father.

The memory of the projection flickers to mind, a reminder of the onyx Burton mentioned in relation to my father, and I can't help but wonder if it's true.

"Creed," he booms as we approach, crooking his finger for me to go to him, and my back stiffens.

Knowing what he did at Pinebrook fills me with both hope and fear. Hope because there's potential that he's the man I've longed for all of this time; he's just hiding underneath the weight of the armor permanently encasing his body. Fear because he was able to play with my mind and body so effortlessly that I was left none the wiser about it.

"I won't be a minute," I murmur, separating from the others to go to him.

I don't look up to meet his gaze straight away, my eyes are obsessively scanning over his armor to see if I can spot anything, but all that greets me is gold, gold, and more gold. Along with the deathly smears of crimson.

"Creed," he repeats, pulling my gaze to his. "Why are you here?"

"Excuse me?"

"What's going on down there?"

"I don't know what you mean," I retort. If Erikel is trying to hide who he is and what he's doing, then why is my father here? Glancing over my shoulder, my father's hand clamps down on my shoulder, forcing my attention back to him, but my eyes slam shut instead and I feel like I'm floating for the briefest moment before I blink up at him.

"No one else but you and your friends have seen me," he explains as if reading my mind. Is he reading my mind?

Shaking his hand off, I take a step back. He looks at me with strained eyes and a flicker of pain furrowing his brows, but he doesn't utter another word. I don't know what's going on with him, and discomfort burns my chest as I walk away to my actual family.

"Are you okay?" Raven asks as I step closer, and I nod.

"I'm fine, why?"

"I don't know, it's just when your eyes closed, your eyebrows…"

I frown at her as we head down the steps, her fingers laced with mine as she strokes her thumb over my knuckles like I've done to her so many times. "What?"

"I don't know, you just looked distressed," she mutters, her eyebrows pinching with concern, and I force a smile to my face.

"I didn't feel that way, I swear." Confused, maybe, but I didn't feel any kind of distress, and that's what's irritating me now. The ability my father has to slip beneath the barriers I have with little to no effort…

Fuck.

My thoughts are interrupted as we step into the room to find the members circling fake Burton and Fitch, who hover by the table.

We step into the crowd, hoping to blend in, but Erikel's gaze immediately tracks us and I notice Fitch's brows furrow when he spots Leila.

"Hey, man," Grave murmurs as he moves to step beside Leila, nodding at me before turning to greet her. They whisper quietly between themselves for a few seconds until Leila giggles at something he says.

"Have you been crying?" he asks, lifting his hand to cup her cheek, and she shakes her head. "Are you sure? Do you want to come back to my place tonight?" he offers, and she nods, nibbling her bottom lip nervously as she tilts her head to look at Raven, who gives her a smile.

"You don't mind?"

"Of course not."

Grave grabs her hand, linking their fingers together, and I'm just as baffled by the pair of them as I am with everything else happening around us. At least Raven won't be worrying about Leila tonight if she's with Grave instead of going home to her father.

"We'll keep things brief," not Burton says, gaining everyone's attention. "I've heard rumors that Erikel is going to lead a march soon. Has anyone else?" He plants his hands on his hips, surveying the crowd, and a resounding no echoes around us.

Is he saying that because he actually is organizing a march, or is he just trying to cut short any rumors that are actually out there? Fuck, now we're going to be second-guessing every last thing.

"I've reached out to The Monarchy a few times on our

behalf, but I'm getting no response. Has anyone else had any luck?" Burton scans the crowd once again as everyone shakes their head. Now he's clearly trying to see if anyone has had any communication with people outside of the academy, and there's no way in Hell any of us are admitting to that. "Okay, we have to stay vigilant and alert. On a final note, a manuscript on magical artifacts is missing from the library. Has anyone here seen it?" Another resounding echo of no's repeats around us, and he sighs with frustration, his knuckles turning white as he clenches his hands. "Are any of you any use at all?" he snaps, his outburst catching everyone by surprise as we gape at him.

That's definitely more of an Erikel trait than a Burton one.

"Professor Burton, are we done with the members for this evening?" Fitch asks, trying to calm the situation, and the Burton impostor waves him off dismissively before storming from the room.

Well then.

"What was the point of even calling a meeting?" Grave mumbles under his breath, and the answer is clear. He simply wanted to know what we knew with regard to topics he deems important. The fact that he just left instead of directing us into a training session only confirms it's not Burton anymore.

The rest of the members disperse, including Leila, who

lets Grave lead her out.

"What do we do now?" Eldon asks, looking as helpless as I feel, and it's Raven who answers.

"We need to reach out to Rhys."

TWENTY SIX

Raven

We tried to sneak into Lyra's office on the way back last night, but there was no answer and the door was locked. It was worth a shot, even if it was a miss, and we will get to try again this morning before classes start.

"Are you sure we can't all go?" Eldon grumbles, swiping his hair back off his face as he pants. The weights are long forgotten, placed at his feet as he gives me those puppy dog eyes.

"Hey, this wasn't my idea, remember?" I retorted.

"No, it was mine. Eldon will get over it. He's just being a pussy," Brax grunts, continuing to lift his weights without breaking a sweat.

"No, he's not. I've seen the most exquisite pussy in all of my life, and it definitely doesn't look like this doofus," Zane states with a grin as he throws his arm around my shoulders.

"Of course you're all smiles; you're the one going with her while the rest of us stay here," Creed adds, planting his hands on his hips.

"Again, blame Brax. This was his idea, and as much as you might not like it, he's right," Zane blasts back quickly, pulling me tighter to his side.

When it was clear we would have to try again this morning, Brax felt it was better for the two of us to go so we didn't draw as much attention to ourselves as the five of us together would do. For Mr. Protective himself to say it only confirms it's the right choice, whether we like it or not.

"Fine, but Brax can sleep on the end of the bed tonight for coming up with such bullshit," Eldon concedes, and I bite back a smile.

These fucking men.

"Quick, let's go, Dove, before he changes his mind," Zane whispers, his lips pressed against my cheek, and I shiver, nodding in agreement.

"We'll meet you outside Lyra's office in an hour. Behave," Brax orders, giving me a pointed look before capturing my chin in his grasp and crashing his lips to mine. He rips away from me far too quickly, his eyes darker than they were a moment ago, and I'm left breathless.

"Yeah, what the big, bad gargoyle said," Eldon adds, cupping my cheek as he kisses me more delicately, but he still steps back more quickly than I would like.

Creed is quick to fill the space he leaves behind, grabbing my tie as he pulls me closer, and Zane's hold on me loosens. "Seriously, keep your wits about you. I want you safe, Raven. Always."

His words shouldn't make me hot, yet here I am. He kisses the corner of my mouth, moving before I can even remotely kiss him back. Acting fast, I grab the front of his t-shirt, pulling him to me this time as I mold our lips together.

Heat tingles over my cheeks and down my spine and I have the pleasure of releasing him far too soon this time. His onyx eyes are wide, his jaw tight as he juts his chin toward the door. "Go, before I change my fucking mind." The snap to his tone only makes me hotter and I nibble on my bottom lip as Zane steers me through the patio doors, across the living room, and out of the front door as quickly as possible.

Zane laces his fingers with mine as we head up the winding pathway, which is a lot quieter than usual due to how early it is. The sound of the breeze rustling the leaves on the trees is all we can hear as we get closer to the main building and it's almost serene.

If I was to close my eyes, I could be anywhere. No enemies, no skinwalkers, nothing. Unfortunately for me, my eyes are open and having to face reality. A reality I hope is over soon. We need to update Rhys on everything we learned last night and pray they're close.

"How are you feeling after last night, Dove?" I look up at him with my eyebrows raised, and he smirks. "I know you've said you're okay one thousand times already, but I don't want you to brush over how you're feeling," he adds, knowing me far too well.

I sigh, focusing on the path ahead as I think. "Honestly, I feel numb to it. My heart hurt when I saw Sebastian and heard what they were saying. The thought of him being under some kind of magic changes things. No matter how much I don't want it to, it does. Is that silly of me?"

"Of course not. The reality of the situation is twisted. You didn't have the best memories of him before you got here, but then he's been nothing but a motherfucker since you stepped foot on campus. That can't be erased, believe me; my desire to put him six feet under hasn't changed in the slightest, but knowing that something else is at play makes me pause. Only time will tell how that will pan out," Zane explains, and I nod in agreement.

It's far less black and white and a whole lot more gray than it was. It's hurting my head.

Zane suddenly stops beside me and I freeze beside him, confused by what's going on, until he nods in the distance.

Sebastian.

He's alone, trudging along the path that cuts across

ours, but he's already farther along than us, so he shouldn't see us unless he turns around. I notice the slight hunch to his back, the tension in his arms, and the way his head is drooped.

Clearly, there's more to the asshole than what sits on the surface, it seems. The question is, do I want to understand it? Good or bad, is it too late?

"Let's hurry," Zane mutters, likely sensing how torn I am.

We do just that, slipping through the double doors and heading inside without a backward glance. Approaching Lyra's door, I take a deep breath before I rap my knuckles on the wood. Tension coils in my veins, but it doesn't last long before the door opens, revealing Lyra on the other side.

"Oh, good. I was going to come looking for you today. Monarch Denver has been trying to reach out," she explains, taking a step back as she waves us into the room. Once the door is closed behind us, she ushers us to the small room hidden in the wall, and I watch with wonder as she makes it appear before our eyes.

She leads the way into the room, which looks the exact same as it did a few days ago. The sofa sits center on the wall straight ahead and she nods for us to take a seat. Once we're comfortable, she smiles. "There's a lockdown on this kind of stuff overnight, so I can't get it working until the ward has lifted, which gives you about twenty minutes, but I had already agreed for him to make contact at that time anyway. Make yourselves comfortable while you wait and I'll seal you in, just to be safe," she adds, and I murmur my thanks before she slips from the room. The door disappears a moment later, just as she explained.

"What are we going to do for twenty minutes?" I ask. My body is pent up with adrenaline from getting across campus and having her stow us away in here so quickly, and now we're going to be sitting for twenty minutes twiddling our thumbs.

"I can easily fill twenty minutes, Dove," Zane says with a wiggle of his eyebrows, and I roll my eyes at him. "Hey, I'm not joking," he insists, his hand landing on my thigh beside him.

"Of course you're not," I mumble, my body tense with desire from such a simple touch.

He doesn't respond with words. Instead, he grabs my waist and pulls me into his lap with a light squeal.

"Are you telling me you don't want me to nudge your panties to the side and slip deep into your pussy right here, right now, Dove?" He quirks a brow at me in question as he flexes his hips up so I can feel his hardening cock beneath his academy-issued pants.

"Fuck," I say with a gasp, and he grins.

"See? I know you too well," he remarks, and I shake

my head at him.

"I'm supposed to be working on my focus and not being distracted by you guys."

"Maybe you should work on that later," he murmurs, brushing his lips over my neck.

"Maybe," I rasp as he pinches my already budding nipple through my shirt and lace bra, making my back arch and a groan fall from my lips.

"It definitely doesn't help that you're so responsive, Dove."

I grind my hips down as I look at him through hooded eyes. "I can't help it."

"Good. Don't ever even bother to try," he states, holding my waist with one hand as he reaches for the fastener on his pants to reveal his thick length.

Hot damn.

"You don't even know when your father is going to appear on the communication," I ramble, clutching on to his shoulders, but he simply shrugs with a smirk running from ear to ear.

"Then we better take fifteen instead of twenty minutes then."

"But—"

"No 'but'. You're going to let me fill you, just like you've let Creed and Eldon. Then I want my cum dripping down your thighs all fucking day." His voice darkens, desire lacing every word.

"Even when we speak with your father?" I rebuke, hoping to throw him off, but his smirk only spreads wider.

"Especially then."

Fuck.

He tucks my panties to the side under my skirt and lines his cock up with my entrance, filling me with one thrust. I can't moan or groan. My throat is tight with desire as he consumes me, inch by inch. I'm at his mercy.

My nails dig into his blazer as I adjust to his size. My whole body is hot as my pussy clenches around him.

"You're like a gift, Raven. Every morning, I get to wake up to you. It's a blessing. I just want to wrap you in me and stamp you with my name so everyone knows you're mine, but I'll settle for branding you with my cum instead." *Fuck.* I rock in his lap, gasping at the combination of his cock and his words. "I know you feel it too, Raven. We all do."

He's not wrong, but I can't find the fucking words.

He moves like lightning in the next breath, lifting me in the air before quickly dropping me back to the sofa, but I'm not on top of him now.

No.

He's above me. His cock still filling me.

Or he was. He disappears suddenly, making me frown, but the firmness of his cock still remains.

"Zane?" I call out, hearing a chuckle in response. "What

are you doing?" I rasp, adrenaline zipping through my body.

"Claiming you as mine in every fucking dimension, Dove."

"If we're invisible, why can't I see you?" I ask. Every other time he's used his magic on me, I've still been able to see him. The chuckle that rumbles from him this time makes me still, and I know what he's going to say before he even opens his mouth.

"You're not invisible, Raven. Just me. You get the pleasure of being fucked by thin air," he murmurs, flexing his hips and making me moan. My legs are spread wide and I can feel his waist and thighs, but there's nothing there to see.

"Fuck, Zane."

Fuck he does. I sink my hands into the arm of the sofa behind my head as he pounds into me, again and again, all while I can't see his body or expressions, but I can hear the pleasure in every moan he gives me.

It's like all the times I've needed to get off but been alone, yet his presence is clear. It's too much and not enough all at once. My spiral comes immediately when I feel the press of something against my clit, likely his thumb, drawing circles in time with his thrusts, and my orgasm rips through me.

Slam after slam, I come apart, sure I'm ripping holes in the sofa as I cling on for dear life.

"Fill me, Zane. I need to feel you too," I plead as he

drags out every drop of my climax before taking me over the edge once more when his jagged movements heat up with force and he fills my pussy with his own release.

"Fuck, yes, Raven. Fuuuck," he groans hoarsely as he reappears and collapses down on me. We're a tangle of sweaty limbs, attempting to catch our breaths as he remains inside of me.

I'm ready to nap, far from prepared for a call with his father, but the stark reminder has me pushing at his chest. "Zane, quickly, in case your father arrives," I whisper like I wasn't just screaming at the top of my lungs.

"Fine. Anything for you, Dove," he breathes, kissing me sweetly on the lips before standing.

I fix my panties back into place, straighten my skirt, and attempt to adjust my blouse and blazer. I'm raking my fingers through my hair as I retie my hair back when Rhys appears before us.

Holy shit, that was close.

"Pops," Zane calls out as he casually drops down on the sofa beside me, throwing his arm out behind me, and I'm certain my cheeks are red.

"I have good news," Rhys declares when he sees us, a huge grin on his face.

"I'm glad someone does," Zane retorts with a huff, making his father frown.

"What happened?" he asks, instantly going into

protective mode, and we don't waste a second catching him up to speed. My embarrassment is quickly forgotten as we explain everything we learned last night, not leaving out a single piece of information.

Once we're done, we fall back against the sofas after talking so animatedly, and I'm left panting for breath.

"Fuck. That's a lot. I'm going to make as many inconspicuous calls as possible. I was going to bring your mother in and let her speak to you, but I don't want her to have wind of this right now. Do you agree?" His attention turns to me, making me pause, but I nod.

"I agree." I would love to see Mama right now. It's instinct for me in these moments to want the figure she's supposed to represent, someone to show me guidance, but the reality is, I don't know if I can trust her, not like I can Rhys. I haven't heard a word from her since she left the night Erikel took over. I know it hasn't been easy for anyone to make contact, but leading up to that point was filled with odd information and what feels like a lot of omissions.

"What's the good news then, Pops?" Zane asks, redirecting the conversation, and I'm thankful. Especially when Rhys's smile returns.

"We're close. Two days and we're going to have you out of there."

TWENTY SEVEN

Eldon

The Monarchy will be here tomorrow.

Tomorrow.

Fuck.

The students at this academy should never have been drawn into a war between realms. The Monarchy should have been the ones facing this the entire time.

Yesterday went by so quickly once Raven and Zane shared the news, but I get the feeling today is going to take its sweet ass time to pass, leaving tomorrow a million miles away.

I close the front door behind everyone as we start up the path to the academy.

We just have to get through today. Whatever it might throw at us, we just have to make it through.

Brax leads the way while Zane and Creed flank Raven

and I hold up the rear. It's strange how we naturally take this formation around her. It's never even been a discussion.

"Raven," Leila calls out, making us pause, and we turn to see her rushing toward us with Grave holding her hand. This is escalating.

"Hey, did you sleep okay?" Raven asks the same question she asked the first time she saw her friend yesterday. Leila nods in response and I notice the way Grave affectionately squeezes her hand.

Raven leaves it at that. She doesn't delve into anything further in Grave's presence and Leila seems happy to talk about anything and everything that's the total opposite of serious in his proximity.

Accompanied the entire way by the sound of the girls' gossip, we arrive at the academy in no time. Grave pulls Leila off to the side and I turn my back to them and focus on my girl instead. She's telling Creed something. I can't hear what she's saying, but the way she moves her hands so animatedly when she talks warms my heart. She's intoxicating. Every last piece of her. I'm addicted.

Leila sidles up beside Raven a few moments later and we all instinctively huddle closer together as we make our way through the academy hallways.

"How has your father been?" Raven asks as quietly as possible.

Leila shrugs. "I didn't go back home. I stayed with Grave."

"What's that about anyway? I didn't want to put a damper on it the other night, but the last time you mentioned him, he was talking about you behind your back," Raven states, and I beam. Trust my girl to ask the question that has been nagging me as well.

"That's what I thought, but one of these guys brought it up to him and he was confused as hell, so we talked it over and realized that when *Genie* is the source of information, said information may not actually be all that reliable."

That's more than true.

"How would Genie have known? Fuck, nevermind. She was probably watching you guys too," Raven says with a scoff, referring to the images she took of all of us with our girl in some compromising positions.

I was ready to tear the entire campus up to make sure no one caught another glimpse of the pictures, but Raven owned it. Just like she does everything else, leaving me speechless and even hotter for her.

As if hearing her name, the she-devil herself appears, placing her hand over Raven's shoulder to push against my chest.

"Do you miss me yet, Eldon?"

What the fuck? I thought we were over this.

I feel Raven stiffen at her closeness, and have exactly zero patience for the idea of entertaining this girl in the slightest. Giving her attention is exactly what she wants, and I never wanted her to begin with, even less than ever now that I believe her father is Erikel.

Instead of confronting her and exposing what we know, I opt for the more childish approach, even if it makes me cringe.

"Can any of you guys smell that? It smells like... shit around here."

I don't even bother trying to knock her hand away as I continue walking, letting it fall off naturally. The smirk on Raven's face makes it all worthwhile, and the sound of Genie stomping her foot on the marble floor a cherry on top.

Without another word, we step into the classroom to find the new institute students already sitting in some of the seats, including ours. I'm trying to decide whether I should be an asshole or just let them sit there when my gaze lands on Ruben, who is sitting on the professor's desk.

My chest feels heavy and my stomach clenches. He killed Burton. He killed Burton when I believed him to be a good guy. It's questionable now, with the information we have learned, but it still drives me insane.

Why would Erikel kill Burton in front of everyone and have Raven bring him back to life, only to off him again and skinwalk around as him? Why not skinwalk as him all of the time so his presence was still on campus? I don't think we'll ever know, but my gut tells me it has something to do with the fact that he enjoys stoking fear in others, and his Burton skin just wouldn't get the job done.

Looking at Ruben now, there's no remorse. Nothing. Not even the smallest inkling.

Brax huffs, and the second he starts walking, I know he's going to cause a scene with the person sitting in his seat, but before he can get halfway there, Fitch walks in and the room goes silent. Leila stiffens, sucking her bottom lip into her mouth nervously as he walks to his desk.

"We'll be taking this class outside today." He grabs something off his desk and heads toward the door again, leaving everyone to follow after him.

Raven's hand reaches for mine and I tug her against my side as we join the moving body of students. Once outside, I expect him to lead us to the changing rooms like usual, but to my surprise, he simply stops on the grass beside the double doors.

"In a real-life battle, you won't have time to change. You will have to fight in exactly what you're wearing at the time. I think we should approach classes like that going forward," he states, folding his arms over his chest as he eyes each of us. I glance at the institute students, noting how their clothing is much more appropriate for this kind of thing, but it won't afford them an advantage over me. I'll make sure of it. "We'll be training today with magic only. No swords allowed."

"What if you're a healer?" a timid girl asks, nervously tucking a tendril of hair behind her ear as she avoids eye contact with the professor.

"Then, at least, you can mend yourself again and again," he retorts with a shrug. Does he seem harsher today? I don't know, but the fact that I truly know who he is and what he's capable of has made me see him in an entirely different light. I have played with the thought that he is also under Erikel's command, as compromised as the rest of them, but for now, he needs to be handled like the enemy until we know for sure. "I'll call out names, and you'll pair off," he continues, not waiting to see if there are any further concerns.

Raven's hand squeezes mine a little harder, and when I glance at her, I find her lips pursed and her eyebrows pinched. Understanding dawns on me. I don't know how, but it's just natural to understand what she's trying to convey.

All anyone knows about her here is that she can bring people back from the dead. They don't know about the mirror magic and my gut tells me she would like to keep it that way.

Fuck.

"Genie and Lucinda. Raven and Leila. Brax and Baron. Creed and Royal. Zane and Idris. Eldon and Ruben." He continues on, but I've stopped listening. Of course, I'm paired with that asshole.

That's perfect. Just perfect.

It's not lost on me that, apart from Raven and Leila, everyone from Silvercrest Academy seems to be paired with someone from Shadowgrim Insititute. Is this to test the strengths and flaws between the two groups of people? Have they been taught differently than we have?

As much as I'm happy to train, instead of using this moment to combine the two academies and create a bond, they're just continuing to pit us against one another. That's purposeful. I'm sure of it.

"Pair off," Fitch orders, and everyone steps away in their couplings.

I squeeze Raven's hand one last time, the worry gone a little from her eyes now that she's with Leila, and I turn to find Ruben waiting expectantly.

"I'm sure you know who I am by now," he states with a smirk. "But I'm having a little trouble placing you. Your name is…"

"You don't have to be polite with me. We both know you're darker than this. Wasting time on names feels silly at this stage." I shrug as I find a good space to face off with him, the pair of us turning to one another head on as his smirk grows.

"You think you know me," he states with a cock of his brow.

"I think you just told me that I do. I'm just saying not to bother," I retort, and he flexes his fingers at his sides.

"Is it because I'm from the Basilica Realm?" he asks, making me frown.

"No. I couldn't give a shit where you're from." And that's the truth. I never batted an eyelid at the fact Raven was from Shadowmoor. You don't get to choose where you come from, but you get to choose who you are as a person. "It's how you carry yourself, like a lap dog waiting for his next order."

I'm provoking him. I know it. I just can't help it. I hate people with smarmy attitudes and holier-than-thou egos. I don't have time for it.

Ruben's hands lift in the next moment, making it clear he doesn't have time for bullshit either, and I just about manage to deflect the ice coming at me. I turn my body temperature up high, fueling my magic through my veins, and watch the ice melt on impact.

"You look a little red. Is that fire magic you have?" Ruben asks, and I'm surprised he's not retreating at the imbalance between us. I can melt off snow and ice all day long. He doesn't give me a chance to offer any kind of response as he aims his magic my way once again. This time, he shoots ice through the air in the form of long spears, two at once.

A fireball is instantly in my hand. I split it in two and toss them both at the incoming missiles. They're longer than I expect, and although my fire melts them, they don't completely melt until they're an inch from my face. It takes everything in me to stand still and not flinch from their close proximity.

Rolling my shoulders back, I aim first, shooting six small balls of fire in his direction, making sure to target different parts of his body to make it harder to deflect. Ruben blocks quickly with ice shields, which manage to slow five of the six fireballs down enough that they burn out before they reach him. The last one does manage to catch his shoulder and he stumbles back a step, a snarl quickly gracing his face.

It's impressive to see him stop five, though. That's more than I expected. I guess I should consider that there's not as much of an imbalance as I initially thought. He put out my fire just as quickly as I melted his ice.

This might actually be fun.

Ice comes barreling toward me a moment later and I bend my knees slightly, getting in the best position to block when my eyes roll to the back of my head. I feel the impact of the ice before I'm knocked to the ground, but everything else fades away as a vision takes hold.

Darkness.

The dripping of water rings out in the distance.

Damp rocks are hard beneath my hands as I push up off the ground.

Blinking does little to clear my vision until it overwhelms me all at once.

Red.

Red everywhere.

It's not blood… it shimmers like jewels in the sun.

Stepping back from the wall, it becomes clear this is a ruby mine. The way they're all a part of the walls, embedded between the stones and shimmering in the darkness is special. I've never seen it before but I know what it is in my soul.

Inching closer, I run my hand over the jagged edges and my eyes fix on one.

It's red. Redder than red, yet it's tinged with what I can only describe as black ink inside it.

Why is it different from the rest?

Poten's Ruby.

Stumbling back a step, I gape around the space. This is where the Poten's Ruby is. Hidden among normal rubies. Where did Burton say he hid it? Ashdale? Fuck. In the caves.

It's hard to make out much more of the space, but a green light seems to flicker in the distance, drawing me closer.

Stumbling over uneven terrain that I can't actually

see, my eyes widen when I get closer to see that the green I'm chasing isn't a light, but another stone...emeralds, and they're positioned more specifically than the rubies, forming an archway in the stone cobbled wall.

A shiver runs down my spine when shadows flutter over the archway, beckoning me closer, but when I look around, there's no one else here with me. Just the rubies and the emeralds.

Red and green.

My eyes startle wide to find Raven hovering over me.

"Are you okay?" she breathes. "I saw your eyes roll, and then the ice hit you, but I couldn't get to you before you fell."

"I'm good," I rasp, more winded than I expected.

"Was it a..." Her whisper trails off as I nod.

"What was that?" Fitch grunts, appearing behind Raven.

"I got lightheaded. I must have been tugging at my magic too much, and then the ice knocked me off my feet," I mutter, standing to find Ruben frowning at me. I don't need his attention right now, so I turn away from him.

"Take him to the medical center," Fitch orders, and when my brothers all appear to help, along with Raven, he quickly shakes his head. "You can't all go. Just one," he grunts before turning away, effectively dismissing me.

"I'll take him," Brax decides, placing his hand on

Raven's shoulder as she frowns at him. "You're safer with two of us around than just one, especially when he's still foggy like this," he explains, and Raven reluctantly agrees with a sigh.

Her lips ghost my cheek for a brief second before she takes a step back. "Be safe and try to give him all of the details," she murmurs, and I smile with a nod.

Brax stays right at my side as we step into the academy building and I take a second to lean back against the wall.

"You good?"

"Yeah, I just need a second."

"What did you see?" he asks, and I blink at him in bewilderment.

"Too much."

CURSED SHADOWS

TWENTY EIGHT

Raven

Eldon reappeared at the end of class and told me all about his vision. A vision I have so many questions about, but I've had to keep them to myself while we've gone from class to class. Now that it's lunchtime, I have them all noted in my mind and I'm ready to pepper him with them.

I hope I don't overwhelm him, but the pointed look he's been giving me ever since tells me he knows and is ready for it.

As if sensing exactly what I'm thinking about, he's at my side when the class is called to an end and we all gather our things.

"Are your questions categorized, or is it going to be a free-for-all?" he asks with a quirked brow and a grin on his face.

Fucker.

"Telling you would give you a heads up and I like keeping you on your toes," I retort, sticking my tongue out for good measure, and he shakes his head at me with a chuckle.

"What's your first one?"

Well, now he's putting me on the spot, but really, it's simple. "What do you think it means?"

He drapes his arm around my shoulder and sighs. "Honestly, I don't know. It feels like the vision was more about the location than a narrative underneath. Which is different. They're usually trying to send me a message, and if that's the case now, I can't see it. Which is annoying as hell."

"Maybe once we've talked it through, it might become a little clearer," I offer, and he smiles.

"That's what I'm hoping for, Little Bird." He kisses the top of my head for the briefest moment as the others join us.

Zane silently reaches for my hand, we all head out into the hallway with Brax up front and Creed a step behind.

"Raven."

I freeze in place, blocking the path of everyone around me, but it's unavoidable.

"Ari? Is everything okay?"

"Figgins is looking for you. Go with her."

"Why, what's going on?" I wait a few seconds, but he doesn't respond. *"Ari?"* Still nothing.

Fuck.

"Raven?" My name on Creed's lips pulls me from my head and I sigh as we step to the side so we're not blocking everyone's path.

"It's Ari. Figgins is looking for me and he wants me to go with her."

"Why?" Zane asks, and I shake my head.

"I don't know. I asked, and he stopped responding."

"And it would definitely be Ari?" Brax clarifies, and I nod.

"It has to be. No one else has ever communicated with me like that before." *It wouldn't be a possibility for someone else to do it... would it?* Shaking my head and clearing my thoughts, I focus on my guys.

"Then we'll all go," Eldon declares, pressing a kiss to my temple this time.

"What about Leila?" I ask, and Brax nods in her direction, where she's cradled under Grave's arm as he guides her toward the dining hall.

"She'll be fine," Creed murmurs, and I nod in agreement. "Where would Figgins be coming from?"

"Uhm, I don't know. Maybe we should head toward her classroom?" I suggest, and the five of us take off in that direction, walking against the flow of students all heading in the opposite direction.

We don't even make it halfway before she comes barreling around the corner, almost walking right into us.

"Oh, you're here. Raven, I'm sorry to—"

"Lead the way," I interject. There's no need for her to get all worked up over-explaining when we're already aware and ready to go.

"Oh, perfect," she mutters, spinning on her heels and turning back in the direction she came from. Wordlessly, Zane takes a step back and I follow beside her as she moves through the halls. Eldon, however, keeps his arm firmly secured around my shoulders. "You don't seem surprised to see me. I'm guessing that's because your magic has grown enough for you to communicate with Ari," she states, tapping her temple.

"Some of the time, but in this case, yeah. Ari reached out, he just didn't explain what for."

She hums in understanding. "It took a while with my familiar too. It'll get there," she says encouragingly, and a question I've been thinking about for a while blurts from my lips.

"Where is your familiar?"

Her gaze drops to the floor, pain flashing in her eyes as she exhales slowly and glances back at me. "I managed to get her through the gateways the night…" Her words trail off, but I know what she means. The night Erikel declared his intentions and rendered us all trapped here.

"How are you holding up without her?" I ask, instantly feeling the pain in my gut. It's hard enough for me right now with Ari, to not be accessible at all is something else entirely. She offers me a wobbly smile, unable to find the words she needs, and I find myself being the comforting one for a change. "You did what you thought was best for her."

"Did I?"

"Is she safe?"

"Yes."

"Then that's all that matters." I try to recall what her familiar is, but if she's told me, I can't remember, and now it feels awkward to ask. So, instead, I change the subject, hoping it will stick. "What are we doing now?"

Figgins clears her throat as we step into her classroom and head straight for the door at the back where her office is. "I heard some of the institute students say they were going to find their familiars in the compound."

"Fuck," I blurt. *Are the creatures Erikel brought familiars with some of his men?*

"Yeah. I don't think it's going to end well when they confirm that some of them are dead, but I also want to see how they're getting in and out of the ward surrounding it. Once I have an understanding of that, then I may be able to adapt it for us too."

My eyes widen in surprise. She really is taking this as seriously as I need her to, and it's a fucking relief to have someone on academy grounds on our side. My heart feels so warm I almost want to let her in on the Monarchy secret, but I keep my mouth shut. Enough people know already, I don't need to add to that list. Besides, being here with her doesn't mean that I trust her, and that's paramount. Not when Erikel's control spreads wider than I would have ever believed.

Instead, I focus on the familiar part again. "If some of those creatures are familiars with the students from Shadowgrim Institute, would they be aware of the… damage Ari has done?" My lips twist nervously as I try to use the right words. Damage probably isn't it, but slaughtering sounded way more sinister than I would prefer.

Figgins tilts her head in my direction, but her eyes aren't settled on me as she thinks. Eldon squeezes my shoulder tentatively in support, but no one utters a word as we wait for her answer.

"I feel like if it was my familiar I would know. Do you?"

I nod. How I feel inside about Ari, the connection of emotions and feelings must run deep enough to know if someone is lost or their life is taken.

"Then let's assume that they do. Although, their tone

didn't suggest so, and there's no telling that their familiar actually is a Drake." I offer her another nod in agreement, and she deems the conversation complete as she spins to face the back of her office again. "We'll go through a gateway from here," she explains, and a moment later I hear the click of her office door locking behind us.

She generates a gateway with her hands, but as soon as it appears, it disappears before our eyes. She frowns, as do the rest of us, before she tries to do it again and comes up just as short.

"What's wrong?" Brax asks, moving to her side, watching her do it a third time with no luck before giving it a try himself. "I don't know what's going on with that," he states, turning to me as Figgins shakes her head in disbelief.

"What—"

Her wonder is cut off by a siren blaring through the room, spiking panic in my veins as adrenaline courses through me.

"What's going on?" I ask, covering my ears. When I see that no one else is, I get even more worried until Zane taps my ear and the cry of the siren dulls. It's still present, but nowhere near as deafening as it had been only moments ago.

You have magic, Raven. Learn to fucking use it.

I roll my eyes at myself as I murmur my thanks while

Figgins unlocks her office door and ushers us outside just as quickly as we came in. I don't know what the fuck is going on, but now isn't the best of times.

Hurried footsteps beyond the classroom draw me toward the doorway, despite my irritation, where students and professors alike rush by.

"The siren is a drill. Everything is shut down and everyone must gather in the courtyard. That's why the portals aren't working," Figgins explains. "Go quickly. I will follow separately," she adds, and I nod before taking off down the hallway with my men in tow.

Following the crowd of both Silvercrest and Shadowgrim students, my steps slow as we enter the courtyard to find Erikel standing at the far end. Creed's father, in his usual golden armor, is standing to his right while Fitch hangs back in the crowd with Leila at his side. Her face is downcast, and I can't see Grave, but that will have to wait until we know what's going on here.

I catch sight of Sebastian stepping in from the right, his pace slow and measured. He glances through the crowd, looking for someone or something, but is quickly distracted as Genie throws herself at him. They're a tangle of arms and lips a moment later and I twist my head in wonder. Is it an act? I don't know, but it's insane either way.

I may be standing here, wondering what the hell is actually happening on so many levels, but I don't think it's possible to get a true answer. Not with so much magic at play, so many people controlled by situations I know nothing about. It's unsettling. And that's an understatement.

While everyone gathers, I turn to Eldon, hoping to distract us from all of this with more talk about his vision, but the second our gazes connect, he discreetly shakes his head before nodding to the side. I follow his line of sight, spotting a few of the institute students beside us.

Damn, there's nowhere for us to talk freely right now. Why is the world against me at the worst possible times? Are there even more suitable times? I don't think so.

Shaking my head, I heed my wandering mind. I need to warn Ari. I'm not going to be getting there any time soon, but hopefully, it means the other students going to see their familiars won't be able to either.

"Ari?" I cross my fingers, praying it works.

"Raven."

Thank goodness he heard me. I sigh with relief.

"Something is going on here. We can't leave the academy right now," I explain, and a tightening takes over my chest as I sense his concern. *"I'm okay. I don't think it will be anything to worry about. I just wanted you to know."*

"Okay, be safe, Raven, or I'll blame those men of yours."

I smile at his remark, focusing back on the present

instead of communicating with him.

"What's this about?" one of the guys beside us asks his friend, and I peer at them from the corner of my eye.

"Fuck knows, man. You know details never get passed down the chain quick enough," his friend retorts with a huff.

"For now, brother. For now. Once everything is said and done, you know it will be different. It was promised."

I want to tell him that promises don't mean shit, especially among those men, but that's not for me to be concerned about. What *is* a slight worry, though, is that they don't know any more than we do, which makes this feel far less planned and way more chaotic. The fact that Erikel's men are so blindly led also baffles me. Maybe it's who I am—the need for all of the information and my obsession with control—I can't understand how people wouldn't want those things too.

Erikel clears his throat, swinging his arms out wide at his sides to gain everyone's attention, and when the courtyard is completely silent, he speaks. "It's been brought to my attention that the peace and tranquility we feel right now will be coming to an end." Everyone frowns, bewildered with where this is going, but he doesn't leave us hanging for long. "The Monarchy is coming to invade us tomorrow." Gasps ring out around us, a mixture of hope and an inkling of horror swirling in the air throughout the crowd. "So we must act today."

Invade? That's a bit fucking dramatic. Are they coming? Yes. Invading? No. Not that I'm aware of at least, and I consider myself very well informed on all things regarding The Monarchy right now. But the semantics don't fucking matter in this moment because the fact remains; he knows. He fucking knows.

How? Fucking *how*?

"Act how?" Ruben asks, catching me by surprise. I thought he would just do as he was told without any questions, but the frown on his face tells a different story. More than that, the question reflects my own. What the hell does Erikel mean we must act today?

"We're going to Ashdale."

TWENTY NINE

Raven

How the fuck does he know about The Monarchy?

I can't get the question out of my head. It's playing on a loop, even as I stare at him, waiting for what comes next.

"When?" Genie asks, unfazed, while the rest of us are frozen in place with shock.

"Now." It's a barked order, a snap of his teeth as his gaze lands on me for a second. I'm certain he's attempting to suck my breath from my very lungs from across the way, but that would be impossible. Though, under his treacherous gaze, it feels like if anyone could do it, it's him.

Fuck.

My back stiffens, and for some reason, my attention is drawn back to Leila, who remains at her father's side with her head bowed.

Head. Bowed.

She didn't...

Did she?

But how else would he have known? There's no other reason for it. Not one.

My heart shreds into a million pieces in my chest.

Fuck. Fuck. Fuck.

I'm angry with myself more than anyone. What a fool I am. I should have listened to my doubts and refrained from trusting her. The pain clinging to my every fiber makes it clear I should have kept her at arm's length. But more so, I'm angry that the hope that was blossoming to full fruition inside of me has been quickly squandered at Erikel's hands again.

"Everybody make your way to the Gauntlet arena, where we will have multiple gateways set up, ready for the mission," Erikel declares.

"What mission?" one of the guys from Shadowgrim Institute beside us asks, and before I can even blink, magic is blasted in his direction, setting him alight in an instant, until nothing remains but black burn marks where he stood moments earlier.

What. The. Fuck?

"Any more questions?" Erikel glances around the courtyard with a smug look firmly in place. My fingers twitch, wishing like hell I had the strength and ability to tear this man down on the spot.

With a reaction like that, he made sure no one dares open their mouth now. When he's certain no one else is going to have an outburst, he waves his hand dismissively.

The crowd starts to move without further question, but I'm heading in the opposite direction.

Shouldering through the crowd, I hear Eldon call out my name, but my sights are set and anger burns in my gut. I grab hold of her arm and shake her.

"Did you do this?" I snarl, not caring if Fitch sees or not. My attention is solely fixed on Leila.

She shakes her head, confusion warring in her eyes, but I'm not falling for that bullshit now. She's clearly too good of an actor for me and I won't fall for it anymore.

"Raven, what are you talking about?" she asks, lifting her hands to my chest as I grab her other arm too. My nails dig into her arms but she doesn't flinch.

"The Monarchy. I want to hear you say it. Tell me. Was. It. You?"

She pushes against my chest and I release my hold on her as she frowns at me with what almost looks like disappointment in her eyes.

"Are you joking with me right now? Of course not. Why would I do that?"

"I don't know, you tell me," I bite, stepping closer, but

I manage to keep my hands to myself this time.

"Raven, I didn't do this," she says calmly, and I scoff.

"Let's go, Dove," Zane murmurs, putting his arm around me and pulling me back against his chest.

I glance over my shoulder at him and spot Creed, Brax, and Eldon all right there too.

Fuck.

I exhale harshly, looking away from my so-called friend.

"Get me out of here," I rasp, looking at Zane pleadingly. He spins me on the spot and starts to follow the remaining members of the crowd heading toward the arena. We don't make it ten steps before a flash of gold stops before us.

Fuck my life right now. How can hurdle after hurdle continue to fall in place before us? I don't want it.

I don't want any of it.

"Son, come." The golden warrior hovers before us, eyes fixed on the younger version of himself, and I notice Creed stiffen under the command.

Like fuck is he ordering him around right now. That's not necessary on top of everything else. My emotions are already heightened and this guy is only making it worse.

"No," I blurt, grabbing Creed's hand and tugging him closer. He steps to my side effortlessly, but the second he's there, his father clamps a hand down on his shoulder. A frown quickly etches into Creed's features at the touch, but a moment later, he nods and takes a step toward him, letting go of my hand in the process.

No. Fucking. Way.

Stumbling over my own feet, I rush around the golden warrior and plant a hand on his armored chest. "What did you do to him?" I snarl, barely containing the rage inside of me.

My eyes are wide, my restraint diminished, and my body stiff with anger and unrelenting tension.

"Move," he orders, ignoring my question as he stares at me with no feelings or emotion in his eyes. So similar to Creed's yet oh-so different without the emotion present.

"No. Tell me what you did to him," I repeat, feeling the presence of my other men behind me. "I won't let you take him anywhere."

I refuse. Not when my gut twists, the wonder of whether my onyx-eyed man is making the decision for himself or not lingering in my mind.

"Raven," Zane murmurs, but I don't look behind me. I'm scared if I turn away, Creed will be gone. Instead, I take a step forward and wave a hand in front of Creed's face.

"What magic do you possess?" My thought rushes past my filter uncontrollably, but it's not him who answers.

"He has mind magic," Creed states, his voice monotone and almost void. It sends a shiver down my spine. His onyx eyes are looking in my direction, but it's like he's not actually seeing me.

Bile rises up, burning the back of my throat. "Are you controlling him right now?" I snap, glancing at the golden warrior, who sighs.

"I won't ask you to move again."

"Good, I'm glad you're not wasting your breath. Release whatever magic you have on him. Now." My nostrils flare, my hands clench at my sides, and my heart races wildly. When he doesn't move an inch, I slam my lips shut and internally growl in frustration. "Do you think you're protecting him? Because you're not. What have you done?" I demand. I'm drowning in air, melting from the icy presence of the golden warrior, and sinking in the hardened ground beneath my feet. All three things should be impossible, but in my mind, the world is colliding around me, and I'm helpless to prevent it.

I wag my finger in front of his face, more than ready to repeat my demand once again, but before either of us can speak, Erikel appears.

"Nice work, warrior, gaining the information about The Monarchy from your son. It's a shame loyalty doesn't run in your bloodline. But he can redeem himself in Ashdale," he snarls before sauntering off just as quickly as he arrived.

Gaping in horror at his retreating form, I'm certain I'm going to pass out as I slowly spin around to face Creed again, who remains in the exact same position he was in a moment earlier.

Creed gave them the information.

Creed did.

When?

How?

Fuck.

My pulse echoes in my ears and thunders in my mind as I let the truth wash over me. If I thought I knew what pain felt like, I was wrong. In comparison to this... fuck.

"What did you do to your son?" I snarl, my chest rising and falling dramatically with every breath as I tremble from head to toe. The golden warrior stares at me bleakly and my gut clenches tighter. "Release him. Now."

A tendril of magic flickers from his fingertips and my heart lurches. I'm ready to grab it, I don't care if my mirror magic is revealed at this point. I need his hands off Creed right the fuck now.

Extending my hand, the warrior tracks my move, and before I get a hold of his magic, he places his hand on Creed's shoulder once more. Creed gasps, tumbling to his knees in one swift move, and when his father takes a step away, I let him, focusing on my onyx-eyed love instead.

"Creed, are you okay?" I rush, falling to my knees in front of him.

"He's alright, Dove. Give him a second," Zane

murmurs, stroking a soothing hand down my spine.

Once again, my vulnerabilities are revealed with my men, and there's nothing I can do about it. Not a single fucking thing. That's another situation for later, though. Now, Creed needs me.

He shakes his head, his hands balling into fists against the ground as Eldon drops down beside me to check on his friend.

"I can't..." Creed croaks, making my heartache. "I can't believe it."

"What can't you believe, man?" Eldon asks, squeezing his shoulder in a silent attempt at support.

Black onyx eyes look up, filled with disdain. "He left me with all of my memories this time and an understanding of what he's done," he breathes, his eyebrows furrowing. If he's confused, we're all fucked.

"What did he do, Creed?" Brax bites, clearly feeling as annoyed as I am.

"His hand... every time he's touched me, he managed to see into my mind and erase his presence all at once." Holy fuck. "Last night, before we went into the guild, he placed his hand on my arm."

That motherfucking asshole.

I'll kill him.

Rushing to my feet, I spin, searching for him, but Brax stops me in my tracks, turning my attention back to the group.

"Wait, so he knows that we know about..." Zane's words trail off and Creed drops his head in defeat.

"Fuck. But if Erikel knew that, I'm sure he would have made us aware," I mutter, confused by all of the information.

Creed shakes his head. "He showed me."

"Showed you what?" I ask, dropping back down beside him. Reaching out to tilt his chin up, I look into his eyes, desperate to understand.

"How Erikel found out, but he also showed me what he did before that." I gulp, waiting for him to explain better. "Erikel reads my father's mind. He doesn't offer the information, the bastard just takes it." Just like the golden warrior does, it seems. "He demanded my father learn of any information I may have, and my father knew he had to give him something. So, he placed the memory of us knowing about Burton in a stone by the entrance and offered him The Monarchy instead."

Fuck. Fuck. Fuck.

"Are you sure? He could just be bullshitting you," Brax grunts, and despite his harsh tone, I agree. This is all so far beyond my understanding, anything is possible now.

"He didn't tell me. He showed me. It doesn't make sense, I know. None of this does, and I don't understand how Erikel isn't able to see that he did that, but I believe him. Despite how much all of this hurts, I do."

"Sometimes our parents are just shitty, though, Creed." I startle at the sound of Leila's voice and my heart drops to my feet.

Shit.

Clambering to my feet, I turn to face her. "Leila, I—"

"Don't apologize, Raven. I understand. I do. But I would never. Not unless someone was able to do to me what they did to Creed. But from a young age, my father taught me how to block people from my mind," she explains, reaching out to stroke her hand down my arm.

Fuck, she shouldn't be comforting me right now. Not when I've been a total bitch. I also need to add it to my immediate to-do list to know how to block people from my mind too. We all do.

"I'm sorry."

She gives me a pointed look for uttering the words she told me not to say, but fuck, she deserves more than that. Especially since the real reason they know is because of Creed, and I'm not getting mad at him like I was at her.

Creed rises, Eldon along with him, and we all turn to face the path to the arena. I don't want to go, I don't think any of us do. Not when we know The Monarchy is so close to coming for us. And especially not when we know what's hidden in Ashdale. Eldon's vision offered us that.

Despite my reluctance, there's no alternative for us in

this moment. No greener grass or glimmer of sunshine on the horizon. Nothing.

Silently, I grasp Creed's hand and the six of us fall into line, joining the students heading toward the same doom as us. It doesn't make sense why we all have to go, but nothing Erikel does makes sense to me. We're definitely wired differently; there's no doubt about that.

As we step into the arena, a chill runs through my body. It shouldn't be colder in here than out there. I glance through the crowd, noting a lot of worry and confusion written on the faces of the students from Silvercrest, while those from Shadowgrim seem calm and collected, but I guess this isn't the first time they've been uprooted.

They're a lot more acclimated to Erikel and his ways, a feeling I hope to never know myself.

We near the portals and Grave appears out of nowhere, standing firmly beside Leila. That's when I realized that I haven't seen Fitch. Which seems odd. He's always protecting her or tearing her away from stuff like this. Why didn't he interject while I was shaking her, either?

"Leila, where did your father disappear to?" I ask, glancing back over my shoulder at her.

"I don't know. He was mad at seeing me with Grave. That's why I was standing with him in the courtyard. He had been in the middle of berating me about my body and my sins when the siren rang."

It still doesn't make sense. There are so many layers to all of this. There's no escaping the carnage.

Confused as hell, I step up to the gateway when it's our turn to pass through. My heart is galloping uncontrollably as I feel the soft sand beneath my academy-issued shoes and a shudder runs down my spine.

I've been here once before at the hands of Sebastian.

The Bishops found me that time. Now they're here with me. Talk about full circle.

Once the last people are through, the gateways disappear and everyone's attention turns back to Erikel, who grins from ear to ear as he addresses us with his arms flung out wide. "We better move fast before the darkness comes."

THIRTY

Raven

"**I**s this fool going to actually explain why we're here?" Leila mutters under her breath, and I bite back the laugh that threatens my lips.

We've been walking across the sand for over an hour, leaving me to wonder why the fuck he didn't have the gateway bring us closer to the cave I assume we're going to, but this isn't my mission and I'm not about to ask. His fur coat stands out in the distance as we trail toward the back of the students, happy to keep as much distance as possible between us and him.

I've spotted a few professors among the crowd, but I haven't seen Figgins or Fitch.

"I'm sure he's leading us to our doom," Grave grunts, and Creed hums in agreement.

I'm perfectly sandwiched between Brax and Eldon

for a change as we all walk in a line. I don't know what's shifted, but apparently, there's no need to protect me as much out here. Not that I'm complaining. I'm actually enjoying it.

We stumble in the sand as we head up the dunes, breathless by the time we get to the top, and that's when the caves appear in the distance. From the sun beaming down from above to the gray skies that loom over the peaks, it definitely feels like we're being led to our doom. Grave might be onto something there.

Everyone keeps moving, watching their step as we trail back down the sand dunes and, as predicted, Erikel doesn't communicate anything further until the opening of the caves is directly behind him. From a distance, they didn't look that big, but now that we're up close, I'm left questioning whether the cave system could be bigger than the entire grounds of the academy.

We're fucked.

My gut twists.

We're going to have to head in there and my gut tells me we're not coming out.

"Upon entering the caves, everyone's priority is to look for a special jewel. It's red, glistens like a ruby, with magic swirling inside the prism. You'll know when you've found it. Whoever finds it will be granted their freedom and released from the academy."

Chatter picks up at his words, excitement buzzing through the crowd as he offers everyone exactly what they want. The only issue with that is he's not a man of his word. I don't think he ever has been, and I don't see this going any differently. He's simply using us to find the Poten's Ruby.

"The clock starts now, but hurry; danger may lurk inside." He steps aside to stand with the golden warrior, watching in amusement as Silvercrest Academy students barge their way inside in the hopes of freedom awaiting them at their success.

Shadowgrim students follow after them, and we continue to lurk amid the masses at the back.

"I think our aim needs to be to find the ruby and destroy it," I murmur as we enter the dark and grim cave system. The walls are damp, the dripping of water echoing in the distance, and coolness wraps around us, sinking deep into my bones.

"I agree," Brax states. "He can't have the ruby. We'll never survive the rest of the night if he does."

Fuck. That's true.

"Do you remember anything about this?" I ask, tilting my face to Eldon's, and he shakes his head.

"No. I remember hearing the water, but it was muffled, dampened by the rubies in the walls. If we can find that, we'll be closer."

Continuing through the cave system, we come to a small area that branches off in different directions. The majority of students are taking the two paths to the left, while a few go for the third trail. That draws me closer to the fourth and final pathway.

Selfishly, I don't wait to see what the others think, I just go, following the damp and dreary path over uneven terrain.

"We're going to try this way," Leila hollers, waiting back at the entrance with Grave and pointing to her left. I nod in acknowledgment, letting my gut continue to guide me.

Another fork in the path appears, and I stand at the split for a moment, hands on my hips as I consider the best route to take. Creed steps forward to offer his advice when a figure appears on the pathway to the left.

The sneer on her lips and the cock of her head are a dead giveaway.

"Fuck off, Genie," I grumble, shaking my head at her sudden appearance. It's unwarranted and unnecessary. Again.

"Oh, honey, when I get this ruby and hand it over, I'll be fucking *all* of the way off while you are left to rot and die. It's going to be fantastic," she says with a little shimmy to her shoulders.

Bitch.

"That sounds great, are you done?" I retort, beyond bored of her presence, but the way she bares her teeth at me tells me she's far from done.

Dammit.

She takes a step toward me, chin high in the air, but Brax quickly steps forward in an attempt to block me from her. Much to her delight, I side step him and face her head on. "Daddy is going to love destroying everyone you love, Raven. Maybe not Eldon, though. *If* you ask me nicely, baby," she breathes, winking at my man, and I'm done with this bitch.

Rearing my arm back, I slam my fist into her face. No magic involved, just raw skin on skin, and as much as my knuckles burn, I'm filled with exhilaration.

"He can kill us all," I hiss, watching as she staggers back with a gasp. She cups her bloody nose for a second before she screams like a banshee.

I watch her energy shift, her magic coming to the forefront, but it's nothing at all like we practiced. Now I'm nervous. But I'm also acting on protective instinct for my men, so before the wisps get any longer, I reach out and grab it.

With her magic locked in my grasp, I start dissecting what her magic can do, but it's too difficult as I'm overcome with the need to just yank at the strand. Before I can consider the consequences, I let my own magic take over and pull as hard as I can.

A scream tears from Genie's lips as she slumps to the floor, breathless. The wisp of magic extends before curling into a ball in my open palm, and I gape at it, trying to understand what the fuck just happened.

"Fuck, I can see it," Zane murmurs, pointing at my palm where the tendrils of magic swirl.

"You can?" I reply in surprise as Genie continues to cry out on the floor.

"What the fuck?" Brax grunts, glancing from my palm to the bitch making all of the noise.

Why can everyone see it? That's not what usually happens.

My pulse rings in my ears, panic and uncertainty kicking in as Creed clears his throat. "Not to alarm anybody, but I think you just took her magic."

I rear back like he's slapped me as my jaw almost grazes the ground.

I didn't... I can't have...

Could I?

"Holy shit, I think he might be right," Eldon murmurs and Genie finally calms down enough to look up at me with loathing blazing in her eyes.

"You have the ruby already. Don't you? You have it," she snaps, staggering to her feet, and I shake my head vigorously.

Brax inches between the pair of us again, but she doesn't try to edge forward this time.

"You can't just leave it floating in your hand, Dove. You need to destroy it or connect with it."

"You mean take it," I repeat, staring at the pale gray color in my hand.

"Yeah, basically."

Fuck.

"Well, I don't want it." That's for certain. Why would I want her magic as well as my own?

No. Fucking. Way.

"Then you have to destroy it," Creed murmurs, and I shake my head in disbelief.

"Yeah, but how the fuck do I do that?"

"You wouldn't dare," Genie yells, her breathing becoming frantic as she claws at her clothes. "Give it back! Give it back right now!" she screeches, and I can't hold onto something that belongs to her for even a second longer.

If she wants it, she can fucking have it.

I blast it back at her, hoping it will just stick, but as everything unravels in slow motion, I don't think that's going to be the case. As the tendril approaches her, she lifts her arms out to her sides, just like her father does, ready to embrace the beauty that is her magic, but instead of connecting and rippling through her body in delight, it collides with her palm and disappears.

Genie stills at the contact, her body going stiff as she topples backward, landing on the ground with a thud. She's locked in place, her arms frozen in the air in front of her as the rest of us wait with bated breath for something to happen.

But nothing does.

She doesn't move, and the tendril of magic doesn't reappear.

Nothing.

"Creed?" I turn to him, pointlessly seeking his help when I know he has no idea either.

He clears his throat, rubbing at the back of his neck before he takes the needed steps forward to hover over Genie. "I think you may have figured out how to destroy the magic... and its original vessel."

I gape at him, knowing he's right.

I just killed her.

Killed. Her.

I mean, she was a bitch, but... fuck.

"I don't understand. I was trying to mirror her magic, but my own kind of..." I don't even know how to describe it so it doesn't sound as vile as it makes me feel.

"Shadow, I think that was another magical ability altogether," Brax states, his eyes soft as he slowly approaches.

"But Genie was right. That was like what the stone can do. I... I don't have the ability to do that." Even as I say it, I know I'm wrong. I know everything has changed once again, and I've revealed another strength, but it somehow feels like a weakness.

"How about we pause all of this right now and circle back to it once we have the ruby taken care of, okay? That'll give you some time to wrap your head around it all," Eldon says, stroking a hand down my cheek, and I nod.

"Let's do that," I mutter, taking tentative steps to avoid Genie the best I can as I take the other pathway from where she lies.

We walk in silence, although my head is loud and clustered with thoughts, fears, and everything in between.

I'm a weapon. I'm a monster. I'm... I don't know what the fuck I am.

I don't know how I manage to keep putting one foot in front of the other as we continue through the cave system. Eldon took the lead shortly after our run in with Genie, attempting to guide us through the darkness until he suddenly comes to a stop.

"Can you hear that?" he asks, and we all listen for a moment, but nothing sounds any different.

Brax shakes his head, confirming what we're all thinking, and Eldon waves his hand dismissively.

"The water, does that dripping sound different to you?"

he asks, being a little more specific this time, but I still don't know what he means.

It's Zane who gives him the resounding no this time, and I expect us to carry on moving, but Eldon can't let it drop. He takes a few steps forward before spinning around and glancing around the small space.

"Down here," he murmurs, dropping to his knees.

Frowning, I move to see what he's talking about and find a small hole in the wall that's hidden by the shadows to our right. He's already going through the gap without a backward glance, and I can't utter a word of complaint because I did the same earlier and he blindly followed. Now it's my turn.

I drop to my knees, cringing at the damp ground beneath me, but I usher through after him and the others follow after me. It's a narrow tunnel that's far longer than I'm expecting, but when Eldon reaches the end, he's able to stand.

He reaches a hand down to me when I get to the end, and when he pulls me to my feet, I gasp.

Holy fuck.

Red shimmers everywhere. Large cuts, tiny jewels, and everything in between twinkles from the wall embedded with rubies.

It's stunning.

"Holy fuck, that's dazzling," Zane says as he stands

beside me, and I nod in agreement. It completely illuminates the room.

"This is where my vision led me. Now we need to find the ruby," Eldon states, racking my body with nerves. We're one step closer to putting a stop to Erikel. I can feel it.

Zane grabs a hold of my hand and pulls me toward the shimmering wall of uncut jewels, and I focus on finding one with black tendrils of magic swirling around inside of it. I sense the others join us, but it's Eldon who gets closer to the wall first.

"In my vision, it was around here," he explains, waving his hand around the shadowed area where the wall meets the ground, which is also embedded with pretty rubies. "Ah, shit. Here. It's here," he says with a scoff of disbelief, and a second later, he's holding a red ruby with black tendrils inside.

I exhale, staring in shock.

We found it. We fucking found it. It feels too good to be true. It feels too good to be true. I repeat the thought for the third time when reality dawns on me.

If it feels too good to be true, it's probably because it is.

"We need to destroy it. Now. I don't have a good feeling about this," I admit, and Eldon looks at me with concern swirling in his blue eyes.

He stares down at the stone for a few moments before

slowly spinning in a circle. He stops with his back to us and points to something in the distance. "Maybe my vision showed me the gate because that's where it should be hidden," he breathes, and when I step around him, I notice the green archway in the distance, just like he had described.

Holy fuck.

"Is that the gate to the Realm of Shadows?" Brax asks, awe in his voice as he blinks repeatedly at it. My heart races for him, remembering how much he's been researching this in an attempt to see his parents again.

My hands shake with nerves as he turns those sweet fucking eyes my way. I see the hope there. A feeling I don't imagine my gargoyle feels very often, if at all, and my heart swells.

"Let's find out," I breathe, a sense of excitement shimmering through us as we look at one another.

Zane claps, chuckling with excitement as we cut the distance to where the green arch stands tall. Eldon keeps a hold of the stone, but he pauses when we get closer. "Be careful, though. In my vision, there were shadows almost dancing over the emeralds," he explains, leaving me breathless.

It sounds like bedtime to me, and just like then, I watch as the silhouettes swirl across the cave wall. I take that as my cue to step up to the door. The shadows have never made me feel unsafe or scared before, I don't expect that to change now. Coming to a stop in front of the door, the dulled brass handle beckons me closer, but before I reach for it, I turn to Brax.

"Are you ready?" I ask, watching as he exhales slowly before giving me a nod.

I take my own deep breath as I latch on to the metal and twist. It swings open effortlessly and all of the shadows slip inside. I frown at first as only a bright light stands before me. A little like a gateway, it doesn't offer me a glimpse of what's inside. I just have to trust it.

A hand grabs mine and I know it's Brax. Clasping on to him tightly, I place one foot in front of the other. My eyes fall closed as the world shifts around me so fast it feels like it takes my breath away.

The sound of birds tweeting in the distance is what greets me first, then a floral scent hits my nose a moment later and I feel like I'm going to drift, a sense of calm serenity washing through me like a gentle ocean wave.

It feels like I'm home.

Which is the weirdest fucking thing ever.

"That's my family's home," Brax murmurs, pulling me from my thoughts, and as I blink my eyes open, I see the house come into view.

"I remember this," Eldon adds, patting his friend on the shoulder as we all stand and stare in surprise.

"Brax? Brax, is that you?" My gargoyle's chin falls to his chest and I watch the weight of the world leave his body at the sound of the woman's voice. She appears a moment later, rushing down the pathway from the porch, both hope and sorrow marring her face as she looks us over. "Brax, honey, you're not supposed to be here yet. What's going on?" Her hand falls to her chest like she has to stop herself from reaching out to touch him.

"I don't know what it means when you say that, but I'm not dreaming this time," he mutters, and her eyebrows rise.

"Then how did you get here? Oh, gosh, did you all… are you all… dead?" she says the final word with a gasp, horror flickering in her eyes.

"No, no. We're fine. I'm fine. We found the gate."

She takes a step back, shaking her head fiercely. "Please tell me you didn't use the gate for the Realm of Shadows, Brax. Please." My spine stiffens, panic clawing at me as she frantically swipes a hand down her face. "No, no, no, no, no," she chants, tears forming, and my gut twists. "Get out. You have to get out right now," she orders, shoving at his chest.

I feel his pain at the first push. The confusion and anguish seeps from him as his mother nudges him away.

"Mo—"

"No, Brax. Get out. Get out *right* now," she yells, and

a man comes rushing from the house.

"Father, will you tell her to stop?" Brax pleads, even as his mother continues to edge us back to the emerald gate that remains open behind us.

"You used the gate," the man murmurs, the color draining from his face. "Not the gate, son."

What the fuck have we done?

"Brax, we need to leave. Right now. Trust them. We need to go," I breathe, looking up at him as he frowns. I can see the war in his eyes, the need to stay and understand, but there's no time for that. "Come on," I encourage, cutting the distance to the still-open doorway.

As I near the archway, I can see the cave system on the other side, and as dark and dingy as it is, his mother is making me feel a lot safer there than here. Even despite the feeling of home I got when I first stepped through.

Her panic is real. Her pain is undeniable.

With hopes of encouraging him back through easier, I step through the archway, feeling my world tip once more as I plant my feet on the ground of the cave. I turn back to the emerald door, expecting to see nothing like last time, but to my surprise, I can see clearly into the Realm of Shadows.

"Brax," I call out, and he glances back at me.

Eldon, Creed, and Zane all step up to the space where I am, but none of them step through while Brax is lingering.

"Why? Please, just explain to me why?"

His mother sobs into her hand uncontrollably before shoving at his shoulders with more force than I expect, and he stumbles through the gateway, landing with a thud at my feet.

Fuck.

"Brax," I start, but he quickly waves me off as he stands, turning to the doorway.

"This is why," his mother cries, pointing at Eldon, Creed, and Zane, who are at her side.

"I don't know what you mean," Brax says, exasperated.

I wave for Eldon to hurry on through, but he shakes his head.

"They've never danced with the shadows before."

"What the fuck does that mean," Brax growls at the top of his lungs as I stare at my fireball, my onyx-eyed love, and my invisible joker.

I understand it before she says it, my heart splinters into a million pieces before she confirms it, and I know there's no surviving this.

"They're trapped."

AFTERWORDS

Do I get a bitch crown for this cliffhanger?

I like crowns, I'll take it.

It wasn't supposed to happen, I swear, but here we are. Oops.

Writing this book made me it's bitch. The words were pouring from me in the most cluster-fuck way ever! To the point where my editor kindly said, for fucks sake KC give them something other than pain and misery haha

Roll on March for the final installment of Raven's story.

THANK YOU

Michael, Michael, Michael. What a man. We love you.

To my angels, I love you more than words to say. Thank you for growing into the most beautiful humans, inside and out, you make me proud beyond words. Everything I do is in hopes that when you're grown you'll be proud of me for trying, even if I don't succeed.

Nicole, Jeni, Tanya. Thank you for holding me together and dealing with my crazy writing pattern during this book. You're all queens!

Kirsty, mate. Thank you for propping me up when all I wanted to do was collapse to the ground and never get up. You're a boss.

To my beta readers, thank you for delving into this world with me, you're top dollar fabulousness and I love you all.

Thank you to Sarah for polishing my words, and to Lily for making every page look like pure art.

ABOUT KC KEAN

KC Kean began her writing journey in 2020 amidst the pandemic and homeschooling... yay! After reading all of the steam, from fade to black, to steamy reads, MM, and reverse harem, she decided to immerse herself in her own worlds too.

When KC isn't hiding away in the writing cave, she is playing Dreamlight Valley, enjoying the limited UK sunshine with her husband, children, and furbabies, or collecting vinyls like it's a competition.

Come and join me over at my Aceholes Reader Group, follow my author's Facebook page, and enjoy Instagram with me.

ALSO BY KC KEAN

Ruthless Brothers MC
(Reverse Harem MC Romance)
Ruthless Rage
Ruthless Rebel
Ruthless Riot

Featherstone Academy
(Reverse Harem Contemporary Romance)
My Bloodline
Your Bloodline
Our Bloodline
Red
Freedom
Redemption

All-Star Series
(Reverse Harem Contemporary Romance)
Toxic Creek
Tainted Creek
Twisted Creek

(Standalone MF)
Burn to Ash

Emerson U Series
(Reverse Harem Contemporary Romance)
Watch Me Fall
Watch Me Rise
Watch Me Reign

Saints Academy
(Reverse Harem Paranormal Romance)
Reckless Souls
Damaged Souls
Vicious Souls
Fearless Souls
Heartless Souls

Silvercrest Academy
(Reverse Harem Paranormal Romance)
Falling Shadows
Destined Shadows
Cursed Shadows
Unchained Shadows

Made in the USA
Columbia, SC
26 February 2024